Swords Reluctant

by

Max Pemberton

Double 9 BOOKS

Swords Reluctant

by Max Pemberton

ISBN: 978-93-70818-74-3

Published by

DOUBLE 9 BOOKS
2/13-B, Ansari Road
Daryaganj, New Delhi – 110002
info@double9books.com
www.double9books.com
Tel. 011-40042856

ABOUT THE AUTHOR

Max Pemberton was an English novelist and publisher, primarily known for his works in the adventure and mystery genres. Born on June 19, 1863, in Paddington, London, Pemberton became a prominent figure in late 19th and early 20th-century literature. His works, which often explored themes of suspense, intrigue, and adventure, were popular among readers of his time. Some of his notable works include The Iron Pirate, a thrilling maritime adventure, and The Garden of Swords, a historical novel set against the backdrop of war. Pemberton's style was marked by vivid storytelling and well-constructed plots, capturing the imagination of his audience. Aside from his writing career, he was also a publisher, which helped him expand his influence in the literary world. He was married to Alice Tussaud, and they spent much of their lives in London. Although his popularity diminished in the mid-20th century as literary tastes shifted, Pemberton's contributions to the adventure and mystery genres continue to be recognized. He passed away on February 22, 1950, at the age of 86, leaving behind a legacy of adventure-filled fiction.

CONTENTS

BOOK I
THE CHALLENGE

CHAPTER I
GABRIELLE SILVESTER WRITES A LETTER

I

Gabrielle returned from the Town Hall where the meeting was held, just after ten o'clock, and was glad to see the fire burning brightly in her room. She remembered that she would never have thought of such a luxury as a fire in her bedroom prior to her visit to New York.

All agreed that it had been a very successful meeting, and that real, convincing work had been done. She herself could say, in the privacy of her own room, that the excitements of such gatherings had become a necessity to her since the strenuous days in America, and perhaps to her father also.

How changed her life since she first set foot on the deck of the *Oceanic* and began to know a wider world! England had seemed but a garden upon her return and its people but half awake. She had a vivid memory of the rush and roar of distant cities, of strange faces and new races, but chiefly of a discovery of self which at once frightened and perplexed her.

Would it be possible to accept without complaint the even tenor of that obscure life in Hampstead which she had suffered willingly but seven months ago? She knew that it would not, and could answer for her father also. A call had come to him and to her. She had been sure of it at the meeting, but of its nature she had yet to be wholly convinced.

Gordon Silvester, the most eloquent preacher among the Congregationalists, had gone to America at the bidding of a famous millionaire, there to bear witness to the brotherhood of man and the bond between the peoples. The achievement of the great treaty between America and the Motherland had drawn together the leading intellects of the two countries, and had culminated in that mighty assemblage in New York which had stood before the altar of the Eternal Peace and closed, as it believed for ever, the Temple of the twin-headed Janus. With the minister had gone Gabrielle, his only child, and thus for the first time during her three and twenty years had she seen any world but that of the suburban parish in which Gordon Silvester laboured.

II

It was a bitter cold night of the memorable winter with which this story is chiefly concerned.

Gabrielle wore furs, which had been purchased in Quebec, and a hat which some upon the steamer had thought a little *outré* for a parson's daughter. These furs she had just laid upon her bed, and was busy unpinning her hat when her father knocked at the door and asked if he might come in. She thought that he was more excited than he was wont to be in the old days, and there were blotches of crimson upon his usually sallow cheeks.

"I am just going to bed," he said in a quiet tone; "if you want anything to eat, let Jane know. The room was very hot, I think—my head is aching."

She turned with her hand still among the curls of her auburn hair, a wonderfully graceful figure for such a scene.

"You must be very tired, dear," she said very gently. "I have never heard anything more beautiful than your speech."

He took a step into the room, his hand upon the door.

"Then you think it was a success, Gabrielle?"

"I don't think at all about it; it was what Mr. Faber would have called 'electrical.'"

He let go the door, and then shut it behind him.

"Ah!" he said, as though thinking upon it, "if we could have had Faber with us."

She laughed, showing the superb whiteness of her teeth.

"The lion and the lamb. Why do you attach any importance to him?"

He crossed the room to an arm-chair and sat there, poking the fire.

"He is one of the men who can make peace or war," he said. "Sir Jules Achon agrees with me. Popular sentiment goes for much, but the men who control the destinies are the financiers."

"But, father, how could Mr. Faber control this particular situation?"

"He could set a great example of forbearance. Is he not rich enough?"

She came and sat by him near the fire. It was yet early in the most memorable winter that England has ever known, but the cold had become intense.

"I saw so little of Mr. Faber on the ship," she said reflectively; "he appeared to me to be a man who could move mountains ... with somebody else's arms, to say nothing of somebody's else's spades."

"Was that your only impression of him?"

"Oh! force—hardly of character, perhaps—that and his restlessness. Why did everyone talk of him? Was it because he is worth eleven millions of money? Was that all that could be said of him?"

"A very good reason nowadays. They say he has a contract with the French Government for five millions of the new rifles. Permissible exaggeration makes him the arbiter of peace or war. Did he not give you that impression?"

"I hardly think so; he was mostly concerned about his boarhound's dinner. As far as I remember, he considers our party just harmless lunatics. I made him confess as much one day."

Silvester passed by the admission.

"He goes on a fearful journey," he said, falling unconsciously to the pulpit manner. "Of course such men know a great deal. He believes that there will be war in Europe in six months' time, and that our country will be concerned. Did he not tell you that?"

"I think not, father. He was too busy asking me to arrange the roses in his cabin."

"Ah! I remember them, pink roses everywhere in early December. What a feminine display!"

"But not a feminine subject. I have never met a man whose character impressed me so clearly. He has only begun in the world—those were his own words."

"Well, then, why should he not begin with us? Sir Jules believes that nothing would make a greater stir than his joining our Committee."

"Then why don't you ask him yourself? He's in London until the end of the week."

Silvester did not speak for some minutes. He seemed to have become a little shy of this outspoken wide-eyed daughter of his, who evaded the issue so cleverly.

"I wish you'd write, Gabrielle."

"To Mr. Faber?"

"Yes; you seemed very good friends on the ship. I believe he'd join if you asked him."

She shook her head.

"I don't believe it would make any difference who asked him. I'll write, if you wish it."

"Yes," he said, rising abruptly, "write now before you go to bed. You're sure you are not hungry?"

Gabrielle laughed lightly.

"I have left all my vices in America," she rejoined, "being hungry in the witching hours is one of them."

III

Her boudoir overlooked the great well wherein London lies. Though the moon was in the first quarter, the night was wonderful in stars, and the air quivered with the virility of frost. She could see St. Paul's and the City spires; the Carlton Hotel lay more to the west, and was hidden behind the slopes of Haverstock Hill. There was no snow, for this frost was black as iron.

Just below, were the winding walks to which the pilgrims came in search of Keats. She had read the sonnets and tried to understand them, but candour compelled her to say that she preferred Tennyson. Sometimes she thought her whole interest in literature to be an affectation; but undoubtedly she was addicted to erotic poetry and the fire of Swinburne would burn in her veins. All this, too, was hidden from her father, who occupied himself but little with her affairs, and believed that her interests were entirely his own.

Girls of twenty-three are usually fervent letter-writers and Gabrielle was no exception. She had furnished folios of gossip that very day for her friend, Eva Achon, who had been her intimate upon the ship. But when it came to writing "John Sebastian Faber, Esq.," her pen trembled upon the paper. How impossible it seemed to say anything to which such a man would listen. She depicted him as she had last seen him upon the deck of the *Oceanic*, stretched on a sofa-chair, and smiling at her philosophy.

"Letters answered themselves," he had said. He got through life on cables and confidence. There was not a private letter in fifty which said anything worth saying. He had proposed a league for the suppression of private correspondence, and begged her to be one of the vice-presidents. She remembered her own disappointment that he had not asked her to write to him.

So it was no easy thing at all to begin, chiefly because she feared his irony and was quite sure that her letter would achieve nothing. Half-a-dozen sheets of good "cream laid" note were destroyed before she could get her craft launched and she was still in harbour so to speak when she heard her name cried out in the street below, and opening the window immediately, discerned Harry Lassett with skates upon his arm.

"Is that you, Gabrielle?"

The cold was intense and filled the room with icy vapour. She shivered where she stood, and drew her dressing-gown close about her white throat.

"Whatever are you doing, Harry? It's nearly eleven o'clock."

"I know that. We've been skating on the Vale. There'll be grand ice to-morrow. Won't you come? You must!"

"I haven't got any skates!"

"Oh, send into town for some. I'll go myself if you'll throw me out an old boot. You don't mean to say you're going to miss it?"

She shook her head and tried to shield herself behind the heavy curtains.

"I fear I'll have to go visiting to-morrow."

"What, those American dollars again! No! They're spoiling you; I thought you had done with that nonsense."

"I did not say they were American. I am going to Richmond to see Eva Achon."

"Oh, hang Eva Achon. We shall have bandy, if it holds. Throw me out that boot, and I'll go away. Your people go to bed in the middle of the day, don't they? It's all locked up like a prison down here."

"I am not in bed, Harry. I am writing a letter."

"American, of course?"

"Of course," and she laughed at him. Then the boot was found, and tossed out.

"How's that?" he asked—a man who had played for Middlesex and the 'Varsities could not have asked any other question.

"Let me know just how much they are, and I will send it round in the afternoon. Father promised me a pair to-night. I'm glad you can get them for me."

"Right oh! We shall skate on the Vale directly I return. Dr. Houghton of Grindelwald wants me to have a pair of his blades. You'd better have the same. They're grand!"

"Anything you like, my dear Harry, if they'll keep me warm. I shall be a pillar of ice if I stand here."

"Like Lot's wife! Was it ice, by the way? Well, good-night, then; or shall I post the letter?"

"That's splendid of you. I'll just finish it. But I'll have to shut the window."

"Imagine me a sentry doing the goose step. Will you be long?"

"Just two minutes, really."

He kissed his hand to her when she shut the window and began to stamp about to warm himself. They had been lovers since children, and were still free. Harry Lassett's three hundred a year "in the funds" just permitted him to play cricket for the county and to spend the best part of the winter at St. Moritz. He had not thought much about marriage.

Gabrielle's two minutes "really" proved to be an exact prophecy. Haste bade her throw both preface and conclusion to the winds. She just wrote:

> "Dear Mr. Faber,
>
> "My father would be very pleased if you would become one of the Vice-Presidents of the International Arbitration League. Will you let me say 'yes' for you?"

And that was the letter Harry carried to the post for her.

Vanity promised her an answer. It would come over the telegraph wires, she thought.

CHAPTER II
A MAN OF DESTINY

John Sebastian Faber had a suite of five rooms at the Savoy Hotel, and, as he said, he lived in four of them most of the time. The room which he did not occupy was devoted to three secretaries.

Gabrielle found him at his desk in an apartment which should have been a drawing-room. The windows looked out upon the Shot Tower and showed him the majesty of Westminster. There was a litter of American journals upon a round table at his back and copies of the English *Times*, much mutilated by cutting. He wore a black morning coat, and would have been called well-dressed by an American tailor.

His was the "clean-limbed" type of man who is such an excellent product of the sister nation—moderately tall, suggesting virility and immense nervous energy. Someone upon the ship said that he "snatched at life," and that was no untrue description of him. But he had also picked up a little sum of eleven millions sterling by the process, and that kind of snatching bears imitation.

A footman brought Gabrielle to the room, and Faber sprang up immediately, brushing back curly brown hair from his forehead. It was evident that he expected a somewhat protracted interview, for he wheeled a low chair near to his own before he held out his hand to her.

"Why, now, I'm glad to see you. Sit down right here and let us talk. A long way in from Hampstead, isn't it? Too hot, perhaps; well, then, we'll have the steam turned off."

"Oh, please!" she said, casting loose her grey furs—he had already regarded her from a man's first aspect and approved the picture—"I have been walking down the Strand and the air is so cold. It's delicious in here—and what roses!"

"Ah! that's where I blush. I always have roses wherever I go; didn't your lady from Banbury Cross do the same thing with the music? Well, I get as far off that as I can—most music. Wagner's good if you're up against a man. You never hear him crying 'Enuf.' Well, now, that's right. So you want me for the I.A.L.—or, rather, your father does. Why didn't he ask me on the ship?"

He swung back in his chair and looked her over from head to foot. She had always been a little afraid of the sensitive eyes, and they did not fail to magnetise her as heretofore. It was possible, however, to be very frank with such a man; she spoke with good assurance when she said:

"Oh! I suppose he didn't think of it."

"You mean that he didn't know enough about me? Why, that's fair. I dare say he heard my name for the first time that night I ran the charity concert for him. Guns and the gospel don't go well together, my dear lady, not in civilized parts. Your father won't want rifles until he goes to China to turn the great god Bud inside out. I'll let him have a consignment cheap when he's starting."

She thought it a little brutal, hardly the thing he should have said; but his good humour was invincible, and she forgave him immediately.

"The fact is," he ran on, "your father is a good man, Miss Silvester, and I'm a merchant. Where we come together is in admiring a certain fellow passenger who ran the ship and will run other ships. There we're on common ground. Now say what you like to me and I'll hear it, for I've just twenty minutes at your disposal, and you may count every one of them. To begin with the I.A.L.—does your father remember that I'm a gunmaker?"

She was vastly puzzled.

"I think he knows it in a vague way. The captain of the *Oceanic* said you were building the new American navy—is that quite true?"

"It would be in a prospectus. My house builds one of the new cruisers, and some of the destroyers. Guns are the bigger line. I've come to Europe to sell guns. Did they tell you that also?"

"Yes, I think everyone knows it."

"Then why come to me? Would you go to the keeper of a saloon and ask him to help you to put down the drink? He'd tell you that drink made George Washington, just as I tell you that guns made your Lord Nelson. Would the Admiral have joined your I.A.L.?"

"Oh," she said, with womanly obstinacy, "then you still think there is no alternative but war?"

He laughed and began to make holes with his pencil in the blotting pad before him.

"It's just as though you asked me if there were no alternative but human nature. Why isn't the world good right through? Why do murder and other crimes still exist on the face of the earth? Would a league suppress them—a decision at Washington that there should be no more sin? I guess not. If a man knocks me down before lunch, I may go to law with him; if it's after and there's been any wine, I'll possibly do my own justice and do it quick. War is as old as human nature, and if we are to believe that a God rules the world, we've got to believe also that man was meant to go to war. Shall I tell you that some of the noblest things done on this earth were done on the battlefield? You wouldn't believe me. Your father thinks George Washington a son of the devil, and Nelson a man of blood. I've heard that sort of thing from the platform, and it's turned me sick. Your I.A.L. is a league for the manufacture of lath-backed men. Do you think the world will be any better when every man turns the other cheek and honour has gone into the pot? If you do, well, I'm on the other side all the time. War may go, but it has got to change human nature first. Tell your father that, and ask him to think about it. I wonder what text he'd take if a troop of cavalry camped in his drawing-room to-night. Would the I.A.L. do much for him? Why, I think not."

She smiled at his wild images, and thought that she would demolish them simply.

"You speak in fables," she said, "it's like the nonsense in the panicky stories. There is no one in England nowadays who seriously believes in that kind of war. I do not think you can do so yourself. Now, really, did you ever see a battlefield in your life, Mr. Faber?"

He looked at her with eyes half shut.

"I was in Port Arthur the night the ships were struck. I saw the big fighting at Liaoyang. Go back farther and I'll tell you stories of Venezuela and the Philippines, which should be written down in red. I'm a child of war—my father died at a barricade in Paris three days before the Commune fell. A diamond of a man saved my mother and took her out to America, where I was born. There's war in the very marrow of my bones—I live for it as other men for women and children. Should you ask such a man to join such a League? I'll put it squarely to you. Now tell me the truth."

The intensity of the appeal startled her. The method of her life in the parsonage at Hampstead would have prompted a platitude of the platforms, some retort about the progress of humanity, and the need for social advance. But it seemed impossible to say such things to John Faber. Her courage ran down as ice before a fire; she was wholly embarrassed and without resource.

"Come," he repeated, "you owe me the admission. Should the request have been made to me?"

"No, indeed—and yet I will not say that anyone would be dishonoured by it."

"Did I suggest the contrary?"

"I think your idols false."

"They are the idols of human nature—not mine."

"We could say the same of the primitive savages. Why should we have advanced beyond the battle-axe and the club?"

"Not the political clubs—see here, is there any real advance when the knife goes deep enough? Suppose a thousand English women were butchered in China—or I'll make it Turkey—would your father be for the I.A.L.? If he were, the people would burn his pulpit!"

"It only means that we must educate."

"We're doing it all the time. Does education make your burglar sing psalms, or does it teach him to use oxygen for burning open the safe? I think nothing of education—that way. Who are the best educated people in Europe? The Germans. Are they coming in to the I.A.L.?"

"My father hopes that much may be done by the understanding between the ministers—"

He laughed rudely, brutally.

"All the sheep baaing together, and the wolf sharpening his teeth on the national grindstone. I've no patience to hear it."

"Then I certainly will not repeat it."

A flush of anger coloured her cheeks, and her heart began to beat fast. She was conscious of a rôle which fitted her but ill, and was no reflection of herself. How much sooner would she have been downstairs among the well-dressed women who were beginning to flock into the restaurant for lunch! This man's brutal logic threatened to shatter her professed ideals, and to leave her vanity defenceless. She remembered at the same time what the meaning of the triumph would be if she won him. All the country would talk of that!

"You are not offended with me?" he said in a gentler tone. "I'm sure you won't be when you get back home and think of it."

"I shall try to think of it as little as possible."

"As your countrymen are doing. If there was more than half-an-ounce of the radium of common sense in this kingdom at the present moment, some people would be thinking very hard, Miss Silvester—"

"Of what?"

He rose from his chair, thrust his hands deep into his trousers pockets, went over to the window and stood looking out.

"They would be thinking of the frost," he said.

"Perhaps it is too cold to think about it!"

He laughed.

"Well said and true. Did you read in the *Times* that there is ice in the English Channel for the first time for twenty years?"

"I never read the *Times*—"

"Then don't begin if you would remain a woman."

"Is she, then, unworthy of it?"

"Not at all—it is unworthy of her. It tells the truth!"

"Oh, I grant that that is embarrassing sometimes. We were speaking of the frost."

"And the fables. The fable, written by a great German, is about to freeze the English Channel and the North Sea! Ice from the Humber to Kiel! Portsmouth frozen up. An ice carnival at the Thames' mouth. Do you believe in fables?"

She stared at him amazed.

"What would happen if this one were true?"

"Oh," he said, "you had better ask the I.A.L."

She was silent a little while, then she said:

"Your bogies are wonderful. Are there many in your life?"

"More than I count."

"They are lucky then?"

"Yes, for one of them sends you to my rooms to-day."

He had never spoken to her in this way before, and the tone of it found her amazed. Hitherto the man of affairs and the woman of the useful vanities had been speaking; but John Faber had changed all that in an instant. She felt his wide eyes focused upon her with a sudden glance which burned. He had taken a step toward her, and for a moment she feared that some mad impulse would drive him to forget the true circumstance of their meeting, and to suppose another. She felt her heart beat rapidly—a true instinct warned her to act upon the defensive.

"I think we were talking of another kind of bogy," she said quickly—"women deserve a new chapter."

He laughed a little hardly, and turned upon his heel.

"The goose awoke and the Capitol is saved. Well, about this frost?"

"Oh, I shall hope for a thaw."

"That's what your I.A.L. is doing all the time. Tell them that John Faber wishes them well, and will sell them a hundred thousand rifles any time they are reconsidering the position. Perhaps I shall meet you when I return from Paris. We can put the contract through then."

She shook her head, trying to hide the annoyance of the rebuff.

"I don't suppose I shall ever see you again," she said.

"I'll bet you a thousand dollars you do, either in Paris or Berlin."

"Why should I go there?"

"Because your little friend Claudine d'Arny will see that you do."

"Oh, that was only an acquaintance on the ship. I had forgotten her."

"My memory is better. I have been chewing her father's name for twenty years."

"Do you know him, then?"

It was his turn to laugh—with the silent anger of a man who remembers.

"He gave the order for my father to be shot. I don't think I'll forget him."

She hardly believed him to be serious. There he stood, smiling softly, one hand deep in his trousers pocket, the other toying with his roses. He had just told her what he would have told no other woman in England, and she thought him a jester.

"Is this one of the fables?"

"Certainly it is. I am going to Paris to write the moral."

She watched his face curiously.

"But, surely, if General d'Arny gave any such order, it was in his official capacity."

"As I shall give mine—in an official capacity."

"Then you have not forgiven him?"

"It is for that very purpose I am going to Paris. That and one other."

"To sell your guns—I read it in the papers."

He smiled—in a kindly way this time.

"I'll give you twenty guesses."

"But I am hopeless at riddles."

"Then I'll solve this one for you. I am going to Paris to give one million dollars to the man who took my mother to America—if I can find him."

"I hope you will succeed—and I wish I knew the man."

He liked this, for it was the first really girlish thing she had said. Perhaps even at that stage Faber read her wholly, and believed that it was good for her to see "common sense in curl papers," as he put it. He might even have led her to talk of her father and her home had not the inexorable secretary knocked upon the door at that very moment. The summons brought him to "attention," as the call of a sergeant to the new recruit.

"Time is unkind to us," he said. "I must go down to Throgmorton Street to make a hundred thousand dollars. Well, we shall meet again in Paris or Berlin. A thousand dollars for your I.A.L. if we don't. Remember me to your father, please. Is he likely to accept that call to Yonkers, by the way?"

"I don't know," she said quite simply; "he is so ignorant about American money."

John Faber smiled at that. Gabrielle went down the Strand blushing furiously, and wondering why she had said anything at once so honest and so foolish.

CHAPTER III
BETWEEN HEAVEN AND EARTH

I

Clad in an alpaca coat, which had long since lost its lining, and in carpet slippers very much too large for him, Gordon Silvester awaited his daughter's return to the house in Well Walk. The luncheon bell had rung a second time, and God alone knew what was in the mind of Agatha, the cook. Silvester feared this woman greatly, especially in those frequently recurring seasons when her madness ran to taking the pledge.

It was a quarter past two when Gabrielle returned, and they should have lunched at half-past one. The minister's anxiety was above all meats, and in his curiosity to know what had happened he forgot the sainted martyr below stairs.

"Well, is he willing, my dear?"

Gabrielle drew a chair to the table; she carried a couple of letters in her hand, and glanced at their envelopes while she spoke.

"Oh, my dear father, it was quite hopeless."

Silvester sighed, and took up his knife and fork. It was a terrible descent from the millennium to mutton; but, after all, he ate but to live.

"I feared it would be so. Well, we have done our best, and that is something. Did he give you any reasons?"

"One tremendous reason—he calls it human nature."

Silvester helped her to a fair cut and himself to two. He was already eating when he took up the subject again.

"This movement will be stronger than his argument," he said. "What people call human nature is often little more than the animal instinct. I can conceive no nobler mission for any man. We cannot expect this particular class of man to see eye to eye with us."

"There was never any chance of it, father. He believes that war is the will of God, and he does not hesitate to say so."

"Would he have us to believe that typhoid fever is the will of God—or smallpox? We are stamping those out. Why not the greater plague?"

Gabrielle sighed.

"I wish you had been there to argue with him, father. A girl is at such a disadvantage."

"Naturally, with such a man. I don't suppose John Faber ever knew one really human weakness since he was a child. Did he say anything about me, by the way?"

"He mentioned you several times. I told him about the call to Yonkers."

The minister's eyes sparkled.

"That is a subject I would gladly take his advice upon. What did he say about it?"

"Very little, I think."

"Was it favourable to my going?"

"I don't think he expressed an opinion either way."

"It would have been a great help to me had he done so. Sometimes I feel that I have a great work to do in America. This Peace Movement is the finest thing in the story of the whole world. Christ Himself has taught us no more beautiful idea—His own, as we must admit. There is a true sentiment in America; but a pretence of it here, I fear."

"Are you quite sure of that, father?"

"Of what, my dear?"

"Of the true sentiment in America. Mr. Faber said on the ship that he hoped to sell five hundred thousand rifles for Mexico before the trouble was over. Is that a true sentiment?"

"I believe it very foreign to the real wishes of the American people."

"He doesn't; neither do the Germans. They say all this talk of arbitration is so much humbug to prevent us adding to our navy, and to allow President Taft to occupy Mexico."

"That is in the yellow press, my dear; you should not listen to it."

"Anyway, Sir Jules Achon thinks it true. May I read Eva's letter? I expect she reminds me of my promise to go there to-day."

"You know that we have a meeting of the Girls' Friendly Committee to-night?"

"Oh, father, can't they do without me for once? I don't often stay away."

He helped himself to an apple tart, and made no reply. Gabrielle read her letter, and her cheeks flamed with excitement.

"What do you think?" she said. "Sir Jules is going on his yacht to Corfu, and he wishes me to go with them."

"To go upon his yacht!" The astonishment was very natural. "That is very kind of him."

"Douglas Renshaw is going, and Dr. Burrall. Eva says they will call at Lisbon and Gibraltar, and perhaps at Genoa. What a splendid trip!"

Her eyes were very bright with the vision, and her lips parted in excitement. Not only was this a respite from the monotonous days, but a respite which she would consider regal. She was going upon a pilgrimage into the old world as she had gone into the new. And with the promise there flashed upon her mind a memory of John Faber's wager. He would meet her in Paris or Berlin!

"It is indeed a very remarkable opportunity," said her father presently. "Sir Jules Achon is a greater man than your American. He has more ballast, and quite as much money."

"And he has not come to Europe to marry an English woman."

The minister looked at her covertly. A secret thought which had sent her to the Savoy Hotel whispered an accusation in his ear, and found him guilty. He would have given much to know just what passed between Gabrielle and John Faber. Perhaps he saw also that his daughter had never looked so well. Undoubtedly she was a beautiful woman.

"Yes," he said at last; "I don't think Sir Jules will marry. You must accept this invitation, Gabrielle."

"But what am I to do for frocks?"

"Can't you wear those you took to America?"

"My dear father, they were mostly summer dresses."

"Well, Corfu is a summer resort. I forget what the winter temperature is—something abnormal. Unfortunately, they have just opened a gambling saloon there. Wherever nature is most beautiful, there men turn their backs upon her."

"Sir Jules is hardly likely to do that. He is going to Corfu to try to meet the German Emperor. You know he has a great idea—the Federation of Europe. He says that commerce is the only key to the peace of the world."

"A faith rather in the Jews than the Divine gospels."

"Oh! I think not—a faith in good common sense, father."

Silvester shook his head.

"He will not associate himself with us," he said, a little sadly. And then, "They tell me he is a very rich man."

"Just the reason why I must have some frocks if I go to Corfu."

II

She was not to leave for Richmond until the end of the week, and when lunch was over she was reminded of Harry Lassett's promise by the advent of that boisterous sportsman and his expressed determination to take her at once to the Vale of Health pond, where the ice was "top-notch." There Gabrielle found herself amid a knot of very suburban but friendly people, whose noisy cordiality forced her to remember that this rather than the other was her true sphere.

Harry Lassett had been down to St. James's Street to get her skates, and they fitted her to perfection. The scene was inspiriting and full of colour. All about them lay the whitened heath; London beneath a veil of sunlit fog in the hollow. So keen was the splendid air that every nerve reverberated at its breath. Such frost had not been known in England since oxen were roasted whole upon the Thames in the early days of the nineteenth century.

She was a good skater, and had often accompanied Eva Achon to Princes during the previous season. Harry Lassett waltzed divinely, and while waltzing upon boards was anathema to Gordon Silvester, waltzing upon the ice seemed to him a harmless diversion. He even came down to the brink of the pond and watched the merry throng at play; but that was before dusk fell and the great bonfire was lighted, and those who had merely clasped hands discovered that a more binding link was necessary. Silvester saw nothing of the outrageous flirtations. He would have been sadly distressed had he known that Gabrielle herself was among the number of the sinners. She was, in fact, one of the ringleaders.

Why should she not have been? What pages of her life written in the dark room of a shabby parsonage forbade that freshet of a young girl's spirit, here gushing from the wells of convention which so long had preserved it? Silvester, all said and done, was just a successful Congregational minister. His sincerity and natural gifts of eloquence had pushed him into the first rank of well-advertised special pleaders. By this cause and that, the doors had been opened to him; and with him went Gabrielle to the ethical fray. If her heart remained with those whom the world would have called "her equals," she was but obeying the fundamental laws of human nature. Millionaires and their palaces; my lord this and my lord that, thrust into the chair of a cause for which they did not care a snap of the fingers—what had Silvester's house in common with them? Reason answered nothing; he himself would never have put the question.

So here was Gabrielle like a child let out of school. The long afternoon found her pirouetting with Harry Lassett, or with other disorderly young men of a like nature; the swift night discovered her in a sentimental mood, with all thought of multi-millionaires gone away to the twinkling stars. A brass band had begun to play by that time, and a man was selling baked chestnuts. A pretty contrast that to the Savoy Hotel.

Their talk had been chiefly ejaculatory during the afternoon, but the twilight found them mellowing. Harry still harped upon America, and with some disdain; and now, at length, his contempt found expression.

"Did you see that American chap all right?" he asked her in an interval of the riot.

She admitted the guilt of it.

"Do you mean Mr. Faber?"

"The fellow you met on the ship—Apollo and the liar; the man who talked about eleven millions sterling."

"Yes, I saw him. How did you know I was going?"

"Oh! I was in the Savoy myself this morning. I'm thinking of buying the place."

"Then you propose to settle down?"

"Or settle up. What did you want from the Stars and Stripes this morning, Gabrielle?"

"An impertinent question. Why should I tell you? Why do you want to know?"

"Because I have the right to know."

"The right, Harry—the right!"

They were over at the eastern corner of the pond, shadows sheltering them. Harry Lassett's "six foot one" towered above her five feet five, and made a woman of her. He had the round, "apple" face of a boy of twenty-four, vast shoulders, limbs of iron. His eyes were clear and lustrous, and his hair jet black. There was every quality which makes a quick, physical appeal to the other sex, and now, perhaps not for the first time, Gabrielle became acutely conscious of it. This was something totally apart from schemes for the world's good; something with which millionaires, were they British or American, had no concern whatever. Ten years of a boy and girl friendship culminated here. She tried to withdraw her fingers from Harry's grasp, but could not release herself; his breath was hot upon her forehead; she quivered at his touch, and then stood very still.

"Why have I not got the right? Who has if I haven't?"

"The right to what?"

"To warn Apollo off. Gabrielle, I'm in love with you—you know it."

She looked up; his eyes devoured her.

"What is the good of our being in love?"

"You don't mean to say you are thinking of the beastly money?"

"Harry!"

"Well, then, don't ask me. I've three hundred a year, and I'm going with Barlean in Throgmorton Street when the cricket season's over. That's a half-commission job, and my cricketing friends will rally round. If I tour Australia next year, they'll pay my expenses, and I'll make them pretty hot. We could be married when I come back, Gabrielle."

She laughed, and half turned her head.

"It's quite like a fairy story. And so mercenary! It's just like a business deal."

"Well, your father will ask for a balance sheet, and there it is—totted up by 'Why not' and audited by 'Expectation.' Why don't you say something about it?"

"Do you want me to say that you will always be my best friend?"

"*Family Reading*—go on. Love and respect and esteem. I'm d—d if I stand it. This is what I think."

He slipped his arms about her, and kissed her hotly upon the lips. She had never been kissed by a man before, and the swift assault found her without argument. She was conscious in a vague way that prudence should have made an end of all this upon the spot. Yet there was a physical magnetism before which she was powerless; an instantaneous revelation of life in its fuller meaning, of a sentiment which had nothing to do with prudence.

"Harry!" she cried, and that was all.

"Gabrielle, you love me—I feel that you do when you are near me."

"How foolish it all is—how mad!"

"I won't have that rot. Why, you are part of my life, Gabrielle."

"Of course, we are very old friends—"

"If you say any word like that I will take you out into the very centre of the pond and kiss you there. Come along and skate now. I feel quite mad."

He caught her in his arms, and they went whirling away. The red-nosed man with the cornet played the "Merry Widow" until his whole body swelled; there were harsh tones of cockneyism, silver laughter of boys and girls, the whirr of good skates cutting the ice. And above all a clear, starless heaven, such as London had not known for many a year.

"How long will you be away with these Achon people, Gabrielle?"

"I don't know; we are going to Corfu to see the German Emperor."

"Don't bring him back with you. He'd never get on with fools. Isn't it all rather out of the picture?"

"What do you mean by that, Harry?"

"Well, your trotting about with millionaires, hanging on to the skirts of other people's ambitions. It can't last. Some day soon, these doors will be shut. There'll be nobody at home when you call."

"That would not trouble me. I go because my father wishes it; and, of course, I like Eva."

"She's rather a jolly girl, isn't she? They're a different class to that Faber man. He's just an adventurer."

"Who has managed to make himself necessary to two continents. I wish you knew him. You'd be the first to bow down."

"To eleven millions! I might if he handed over one of them. That must be the fly in his ointment. I don't suppose he has a friend in the world who doesn't want to get something out of him."

"Do you include me in that category?"

"Well, you wanted his name. I knew he'd laugh at all that peace rot. It's the greatest humbug of the twentieth century, and I admire the German Emperor for his courage. He and Kitchener are the two greatest men in the world to-day. Now, don't you think so?"

"I don't think anything of the kind. If there is any one conviction in my life that is sincere it is this. You know it, Harry."

She was very earnest, and he would not wound her. Gabrielle Silvester could dream dreams, and some of them would put great intellects to shame. Harry knew this and admired her in the mood; he altered his own course at once.

"Of course I know it. But tell me, what did Faber say?"

"Oh, very little—he spoke about the frost."

"Wants to skate with you, eh?"

"I think not. He is full of bogies. The English Channel and the North Sea are to be frozen over."

"Great idea that. We shall skate all the way to Paris! Dine at the Ritz and curl afterwards. What a man!"

"No, really—what he fears is a panic in England if the sea should really freeze."

Harry thought about it for some minutes in silence. Presently he said:

"I don't believe it could happen. He was chaffing you."

"I think he was."

"But if it did happen—by gad! what a funk some people would be in!"

"The valiant people—who believe in war in the abstract."

"Now you're ironical, Gabrielle."

"No," she said; "I'm only hungry."

III

It was very dark in Well Walk when they arrived before her father's house.

Harry had fallen to a sentimental mood, and would talk about their future just as though it had all been settled in the beginning of things, and was as unalterable as the course of the planets. She began to think that his love for her was very real, and not a mere ebullition of a boyish sentiment. Long years of her childhood seemed to be lived again as he put his arm about her and told her of his happiness.

"You knew it all the time, Gabrielle. You never had any doubt about it. Of course, I loved you. Tell me so yourself. Let me see it in your eyes."

She laughed, and told him, as the situation seemed to require, not to be foolish.

"Father will be waiting for me. What shall I say to him?"

"That I am going to marry you directly I return from the Australian tour."

"Why frighten him prematurely? There are thousands of pretty girls in Australia."

"That's beastly of you. Deny it, or I will kiss you again."

"Oh, Harry, my cheeks will be so red."

"Say it's the frost. I must kiss you, Gabrielle. There—little cat! Why do you wrestle with me?"

"Because I feel that we are just two children playing."

"But you'll never play with any other child—swear that to me, Gabrielle."

"My dear Harry, that would be the most childish thing of all. Now, you must say good-night, I hear my father."

He held her for an instant in his arms, and she trembled. When at length he strode off in his masterful and imperious way, her father stood in the porch and called her. He had seen nothing of this curiously "worldly" scene, and was full of a letter he had just received from the Archbishop of Canterbury. This invited him to a Conference at the Mansion House, and he pointed out with satisfaction that it had been written at the archiepiscopal palace at Lambeth.

"This movement may not bring all the nations in, or make them dwell together in harmony and peace, he said, "but it will certainly bring peace to the churches. Of course, they will ask me to speak, Gabrielle."

"When is it for, father?" she asked him.

"In ten days' time—at the Mansion House."

"You will have to get a typewriter; I shall be at Richmond."

"I think it is better. I should not like Sir Jules or Mr. Faber to know that you do such work, Gabrielle."

"Oh," she said with a light laugh, "I don't think they would be shocked, father. They are both self-made men."

"Yes, but self-made men rarely like self-made women. It's the way of the world. If we go to America—"

"But you do not intend to accept the call from Yonkers, father?"

He shook his head.

"A man might do a great work over there. My imagination is sorely tempted. I am altogether at a loss."

She was too tired to take up the ancient arguments which this threadbare question had provoked. Later on, in her own bedroom, she sat before a brisk fire, and tried to take stock of the varied events of that busy day.

Vaguely out of the mists there emerged the truth, that two men had made love to her, and that one was a man who might presently rule the Western world. She could look down a vista of fable land to a future surpassing all expectations of her dreams, and believe that at a word she might enter in. The obverse of the medal was Harry Lassett and the story of her youth. This lad had crept into the secret places of her heart. She still trembled at a memory of his kisses. With him, life would be meticulous—a villa and a trim maidservant. His scheme of things could embrace no great idea; and yet he, too, was a popular hero, and great throngs would go to Lords to see him play. Gabrielle knew that she loved him; but she doubted if her love would prove as strong as the dreams.

It was midnight when she undressed.

The weather had turned much warmer. She opened her window to discover that it was snowing, and that the snow melted as it fell.

The fables were already discredited. It seemed almost an omen.

CHAPTER IV
THE BEGINNING OF THE ODYSSEY

I

Bertie Morris was a very fair type of the American journalist, whose body goes to Paris while he lives, whatever may happen to his soul at a later period.

Thirty-one years of age, he knew the world backwards; was as much at home in Port Said as in Philadelphia; wrote as though kings were his boon companions and had settled the hash of more than one intrepid lady with polyandric tendencies. The product is purely twentieth century, and frequently has flaxen hair. Bertie was becoming bald in the services of the *New York Mitre*. He was blessed with a proprietor who would have drawn blood out of a stone and then complained of its quality.

When John Faber left London, he went straight through to Paris, and there chose Bertie Morris for his guide. This young man had specialised in the Franco-German war, and knew the whole story of the Paris Commune intimately. Fired by the splendid opportunity of hob-nobbing with one of the richest men in the world (and of eating his dinners), Bertie set out gaily upon his fortunate pilgrimage. He had hired an old soldier, by name Picard, who had served under General d'Arny when that worthy shot down the revolutionaries as though they had been French partridges; and with this fellow for a guide, he and John Faber set off for Belleville and Vincennes.

Bertie's vocabulary, it should be said, was chiefly exclamatory when he was not translating. He was a fluent Frenchman, and had an uncommonly sound knowledge of his subject. Listening to him in more restrained moods, Faber lived again those bloody days which had cost his father his life, and indirectly had established his own fortune. All the ferocity, the savage brutality, the hopeless idealism of the Commune came to be understood by him. Here had the trade by which he lived prospered greatly. It had dyed those stones with blood some forty years ago.

"Say, shall we begin with Belleville or the Bois?" Morris had asked him. He thought that it would be best to work round the city to his father's old house near the Jardin du Luxembourg. But first he had a question to put.

"What I want to know is this," he asked: "How did it all begin? What set a handful of red republicans trying to fight a country? It's a big thing to have done, anyway. What put it into their heads?"

Bertie Morris liked the subject, and entered upon it with true American zest.

"Why," he said, "war was at the back of it. You've seen the same thing in Russia. Peace keeps the lid on the pot of revolution; war spills the stew. There were just two or three hundred thousand descendants of the old Jacobins in Paris, and when Napoleon III. was sent into Germany, they made up their minds to keep him there. Directly peace with Germany was signed, all the wild men came out. You had every kind of crank and others. There were big men and little, dreamers and red devils; they meant to govern Paris on the 'help yourself' plan, and they didn't begin so badly. But for Thiers and a few million sane folk behind him, I don't doubt they would have enjoyed themselves finely. As it was, what they divided were bayonets, and there were plenty to go round."

He rattled on, appealing often to the old soldier Picard and proud of his staccato knowledge. Faber listened with interest but said very little. He was trying, while they drove through the narrow streets to Père la Chaise, to realise what this Paris had been when his father lived and worked in it during the fateful years before the war of 1870. The first John Faber also had been something of a republican; had dreamed dreams of the millennium and of the rights of the proletariat. And the French had dragged him out and shot him for his pains. He had died protesting that he was an American citizen.

A big Mercédès car carried the pilgrims upon this journey, and its welcome in the black streets of Belleville was not blandly enthusiastic. Blue blouses at the doors of the wine shops spat upon the pavement and cursed the bourgeoisie; coarse women with skirts hanging about them like rags laughed brutalities and flung indecencies after them. There were pale-faced Apaches and white and callous children. It was inevitable that these should suggest their forbears of 1870, and even the old soldier remarked the fact:

"They would burn Paris again to-morrow, messieurs—as I have seen it burned already. Ah! the terrible days!"

He tried to give them a picture of the fateful week—the last of the month of May and of the Commune. The Communards had been driven into the eastern labyrinth of the city then, he said, and in the anger of defeat had sent their women forth to burn this Paris which could not defend them. Since Nero fiddled, no such spectacle had been seen in Europe. The old man told them the story with eyes uplifted and hands clenched. He had become as a child, and these were the scenes of his youth.

"It was on the Tuesday night that they burned the palace of the Tuileries," he said. "The women went out with naphtha; I saw them running like devils through the streets and crying to one another to fire the houses. The day before that, the Hôtel de Ville flamed up. They say it was an accident, but—God knows. The 'Council of State,' the Bank, the Bourse, the Church of St. Eustache, all were burned those terrible days. There was one bank of the river a wall of fire on the Wednesday night; a man could have read his paper at Passy. It was as light as day, they told me, in the park at Versailles. All the streets were full of wild, screaming people; but if you went a little way toward the Bois you heard the cannon, you stumbled over the dead. What a butchery was that, messieurs! God help those who went out of their houses to see what the soldiers were doing! Ladmirault, Galifet, Vinot, Cissey—those were the names of the generals. They held their courts under the trees, in the cafés, at the street corners. It was sufficient to have worn a blouse, to be sorry for the dead, to express displeasure at what was being done—away went such a man or woman to the nearest wall. We are now coming to the Rue Lafayette. I was in this very street when my company seized the Communard, Varlin, and dragged him up to the Buttes Montmartre. They tied his hands behind his back and cut his face with their sabres while he walked. It was a horrible thing to see, messieurs! When he could no longer walk, they carried him until someone thought it time to kill him with the butt end of a musket. They say he was the cleverest member of the Commune—I do not know; I was only of the infantry of the line, and their politics did not concern me."

Faber listened to all this with the interest of a man who is obsessed by one dominating idea. This Commune had been the first attempt in modern times to set up the socialism of Marx—and in what had it ended? In a deluge of blood, and the derision of all sane people. He wondered what would have been the modern story of Paris if Félix Pyat and his fellows had been stronger than Thiers and the Versaillese. A consummate knowledge of modern politics reminded him that the blue blouses of France were still socialistic to the core, and that individualism sat upon a throne of straw. He had often thought that such fortunes as his own would never be made by generations to come; but that concerned him little, for he had no children. The reflection brought an image of Gabrielle Silvester to his mind. It was odd that he should think of her while the old soldier related these bloody scenes.

Bertie Morris, on the other hand, enjoyed himself immensely. He drove his tame millionaire as far up the Butte as he could, and even took him to the Rue Lepic and the Moulin de la Galette. He was a prize to be shown to artists and authors, poor devils who would dine that night for fifty sous and sell their masterpieces for as many to-morrow. This pilgrimage of the ateliers was not unwelcome to Faber, and was made at his own request.

"I want to hear of a man," he said, "Louis de Paleologue is his name."

"Where do you think he hides up?" Bertie asked.

Faber said that he had no idea.

"He was drawing for Gavarnie some forty years ago. I've never heard of him since, and I wasn't born then."

"Say, that's simple. Has he any grandfathers alive?"

"It's a fine story," was the quiet response. "I only learned it a year or two back, when I found some of my mother's papers. Louis de Paleologue was the man who took her over to America when General d'Arny shot my father. There was a pile of correspondence between them, and it does the man great credit. If I find him living I'll give him a million dollars, if he'll take them."

Bertie Morris whistled.

"You don't suggest a preliminary canter. Why not try it on the dog? He's willing."

"Most dogs are. My world is all barking. You find Paleologue for me, and see what Father Christmas puts in your stocking. He's the only man in Europe I ever did want to see outside my own business. It's natural that I can't find him."

"Can you tell me anything about him? Where did he live? What was he? For whom did he work? I'm right out for this, Mr. Faber."

Faber smiled.

"He was an artist who drew small pictures with a large genius. They say he worked for Hachette. The last letters speaks of his marriage—it must have been written many years ago. I cabled to Paris when it came into my hands, and the answer back from your office was that he had gone to the East. That means Paleologue was a Roumanian, and he's gone home. I suppose I shall have to follow him."

"It would be a bully trip, anyway. Why not do the Balkans in a motor? There was a chap here last month who had just come back. They didn't shoot him this time."

"Well, I guess they won't shoot me, either. I'm buying a yacht directly. Now, let's go and lunch. Your young Raphaels are rather greasy. I think I'd like to wash."

II

They lunched near the Bourse, in a flaring café whither the jobbers resorted. There were a few conspicuous women of the company, loudly dressed and aggressive in the true spirit of their commercial patrons. These liked neither English nor Americans, and said so by face and gesture. The jobbers themselves looked a gloomy troop, though whether depressed by their hopes of gain or surety of loss it would have been difficult to say. Had they known that John Sebastian Faber sat cheek by jowl with them, it would have been another story. How many a time had he, from his distant office in New York, set that same market hoarse with excitement, filled the streets with bawling madmen, and put ropes of pearls about the necks of the cocottes who now made inelegant grimaces at him when the clients had their backs turned. He thought of it with some pleasure over a *sole meringue*. They would have been down upon him like a pack of wolves had they known him.

Bertie Morris enjoyed his *déjeuner* with the satisfaction of a man who knows he is not paying for it. He had a programme for the afternoon, which was to be capped by a dinner at the Ritz Hotel, also at Faber's expense. It never occurred to him that he was not putting his companion under a large obligation, and the whole tone of his talk was autocratic, as one who should say, "I open all doors."

"We'll trot out to the Avenue de Nancy and see where the Versaillese came in," he put it cheerfully. "It was on a Sunday, Picard tells me, and the fraternity lot got a few shells for breakfast. They had just made up their minds that the millennium had come, when Vinot and Ladmirault turned up with the cannon. They had a good deal in common afterwards—chiefly explosive. I'll show you a house at Passy with a shell in the wall over the front door. The owner won't have it touched. It's right there, just where the Versaillese put it."

"A kind of keepsake. Do they remember anything about all this in Paris nowadays?"

"On the first of May, before they get drunk. I don't think it comes up at any other time. The century isn't interested overmuch in yesterday. It's all 'to-morrow' nowadays."

"I don't know that I quarrel with that. Half the people would commit suicide if it wasn't for to-morrow. We're a sort of recurring decimal, but we don't believe it."

"Say, then you don't believe overmuch in the 'destiny' department?"

"I do not. A few things are going on all the time—very few. The civilization of Babylon was pretty much the civilization of Rome; while Rome wasn't so very different from ourselves. There's a little levelling of the classes; but there's no longer a goal, either in heaven or hell. That means a soulless people."

"But it marches all the same."

"Where science leads it. There's the only clear thinking. What's the good of talking when men don't know why they're here, or what they are? When they had heaven and hell, they thought clearly enough. Your new gospel leads them into a morass. It couldn't very well lead them anywhere else. The things that go on evolve as we ourselves have evolved. All the politicians, parliaments, philosophers don't help them a jot. They were saying the same thing on the top of monoliths before the flood. We are driven—but we don't know why or whither unless we believe, as all but the fools have believed, by Almighty God."

Bertie Morris helped himself to an orange salad.

"Say, why don't you write all this?"

"Because I've something better to do. My business is to make guns and to sell 'em."

The journalist pricked up his ears.

"There was some talk of a big contract of yours going through here. Is that right?"

"Ah! you'd pay something to know—and a good many more. Did they couple d'Arny to the talk?"

"Well, it's chiefly up to him. He's a lot of backers up against him in the Chambers. Jaurés says he's corrupt."

"He'd have to be in his job. We're all corrupt, for that matter. I believe that Walpole's right. I'd buy any man body and soul for a price."

"And women too—I don't think."

Faber laughed.

"No money is too much for a good woman," he said.

III

They followed the programme afterwards, driving right round the Bois and returning to the Jardin du Luxembourg.

The day had fallen bitterly cold again, and a light snow whitened the trees in the famous avenues. Paris took a romantic mantle and covered her pretty shoulders daintily. Habitués fled to the cafés and ensconced themselves in warm corners; fur-clad women sank deep in the cushions of their motors; there were ridiculously dressed children scampering about the Bois and crying, *"Dieu, comme il fait froid"*—a fairy-like scene quite characteristic of a city which is rarely serious, and then tragically so. Through this Faber passed to his father's house. He had become silent and preoccupied—a man of few emotions, but of one which had never been absent from his life.

His father! How often he had tried to create the living man from the insufficient pictures of that time!

They had told him that John Faber was tall and Saxon haired—a cheery, business-like, unobtrusive fellow, very generous, far-seeing beyond his epoch. He had founded the house of Faber at Charleston, and had come over to Europe to learn Eastern methods. He was in Paris for the purpose of studying the new French artillery when the war broke out, and had lived for three months there, in the little house overlooking the gardens of the Luxembourg. Such was the man whom General d'Arny had shot in that very street, swearing he was of the Communards. A fever of anger fell suddenly upon the son as he remembered his mother's story. Good God, his own father! What years of affection they would have spent together but for that mad ferocity of the Commune! How the one would have helped the other! And the fortune—he would have poured it into his father's lap and waited for his words of pride. His father—shot there in that silent street—the man whom his mother had loved as woman rarely has loved in the human story.

He left the car at the corner by the Catholic Institute and walked down the Rue d'Assas to its junction with the Rue de Fleurus. Naturally, the condition of things had altered very much, and there were many new buildings in the vicinity. He discovered certain landmarks, but others had vanished into the limbo of the municipal gods and trim modern "blocks" had taken their places. For all that, he believed that he could identify the actual house in which these things had happened, and when he had located it, he knocked upon the door, and was answered by a trim old woman, who seemed much put out at the occurrence. Bertie Morris was quite equal to such an occasion. "Give her five francs," he said. It was done immediately.

"Who lives here now, madame?"

"Monsieur Brocas, the advocate—for many years, he and his mother."

"Is he at home?"

"He is at Lyons, m'sieur."

"And madame?"

"She is in the south."

"This gentleman with me is an American. His father and mother lived here forty years ago—before the war. Naturally, he would very much like to see the house."

"What is his name, m'sieur?"

Faber told her himself, and the tone of his voice seemed to awaken memories. She began to mumble something in the argot of the "Boul. Mich," and then bade him come in. The room clearly belonged to people who were fond of books when at home, and neglectful of them when away. It was all very untidy and dusty; the furniture handsome, but shown to poor advantage. The very first thing Faber set his hand upon was a volume of Hawthorne's "House of the Seven Gables." His father's name was written beneath an English book-plate.

"Tell her," he said to Morris, "that this was once my father's property."

She did not seem at all interested, but she avoided their glances nevertheless, and seemed strangely afraid of them.

"You understand?" said Faber at last. "My father's book."

She nodded and answered him, to his surprise, in broken but comprehensible English.

"I was your mother's servant three years, m'sieur—a very little child. I am nearly sixty years old, but my memory is good."

"You remember my father, then?"

"If I remember him! Do children forget such things?"

"Were you here when he died, madame?"

She clasped her hands together almost as one in prayer. Her voice was a sing-song, like that of a child reciting a learned lesson.

"It was at nine o'clock on the Friday night. Ah! what a day, m'sieur! There had been cannon since the Sunday, and the streets full of mad people. I looked down from my window and saw the dead carried away. I was cold with a child's curiosity. When night came, m'sieur would not dine. He had been out all day helping the wounded, and all he would take was a little soup and wine. Then he went out again while madame and I were up in the front room watching the fires burn and listening to the cannon. M'sieur, the heavens opened that night! My soul shrank at the sight; I thought the end of the world had come. And I was but a child, and had lived such a little while."

She paused and breathed almost convulsively, as though suffering the terrible hours again. Faber watched her without flinching. His swift imagination moved out there in the streets where his father worked amid the wounded.

"And afterwards, madame—afterwards?" said Bertie Morris in French.

She looked up at him almost angrily, the thread of the inspiration of memory broken.

"It is so many years ago, m'sieur. I remember badly."

Faber stepped across the room and laid his hand upon her arm.

"How did my father die, madame? Remember, I am his son."

"So very like him, m'sieur; he seems to stand beside me once more."

"You remember the night—you cannot have forgotten it?"

"No, no; it is all here. The heart knows, but the tongue will not speak."

"Did you see him when they brought him in?"

She quivered, as though the scene had been yester-night.

"M'sieur, it passed so swiftly—death came to him while he walked. I saw Captain d'Arny upon a white horse—I heard m'sieur's voice—how well I knew it! Then someone spoke in anger, a rifle was fired, madame ran from me, her tears choking her so that she could not speak to me. They brought monsieur in and laid him on the sofa; your hand is touching it now. I remember that his hand was in madame's, his eyes hurt by the bright light of the chandelier. He begged for a little wine and I went to the buffet; my hand shook, and I could not open the bottle. When we had found a glass m'sieur was dead. How shall I tell you more?—m'sieur was dead."

Her voice died down almost to a whisper; none of the others spoke for some minutes. It was still snowing, and a black cloud was over the city. Faber thought that it must have been just such a day when the Versaillese, drunk with victory, entered the Rue de Fleurus and found his father there.

Some of them still lived and remembered the night. General d'Arny was such a one, and they were to meet to-morrow.

IV

At the Ritz Hotel a few hours later, Bertie Morris studied a fine company with a critic's eye. He knew most of the people in the famous *salle à manger*, and put himself up several pegs on the strength of his knowledge.

"Say, there are some glad frocks—what?"

Faber, who had a little bundle of papers in his hand, looked round and about for the first time. "All friends of yours?" he asked slyly.

Bertie showed a row of gold-rimmed teeth.

"Know most of them. Newspaper people must. That's young Mrs. Vanderbilt; the Countess Sobenski's next to her. Of course, you recognize Steel—and the Great Man. He's as good as he's great—a hundred and forty papers and more than one Cabinet Minister pretty fond of him. Beyond him is Sir Charles. Did you ever hear him speak? About the best hindleg man they've got over yonder. Oughtn't to have been an actor—he'd have run Canterbury better. Who the next lot are, can't say. The flaxen-haired one is a d—d fine girl—I don't think. Wonder who she is?"

Faber smiled. "She's a parson's daughter—no good to you. There's Sir Jules Achon and his daughter, but who the little girl in black may be, I don't know; she looks like a French girl."

"I'll ask Ellis; he's a 'Who's Who' here. Fine chap, Ellis, ought to have got the K.G.G. when he was in London."

"What's the K.G.G. anyway?"

"The Knight of the Grand Gorge—two pots crossed and a tumbler rampant. Puts Pommery in your thoughts. Suppose we do?"

Faber gave the order and the wine was served. Accustomed to the immense hotels of New York, he found the Ritz interesting chiefly by reason of its guests. The women were magnificently gowned, and many of them very pretty. Such a cosmopolitan company could hardly be found in any other hotel on the Continent; its united wealth would have financed a kingdom. Faber reflected with satisfaction that he had the right to be there. His brains had earned him the title.

"About this parson's daughter," Bertie asked; "what's she doing in such a place as this?" He had grown curious, for Gabrielle Silvester was quite the most beautiful woman in the room.

"She appears to be eating at present."

"Yes, I know; but who are her friends?"

"The man is Sir Jules Achon. He's a big man—those who come after will hear of him. Have you read nothing of the Federation of Europe?"

"Not as much as the top dot of a semicolon. Who's going to federate?"

"It's his own idea. Kill war by commerce—you can't kill it any other way. Europe's paying ten per cent taxation as against America for her armies and navies. Make one federated state with no commercial barriers, and you knock the ten per cent down to two. That's Sir Jules's notion."

"You don't think there's anything in it?"

"So much that if I was British born, I'd give him a headline in dollars which would set the town talking. There's everything in it except the men. He's got the German Emperor, and he'll get the Tsar. It's the smaller fry who don't listen."

Bertie smiled.

"Your Venus with the tow-coloured topknot seems to be in that boat. She's looking at you all the time."

"Do you quarrel with her taste?"

"No; but you know her pretty well, then?"

"An impertinent question. She came over on the ship with me."

"And wants to go back the same way—eh, what? Well, I'd like to interview Sir Jules anyway. There ought to be a column story in him."

"Yes, he ought to be worth fifty dollars."

"Did you say he'd got the German Emperor?"

"I understand that's so; he's going down to Corfu to see him again. He'll get the thing through if I don't upset it."

"Why should you upset it?"

"Rattle up your brains and see the reason. I'm here to sell guns. While that man is dangling about an anteroom, kow-towing to menials, I shall be inside with the chief. It's common sense. I'm here to do business—he's here to prevent that kind of business being done."

"Is he going to take the peerless Saxon with him?"

"You seem rather hot on that scent."

"A d—d fine woman! Look at her arms! She's got a style you don't often find among Englishwomen. I can't see her feet."

"Ask the waiter to take away the table."

"I'll bet she takes fives. Her eyes are of the 'get there' sort. Can't you feel her looking this way?"

"I'm not conscious of any rise of temperature. If you've done looking, perhaps we'll smoke. They'll be coming out immediately."

"Then you'll introduce me?"

"Ah! I didn't say that. Is it brandy or Kümmel?"

"Oh, brandy—if you've got to talk to women."

They passed out into the corridor, and sat there near the band. The place was deliciously warm; it glowed with soft lights, and was redolent of the odours of flowers. Superbly dressed women rustled by them; men, who had dined well, lurched past with their hands in their pockets and cigarettes in their mouths. The Hungarians played one of Lehar's waltzes—a scene of colour and of life reflecting the holy of social holies and of the almighty dollar. Presently Sir Jules Achon came out, followed by the three girls. Now, Faber recognised the third. She was Claudine d'Arny, General d'Arny's daughter.

The party was almost gone by before Gabrielle discovered him. She turned at once and held out her gloved hand.

"The wager," she said, looking at him very earnestly; "I appear to have lost."

"Well, there's nothing to pay anyway. Are you going through to the yacht?"

"Yes, to Naples. Sir Jules wishes me to see Italy and then the Adriatic."

"Full of pirates and wild men," said Eva Achon, who was by Gabrielle's side. "We shall all be carried away to a cave."

"I didn't know they had so much taste. How do you do, Sir Jules?"

Sir Jules was a little man with a wonderful head. He was sixty-four years old, but had the intellectual energy of a man of twenty. The East and the West were strangely blended in a countenance full of power and quiet dignity. A softer voice Faber had never heard.

"Very well, Mr. Faber. And you?"

"Always well—on paper. You are going through to Italy, I hear—you'll catch the Emperor, I think."

"I hope so. The promises encourage me."

"But the performances will be better. Any old fool of a minister can promise; it is a king who performs."

"You have read my pamphlet, Mr. Faber?"

"Every line—the greatest peace scheme—I was going to say, on earth. I'll change that: Out of heaven's nearer it!"

"Of course, it must come slowly, if it comes."

"All the best things come slowly. Man was about a million years about before he thought of microbes—this is a great affair; none greater. It would be the coup of the century if you brought it off. There could be nothing greater."

"I hope to do so. Are you staying here long?"

"As many hours as it will take me to teach a man my name. I may be at Corfu myself afterwards. I'm imitating you, and buying a yacht."

"The one luxury in the world—get a good one."

"There won't be any better when I begin."

The group passed on; Faber shook hands with Eva, but not with Claudine d'Arny. When Gabrielle's turn came, he held her hand in his for a brief instant and said:

"Well, how's the I.A.L.?"

"Waiting for your name," she replied. But she did not withdraw her hand.

"Will you give me the top of the bill?"

"In gold and purple."

"And printed on fine linen? Well, I'm not tempted."

"The day will come—"

He laughed and dropped her hand.

"That's Booth, the actor. Well, most of you are play-acting, anyway. Good-night, Miss Silvester, don't forget what I say."

She laughed and spoke in a lower tone.

"I will remind you of it at Corfu," she said.

The men watched them down the corridor before Bertie Morris became eloquent. He was not a little piqued that the girls had ignored him, while even Sir Jules had regarded him as one regards an ugly piece of china in a glass-case. A poor tribute, he thought, to the might of the pen.

"Well?" said Faber.

"A d—d fine girl, but cold as marble!"

"What makes you think so?"

"Voice, gesture, everything. Give her a chance, and she'd be up on a platform spouting."

"I don't think so. She's going to have many chances. What about the others?"

"The old man's daughter is just a bread-and-butter miss. I liked little Claudine d'Arny—as ugly as sin, but passion enough for a nautch girl."

"You remind me of her father. See here: I had a letter from him to-day. What would happen to-morrow if I published it—by accident? Here's a note of it."

Bertie read it carelessly; then with a journalistic interest:

"If you published that—"

"Or you did—"

"Same thing—I guess he'd be out of Paris in four-and-twenty hours."

"Ah, then I mustn't publish it—don't you be playing any journalistic tricks on me!"

"I don't think," said Bertie Morris.

And their eyes met.

CHAPTER V
GENERAL D'ARNY AND HIS DAUGHTER

I

General d'Arny lived in an old house in the Boulevard St. Germain, one of the few monuments still existing to the golden age of Récamier and the salons. He did not care a scudo for the literary and artistic associations of this gloomy mansion, but much for the fact that he paid little rent. Beaumarchais had lived there on the eve of his flight to Holland; the great rooms had known Fleury and his fellows, Balzac and Saint-Beuve—a very panel of genius written across the centuries.

It all meant very little to Hubert d'Arny, the bulk of whose fortune went into the trough at Panama; the residue into the hands of the jobbers on the Bourse. The general was notoriously a financial derelict; as notoriously a suspect to his many enemies in the Chamber.

He had married late in life—some years after the war—and his wife died in childbirth. One daughter, Claudine, was alternately the object of a maudlin affection and of sentimental regret. She cost a great deal of money, and had the indecency to arrive at a marriageable age. When Captain Issy-Ferrault, a son of one of the oldest aristocracies in France, came forward, the general assented in spite of his democratic principles. The business of providing for the girl aged him pathetically. The newspapers said it was Morocco; but the trouble lay much nearer home.

As it chanced, John Faber arrived in Paris in the midst of the preparations for Claudine's wedding. He knew nothing of it; no one had guessed that he had any interest in the daughter of the French Minister of Artillery, or she in him. Claudine went to America at the invitation of the French Ambassador, whose children were her friends. When Faber was introduced to her upon the ship, she said frankly that she did not like him. His manners were *gauche*, and his eyes inquisitive. She avoided him with a sure instinct, being ignorant that he knew anything of her or her family.

This was a great misfortune, for she had many qualities which appeal to men, and Faber was not the kind of man to remain insensible to them.

In Paris, upon her return, she entered the promised land of preparation. The general swore loudly while he signed the cheques, but signed them none the less. Dressmakers flocked to the Boulevard St. Germain, and their mouths were full of pins. Claudine was of a romantic temperament, but it could stoop to laces and fine linen. She argle-bargled with her father like a wench at a fair, and when he discounted the list, she declared that she would not be married at all. A scandal was the potent weapon in her armament. He could not have a scandal.

This extravagance of idea filled her bedroom to overflowing; to say nothing of other bedrooms. She would sit curled up amid a tangle of the most delicate draperies—transparencies which should have come from a fairy godmother; masterpieces in velvets and satins—she would wonder if life were long enough to wear them all. These things were hidden in her virgin holy of holies, but she ticked off the days which shut the door against the One Unknown, and often fell to a young girl's awe in the presence of the mysteries. Then came the last night of all—the maids had left her; the house was at rest. A dirty fluff of snow fell upon the streets of Paris. She was to be married at St. Eustache to-morrow!

Claudine undressed herself, and putting on the most wonderful of lace robes, she sat before a fire of wood and warmed her pink and white feet at the blaze. There should have been regrets at the life she was leaving: she might have dwelt with some affection upon her passing girlhood, and the home which had sheltered her. But she did nothing of the kind. Her thoughts were entirely devoted to St. Eustache and afterwards. What an exciting day it must be! Every friend she had would be in the church. One of the canons was to marry them, and afterwards there would be a great feast and many speeches in the old ballroom downstairs. At four in the afternoon, Justin's motor-car was to take them to the old château, near Rambouillet, where the first week was to be spent. She pictured the lonely drive over the whitened roads, through the forests—then the château, grim, old and moated. They would dine together—and then—then she would know what love was!

Her ideas were truly French, and English sentiment could have offered them little sympathy. Perhaps Captain Issy-Ferrault stood to her less for *the* man than for *a* man. She had been educated in convents where saintly women shuddered at the mere footsteps of their common enemy and provoked a thousand curiosities by their very holiness. Then had come a few short years of the world—it had taught Claudine that all life began from the hour when a man first took a woman into his arms and the Church blessed the proceeding. Afterwards there were other things. The first step was sufficient for her vigil that night.

Her wedding dress had been laid upon a little bed in the adjoining room. She went there on tip-toe as though afraid that someone might spy upon her while she touched the satin and laces with delighted fingers. Strong scents perfumed the room and the odour of blossoms. Claudine went and stood before a long mirror of the wardrobe and studied herself in many attitudes. She did not know whether she was really pretty. Justin, her fiancé, had paid her many compliments, and she tried to believe them. A greater source of encouragement was her figure—the fine rounded limbs, the pink and white of a young girl's skin. For an instant she remembered the ordeal of discovery which awaited her to-morrow; then with a light laugh, she returned to her bedroom. Other brides had suffered and survived—she took courage.

The priest had told her to say many things in her prayers—good man, he said them in his—but they were clean gone from her head at this time. The girlish romance of an English wedding was not for her. No gifts of sweet and silent hours were hers. She knew very little of Justin—he, less of her. He had kissed her but twice, and then apologetically. Yet to-morrow she would be his wife.

Stay, but was it to-morrow? She listened at the window and counted the church bells chiming the hour.

Twelve o'clock.

Her wedding was to-day.

II

The afternoon of the same day had found General d'Arny closeted with John Faber in a little room in the Avenue de l'Opéra. Here was the Paris agency of the great Charleston Company, and hither came d'Arny at his own suggestion.

A bent old man, not lacking dignity in a common way—dignity had gone to the journalistic dogs that afternoon. He entered the office trembling with excitement; he could not speak for some minutes, and when he did so, his tones rolled like thunder.

"It is finished," he said. "Read!" And he held out a paper with quivering fingers.

Faber watched him with half-closed eyes. He was thinking of another day, when this man, a mere captain of the Chasseurs-à-Cheval then, had ridden down the Rue de Fleurus and commanded his men to hunt out the Communards. Some forty years ago, and no doubt the soldier had forgotten every hour of it. None the less, the sword of destiny was poised and would fall.

"What shall I read?" Faber rejoined, after a little spell of waiting. He knew every word his friend Bertie Morris had cabled to America, but his face was void of knowledge.

"Some talk of the deal," he ran on. "Well, I guess we expect it. Why should they keep quiet?"

The soldier pulled himself together, and taking the paper from the outstretched hand, he began to turn the leaves quickly.

"It is on,"above pages he said. "Yes, that is it, if you would be good enough to read."

The clock ticked in a silent room for some minutes. Faber read the article to the end without moving a muscle of his usually expressive face. A great business man is often a great actor. He was one.

"There seems to have been a leakage," he said presently, and then, looking up, "Whom do you suspect?"

"I suspect! God in Heaven, what has suspicion to do with me?"

"I should have thought you were in the way of it—that is, if you take it seriously this side."

The old man wormed with impatience.

"The *Soir* has it; there will not be a paper in Paris without it to-morrow. Do you not see that it is, in effect, the letter I wrote to you on Tuesday last?"

"Who's to blame for that? I told you at the beginning not to write."

"Is it to be imagined that you cannot receive letters?"

Faber leaned over the table, and began to speak with some warmth.

"See here," he said, "you're a Minister of Artillery in Paris. You receive, I suppose, some three or four hundred letters a day? Can you be responsible for them all?"

"But this was sent to you privately at your hotel."

"A foolish kind of letter at the best—I remember every word of it. You admit in so many words that our deal is for forty thousand francs, and stipulate that Captain Clearnay must have ten. Why couldn't you come round to me and say so?"

"I was three times at the hotel that day; you were absent on each occasion. It was urgent that Clearnay should be dealt with if the contract was to go through."

"Exactly what this newspaper man says. He calls it a second Ollivier case, I see. Well, I shouldn't wonder if it made as much noise."

D'Arny tortured himself into new attitudes.

"Good God!" he cried. "Don't you see my position?"

"Perfectly. I saw it from the beginning. You'll have to leave Paris awhile."

"Then the contract is lost?"

"I never thought it would go through, General. I wasn't such a d—d fool."

"But at least a word from you will save my name. You can deny the letter."

"I could deny it."

"Are you wishing to tell me that there is any doubt?"

"No doubt at all. Unfortunately, it was read, by mistake, in the Hotel Ritz the night it reached me. You should see Morris, of the *New York Mitre*. He might do something for you."

The man rose, white as a sheet and broken. He may or may not have understood the nature of the trap into which he had fallen, but it was clear to him that John Faber could or would do little for him. He went out into the street to be offered a copy of *La Guêpe*, and to hear the newsboy cry the latest news of this surpassing jobbery.

A less consummate artist than Faber would have spoken of the Rue de Fleurus, and of what happened there forty years ago. Hubert d'Arny had not the remotest notion that the man who had ruined him was the son of that American citizen who had been shot by his orders at the crisis of the great debacle.

III

Paris licked its lips over the scandal, and then stood aghast.

The tragedy surpassed all expectation, and yet all admitted that there was no other course.

Hubert d'Arny was found dead in a little hotel at Passy that very night. He had blown out his brains upon the eve of his daughter's wedding. People thought rather of Claudine than of him. Much that would have been written and said was obliterated or hushed when she was mentioned. Who would break it to her? Such a blow had not been struck at the Republic since the Humbert scandal.

Faber knew nothing of the coming wedding, and he heard the news of Hubert d'Arny's death without emotion. There were primitive traits in his character which this affair made dominant. If pity urged claims, he thrust them aside when he remembered his dead father. "An eye for an eye—and for death, the dead." A sense of power and authority nerved his will and flattered a well-balanced vanity. After all, his brains and money had won this victory against all the shining armour of France. He perceived that the financier was, after all, the most considerable power in the world to-day. Kings can make war when the bankers will pay for it. He had been his own general and his money was his army. A stroke of the pen had laid one of the most powerful men in Paris dead at his feet—as vulgar tragedy would put it. A mind that had little subtlety and much common sense rose to no analytical attitudes. He had killed the man just as a Southerner shoots down a nigger—and of the two the nigger was perhaps the more deserving.

In this frame of mind, he was greatly astonished to receive a visit from Gabrielle Silvester very early on the following morning. He had even forgotten that she knew anything of his dealings with General d'Arny, nor did he immediately connect her with the tragedy of which all Paris was talking. She had come to tell him that the yacht was sailing, he thought; then he noticed that she did not offer him her hand, while her manner toward him was utterly changed—a chill womanly manner he could not mistake.

"Why!" he said. "Still in Paris?"

She avoided the question, and went straight to the heart of the matter.

"I have come to ask you, Mr. Faber, if you knew that Claudine d'Arny was to have been married to-day?"

He stepped back a pace and looked her full in the face. Rarely in his life had he flinched before man or woman, but the accusation stunned him.

"Was I aware? But how should I be aware?"

She drew nearer, her face aflame and her heart beating wildly.

"I must know this—please bear with me. I must have your answer!"

"It has been given you. I knew nothing."

She seemed dazed and not a little helpless now. Seating herself upon the edge of a chair near the fireplace, she began to speak her thoughts aloud.

"The secret is yours and mine. I would have told nobody. For you, it must be a hard thought to the end of your life. She was to have been married to-day. Will you tell me that if you had known it, it would have made a difference?"

He debated that, standing with his hands in his pockets, but his face grave enough.

"Nothing would have made any difference between that man and me. He shot my father. Very well—he had to pay, sooner or later. But I don't think it would have been to-day, if I had known."

She was silent a little while. Then she said:

"I can think of nothing but such simple things. If I had stopped to tell you in the hall of the hotel—just that—there would not have been to-day! It was one of those chances that do not recur. I thought everyone knew that Claudine was to be married."

"The last thing a man knows about any woman who is a mere acquaintance. Have you seen her to-day?"

She shivered.

"I dare not go—I dare not!"

"She has relatives in Paris?"

"I suppose so—friends would put her to shame. Does it matter when he is dead?"

"He was a rogue, or I would have spared him. He tried to cheat me from the start. I found nothing I could fix upon—and I looked for it!"

She would not consider it from that point of view.

"This will always be in your life and Claudine's. Time cannot alter judgments of this kind. It will grow with the years. I am very sorry for you, Mr. Faber."

He resented it; the patronage of women rarely failed to anger him.

"Leave me to my own affairs. I take the responsibility. I've taken a good many in my time. The girl's to be thought of. Who was she going to marry?"

"Captain Issy-Ferrault. I hardly know him: an officer of cavalry, they say."

"Poor, I suppose, as most of the kind?"

"I cannot tell you."

"When will she marry him now?"

"Oh, surely, you understand?"

"I understand one thing: he's going to marry her."

"A child would know that it's impossible!"

"Then I am wiser than a child. Will you let me have his address—to-morrow, say?"

"I am leaving Paris to-morrow."

"Then one of my clerks will get it. Shall we meet at Corfu?"

"I don't know," she said. "I came to tell you that I never wished to see you again."

"You haven't told me so. It shall be at Corfu."

She did not answer or hold out her hand. He knew that a barrier had risen up between them and his pride was quickened.

He would marry this woman because she had judged him.

BOOK II
THE PLAYERS

CHAPTER I
A RACE FOR AN EMPEROR

I

There were two yachts on the Adriatic Sea waiting for an emperor.

One lay in the harbour of Fiume; the other at Trieste. The emperor himself was still at Potsdam, and none of the newspapers seemed to know when he would sail.

Sir Jules Achon was a man of infinite patience and superb tenacity. Few but his intimate friends knew much about him. He had amassed a great fortune as a shipbroker, and now with advancing years, he devoted the bulk of that fortune to this tremendous project of European Federation. Yet it was all done without any claptrap whatever. The newspapers had hardly heard of it. There was no writer of eminence to take it up. Sir Jules worked in great places, but he worked silently. Already his scheme had the approval of kings and emperors. He had gone to St. Petersburg with a recommendation to the English Ambassador which opened all doors. But for a dramatic accident of destiny, the Tsar would have been his first patron. Three ministers knew his scheme, and two of them were warm supporters of such a transcendent project. The third saw in it a danger to the diplomatists, which self interest could not tolerate. "This will make an end of us," he had said. Sir Jules agreed that it was so. That very night Ivolsky obtained an audience of the Emperor, and besought him to withdraw his patronage. The others were too late by a few hours, and who shall say how far that accident of time and space has affected the immediate destinies of Europe?

For the common peace projects, beating of pacific drums and waving of fraternal flags, Sir Jules cared not at all. He believed that international peace could come only upon a basis of common European interests. His scheme would have established free trade between the kingdoms. Wars arise chiefly from commercial disputes; commercial disputes are the first fruits of tariffs. Let the commercial incentive be wanting and disarmament may begin. A gradual process needed many years for full attainment—but it could begin to-morrow if the conditions were fulfilled.

He talked very little of all this to those with him on the yacht. It was, in effect, a young people's party and a merry one at that. Dr. Joe Burrall had come from Putney, a braw man of thirty, who had rowed for Cambridge. Douglas Renshaw, a gunner whose occupation had gone, came because he was asked, and was asked because he was sure to come. He had taken to the Stock Exchange recently as a wire-haired terrier to the gorse, and Sir Jules had put a small fortune into his pocket. He knew a little geology, and declared his intention of studying Slav. So far the only word he had picked up was "hijar," and he was not very sure to what tongue it belonged, though he used it frequently as an expression of joy.

These two with Gabrielle Silvester were the guests of Sir Jules and his daughter upon the *Wanderer*, the fine steam yacht which had so often invaded the superb mysteries of the Western Mediterranean. They understood their host's ambitions, but rarely spoke of them. When it was learned that there was a doubt about the Emperor going to Corfu after all, they looked upon it as a personal rebuff, but did not discuss it except apart. All kinds of excursions kept them busy. They visited the unsurpassable islands of the Adriatic, became learned about Zara and Sebenico and matchless Ragusa, the incomparable Republic, defying East and West alike during the centuries. Local interests attracted them; they saw much of these savage peoples; were ashore for many a frolic; lived in a blaze of sunshine and an atmosphere wholly medieval.

Gabrielle's voyage to America had been her first world experience beyond the walls of meticulous suburbia. This new adventure fascinated her beyond measure. She felt that she had really begun to live. It were as though the passion of the East stirred in her normally cold blood and left her panting. Destiny had snatched her up from the ruck to put her in high places. Far from surrendering to the enervating suggestions of this sunny sea, they forced her mind to considerable ambitions—and with them all the name of John Faber would associate itself despite the memories. This was contrary to all she had determined in Paris, and put her to some shame. She felt that she had no right to see such a man again, that he was a social pariah, without pity or any title to the meanest respect. And yet he would creep into the scheme of her ambitions, and she understood in some way that without him they were meaningless.

II

It was a great surprise to Gabrielle when the launch returned to the yacht one afternoon in the second week in December with her father and Harry Lassett on board. This was one of Sir Jules' great surprises—one in which Eva had a part. Silvester was very tired after his long journey across Europe, but Harry was very full of it. They were greeted by Douglas Renshaw with a "hijar"; by Sir Jules with that quiet smile which betokened pleasure in the company of his friends.

"I had no idea you could get away," he said, "or I would have asked you in London."

Silvester said that he had no idea of it either; an American had come over from Yonkers and was taking his services for a fortnight. Harry admitted that for his part he could always get away, which, as Joe Burrall remarked, was an advantage as useful in debt as in matrimony.

This was a sunny day, an ideal day of southern winter, and they all took tea beneath the awning of the promenade deck. With Harry, Gabrielle was a little constrained and uneasy. She was glad to have him there, and yet felt that in some way his presence was a douche upon her schemes. He spoke of the little world of outer London, not of the wider horizon to which she looked. She had built a tower of her imagination which Harry Lassett would never climb. Indeed, he would have derided it as he had done her American friendship. With her father it was different. She had a long talk with him in his cabin before dinner and she learned again how much importance he had attached to her diplomatic success with John Faber.

"It would send me to Yonkers with better credentials than any Englishman ever carried across the seas," he said. "Think of it—John Faber with us! The man who has done more than anyone alive to make war possible in our time."

"You will never get him, father. It would be a great wrong against the truth if he came in."

"Why should it be wrong, Gabrielle?"

"For many reasons. He believes that all our dreams are sentimental moonshine; he never could be in earnest—how should he be when he does not believe?"

"Is it not possible to put our view so convincingly that he must believe?

"Are we convinced ourselves? Is it very real to us?"

"It is very real to me. I think it must be to every man of culture."

"How many that would exclude. Nelson could not have been a man of culture."

He looked up, pained.

"Faber has been talking to you."

"No, I have been talking to myself. I think with you that war is a very great crime against humanity, but, after all, God allows it."

He sighed and began to sort out his papers.

"There is a great deal which seems to be permitted. It is another way of saying that mankind has been left a great work to do. We are fortunate if we are called to bear the smallest burden. I think disappointments should be numbered among them."

"Oh! I agree with you. And, of course, I shall still hope for Mr. Faber's name."

"If you think it a wrong, that would be an inconsistency."

"Not altogether; it might be a great victory. He is a man with whom you can argue."

"Then I hope you will see him again at Corfu."

Gabrielle did not answer that. Her own words accused her in some way.

A great victory! A woman's victory! What would that mean in this case? For the moment she let ambition run away with her and imagination reared fine castles. They went down with a crash when she heard Harry Lassett calling her. She made some excuse and went out—just as she had gone when Harry called below her window at Hampstead.

III

A superb night with a fine round moon found them aft upon the deck, gazing over the lights of Fiume to the vine-clad hills beyond. A wonderful stillness upon land and water gave place from time to time to sounds most musical—the lingering notes of sonorous bells, the lilt of Italian song, the splash of unseen oars, and the music of ships. Lanterns shone about them, the lanterns of steamers at anchor and of the Austrian fleet. Against a glorious horizon the sails of feluccas would take fantastic shapes; the stars grouped themselves in joyous brilliancy. There were many houses upon the distant hillside and they stood there as beacons, speaking to the ships and the sea in a tongue which all understood.

Sir Jules and Silvester were in the smoking-room at this time having what Harry called "a pow-wow." Eva played sentimental themes upon the great organ in the drawing-room; the doctor and Douglas Renshaw were ashore for the good of the populace. Gabrielle, herself, set deep in a deck chair with Harry Lassett at her feet. He smoked a great pipe and talked St. Moritz. There had been trouble with his trustees, and he was not sure he could get out there this year.

"So, you see," he said, "I came along when the old chap asked me."

"A most candid way of putting it; there could have been no other reason in the world."

"Oh, I say, puss! That's nasty now."

"Not at all. To qualify candour is a crime. Well, you can't go to St. Moritz. What then?"

"I didn't say I couldn't go. I said that old Ben Stuart, my trustee, was playing the fox with me. He says I overdrew a hundred and ninety last year, and it can't go on. As if it was his own money!"

"Do you disagree with his accounts?"

He laughed.

"Arithmetic's no good to me. I was a bit of a flier at Ananias and Dido at school, but I could add up a column every time and make it different. I ought to be Chancellor of the Exchequer—eh, what? Surely, you don't mind?"

He nestled his head against her knees as though this kind of comfort were some solatium. Gabrielle was thinking of John Faber and of what his opinion would have been of such an admission.

"I suppose life isn't worth living unless you go to St. Moritz?"

He detected no irony.

"How's a man to keep fit in our beastly country?—then, there's habit. I believe in doing to-morrow what you did yesterday—don't you? If I stop in England, it's covered court tennis, nothing more! How's a man to go through the winter on covered court tennis?"

"The survival of the fittest. Whatever will become of you on the yacht?"

He puffed stolidly.

"That's vegetation. I can lie on my back with any man—I'm a plus two at it. A man's year should include a month of it. Then I'm orderly; I know just what I'm going to do during the next two seasons, as sure as the moon and stars: cricket, four months; two months' shooting; a bit of hunting if I can get it in, and if I can't, then some pat ball on the links. What more do you want?"

"Are you putting the question to me?"

"I wasn't—but I will!"

"Oh, I should want a lot more: to begin with, a definite object."

"Ah, you're a girl. My opinion of men with definite objects is that they are generally bores."

"But the country would not get on without them, would it?"

"Don't believe such nonsense, puss. Who's the greater man: Asquith or Foster? Would you sooner be Lloyd George or Bobs? Who's doing more for England—the man who helps to beat the Australians, or the lawyers who put threepence on the income tax? You ask the average man, and see what he says."

"The average man has not much brains; he is the servant in the house of intellect. I should never consult him about anything."

"Puss, I know what you're thinking about—it's that popgun man."

"Rather inconsequent, isn't it? You wouldn't average Mr. Faber?"

"No, I suppose he's clever enough. He makes money. Old Baker, our head at school, always used to say that the faculty of making money was one of the most contemptible. But it's useful, I admit."

"Oh, yes, we all admit that, and show our contempt of the faculty by worshipping the possessor."

"Do you worship John Faber?"

"Collectively, yes; individually, not at all."

He thought upon it.

"I suppose you had a jolly time with him in Paris?"

"Oh, my dear Harry, what next? I saw him twice: once in the corridor of the hotel, then in his own rooms."

"In his rooms!"

"Yes; to tell him I never wished to see him again."

"Oh, you brick; that's the best thing I've heard. Of course, I knew you would. There's never been anything said, but you owed that to me—now, didn't you, puss?"

She would not answer him. They passed to the vague intimacies of an incomplete amour, in which their whispers were inaudible and the sound of voices in the cabin a warning discord. Eva still played an intolerable waltz. The harbour waves sported about the dinghy, tethered astern. Gabrielle wondered why it was that she was incapable of resisting all this; that she suffered this quite brainless boy to kiss her at his pleasure—a great bear with fearsome limbs cuddling her. Was it because of her twenty-three years of Suburbia? Because of an inherited instinct for the commonplace of the natural life—such a life as all about her lived, and would live in that little world of Hampstead? Or was it purely the call of sex—more potent than a thousand theories, imperious beyond all the laws of emperors and kings?

The latter thought did not occur to her. She suffered the spell of the scene, the soft airs of night, the shining stars, the harbour lights, the waxing and waning chords of distant music. Harry's passionate whispers were like a message from afar. She submitted to him as though thus was her destiny written.

CHAPTER II
LOUIS DE PALEOLOGUE

I

Do you know Ragusa—Ragusa, the Pearl of the Adriatic?

It was here that the Imperial yacht carried the Emperor when at last he sailed from Trieste—here that John Faber saw him within three hours of his going ashore.

Here also Faber found the man he had sought so many years. Louis de Paleologue, who had taken his mother to America after his father's death in Paris.

Ragusa—what city is like to this of all that border the incomparable shore? Sebenico, Zara, Spalato—who cares if they perish while Ragusa remains?

Consider how through the centuries this little republic shut the gates of her sanctuary in the face alike of Moslem and of Christian; how she defied now the Turk, now the Servian, even the mighty power of Venice at its zenith. Neither friend nor foe coming to her for shelter was refused. She protected Stephen Nemanja, who fought her allies of the Byzantine Empire; she opened her gates to Queen Margarita, and defended them against the King of Dalmatia. The "winged lion" writes no shame upon her citadel. She fell at last, not to man, but to the very earth which opened and swallowed her up. There was never a history of Ragusa after that fateful year 1667. The great earthquake ended a story—Napoleon wrote but a sorry epitaph.

What a cosmopolitan company is that which gathers every day within the tremendous walls of this fallen citadel. All the colours of the Balkan peoples are to be seen here—the flag and turban of the Turk; the white breeches of the Albanian—Joseph's coat upon the back of the son of the Black Mountain. Servians are here: Bosnians and men of Herzegovina; Italians who have drifted down from northern towns; Austrians in possession. Crimson clashes with the sky-blue tunics of the Austrian officers—there are deep reds and glowing tints of orange—all moving in kaleidoscopic splendour through streets which the extended arms may measure; by churches and palaces, which are matchless in their art. A city girded by the libidinous foliage of the south; a city of half-lights and shaded cloisters; of a fortress running out into the blue Adriatic, lifting mighty walls to the caress of the kindly seas.

II

Louis de Paleologue had taken up his abode in a veritable hole in the wall near the Dominican monastery. The place was dark and cavernous, and might have been (but for its monstrous stones) a booth in an Eastern bazaar. When he worked it was in the cool of the monastery gardens, the monks stealing looks over his shoulder at wonderful forms in bewitching *négligé*—or even at terpsichoreal advertisements of pills and powder. For despite his sixty-two years, and the fact that he was a prince in his own country, Louis still earned his living by the advertisers, and was held to be the cleverest draughtsman at the business.

One grievance he had, and one joy—his daughter Maryska, nineteen upon her last birthday, and still a child. Maryska like her father (and another celebrity who has had a statue raised to him) never grew up. She was the youngest woman of nineteen in the whole wide world, and when father and daughter went for "a rag" together, it was wonderful that anything at all was left in the Cantina—as he had named the house.

Such days they passed! Louis, prone in the sun with a cigarette in his mouth; Maryska, flitting about the scene like a schoolgirl at play! They went hand in hand everywhere like sworn friends in an academy for young ladies. What money they earned would be sometimes in his pocket, sometimes in hers. They quarrelled babyishly—the man shedding tears more often than the girl. Yet he would have put his knife into the heart of any who did her injury, with as little thought as he would have killed a stray dog at his door. There had been one such tragedy at Zara—the body was found in the harbour some days afterwards.

Maryska was a cosmopolitan. She had starved in New York, in London, in Paris, in Berlin. Now she starved in Ragusa—except upon those splendid occasions when a cheque came from England. Then the Austrian banker would be fetched out of bed or café to cash it. They were rare days, for Louis would knock down the bottles like ninepins, and never turn a hair whatever their number. Maryska drank just as much as she could, and then fell asleep. He used to shout and swear because she would not wake up to draw another cork for him.

Latterly, it had been the devil to pay at the Cantina. Louis had lived in prospective upon six disorderly nymphs—all décolleté—who were to have proclaimed the merits, *urbi et orbi*, of a new suspender for ladies of fashion. These drawings were quite wonderful. The prior of the monastery who no doubt, may have imagined that they were part of a scheme for a stained glass window, thought very highly of them. The Austrian officers begged for copies of the paper. The governor laughed and had a fit of coughing. He wanted to know where the models came from. Louis would not tell him that, except to say that they were memories of Paris and New York. He rarely drew the beautiful dark face of Maryska—but there is a portrait of her in the church of St. John the Divine in London, and many would swear it is a madonna of an old master. Louis painted it for the priest, who used to tell him he was a scoundrel. It was so very true.

Well, the pictures were drawn and dispatched to London; and then a dreadful thing happened. The firm, which understood the female mysteries so well, treated the financial verities with a contempt which quickly ended in Carey Street. No cheque came to that hole in the wall at Ragusa. Squat-legged and patient, Louis smoked his cigarette and listened to Maryska's wholly unmelodious music. There was bread in the house, but no wine. Well, wine would come presently.

Wine did not come, but in its place came John Faber. For a moment, Louis thought that a customer had crossed the seas to buy his pictures. Then he said that the firm, which was suspended because of its suspenders, had sent an embassy with the cash. However it might be, he determined to borrow five crowns of the stranger, and saluted him with princely politeness.

Maryska, meanwhile, stood up ready to go to the wine-shop.

III

Faber took off his hat at the entrance to the cavern, and blinked in the darkness. He saw a handsome man squatting on the floor, and behind him a pair of eyes which glowed as a cat's. They belonged to Maryska; but he did not know, indeed, he wondered if there were wild beasts in the place.

"Say, does anyone named Louis de Paleologue live here?"

The accent transplanted father and daughter to New York in an instant. What years they had lived there! How they regretted them!

"He does, sir, and what then?"

"You are Mr. Paleologue?"

"That is so. My daughter—she doesn't bite—at least, only me!"

Maryska's teeth were to be counted on the instant. She laughed as the Italians laugh, without reservations.

"*Accidenti!*" she cried, and then coming out into the light, "*caro mio*—he is too tough, poppa, I should spoil my teeth!"

Faber saluted her in a way he intended to be Continental.

"You have been in New York, signorina?"

"Five years, mister. I am all Americano!"

"Then I'll walk right in, if I may."

He did not wait for permission, but entered the cavern. It was evident that he would have liked a chair, but seeing none, he accepted a mat which she offered.

"Poppa burned all the chairs long ago. Can you sit down on nothing, mister?"

He said that he could, looking at Maryska all the while. Louis took a box of Bosnian cigarettes from the floor and passed it over.

"Say, are you thirsty, boss?"

Faber smiled at that.

"Well, this is thirsty ground. As the governor said—but I guess ye don't know what the governor—"

"Bet you!" He said. "'Don't let it be long between the drinks.' There's a wine-shop two blocks away."

Maryska stepped forward, as keen as a hound. She held out her hand for the money without any shame at all—she and her father had been holding it out for years—yet some of Louis' gifts in return had been more precious than gold.

"How much shall I give you?" Faber asked. She replied that a kronen would be ample. He gave it her, and she was away in a flash.

They smoked a space in silence when she was gone. Presently Faber said: "Business good down this way?"

Louis did not like the tone of it, and the quills of his pride stiffened. "What's that to you?"

"Might be a good deal—I'm in dead earnest."

"What's your line—pills or powder?"

"I'm neither. I make guns."

"Want me to fire 'em off—well, I'm ready. What's the size?"

Faber smiled.

"Not quite it," he said; and then wandering right away from the subject, "I wish I'd known you were in New York. You didn't work under your own name there."

"That's so. I used to sign just 'Louis.'"

"Will you draw me a picture of Maryska—for my house? A thousand dollars now and another thousand when it's delivered?"

Louis drew back a little.

"Why the girl?"

"You must know why. There couldn't be a better subject."

"Yes; but if I do not choose to do it, what then?"

"Why, then I'm beaten."

He threw away the stump of his cigarette and took another. Presently Maryska returned with the flask of white wine and the glasses were chinked. The child drank a draught which would have put a vintner to shame. Then she showed her pretty teeth.

"Oh, how good!" she said, and then with a heavenly sigh, "*Ecco c'e vuoto.*"

"Think you could do another?" Faber asked Louis. The reply was quite stately.

"Sir, I am at your disposition."

Maryska went off with five crowns this time. When she was gone, her father thawed a little.

"Have you seen much of this place?"

"Just as much as the harbour showed me."

"Staying here long?"

"Why, as to that—why stay?"

Paleologue knocked the ashes off his cigarette with magnificent dignity.

"You make guns; why not see some of them go off?"

"Do you suggest fighting?"

"That's so. I'm going up to Podgorica in three days' time, afterwards on to the frontier. There'll be riot, rape and pillage. Like to come along?"

Faber was a little nonplussed.

"Do you go alone?" he asked.

"The girl and I, certainly. We can talk business on the road. Why not?"

"Oh, I'll come! Here's the wine, I see. She's a wonder that girl of yours."

Louis assented.

"Her bringing up; she has forgotten how to read and write. It is education which is the matter nowadays. I believe the Greeks knew women. Come here, wild cat, and tell the stranger you can't read or write."

Maryska reddened at this and cried "Beast!" with real anger. She sulked for quite a long time, hiding in the dark corner where only her glowing eyes could be seen. Louis took no notice of her tantrums; he had begun to be rather interested in the stranger.

"Say, you know the fighting may be a bit lively. I'm bound for Ranovica—want to see it burned. There was a man here yesterday from the London illustrated papers. He's out for fancy pictures and put me on. He's mighty anxious after the rape and pillage. I guess we'll see something of that at Ranovica."

Faber looked at the girl; she did not seem to be listening.

"Aren't you imprudent? Isn't it better to leave your daughter here?" he asked in a low voice.

Louis did not understand him. "Where I go, she goes. Besides, they know me very well, these people. You are not afraid, mister?"

"Afraid! How do we go?"

"Steamer to Antivari."

"I'll take you on my yacht."

Louis expressed no surprise. If his guest had promised a warship with golden plates his sphinx-like attitude would have been unchanged.

"Just as you like," he said. "We take the horses at Scutari anyway."

To which Faber responded with a further offer. "I've a car on my ship; we'll put her ashore and try that road."

Louis shook his head. "No good at all; there isn't any damned road. To-day's Saturday; shall we say to-morrow morning at ten?"

"But it was to be three days' time."

Louis yawned. "Oh, d—n time!" he said. "I never think of it."

"Then we'll start to-morrow at ten."

He drank off his wine and turned to look at Maryska. She had crept nearer while they talked, and her head was bent to the floor that she might not miss a word. When Faber held out his hand to her she leaned upon her elbows and looked at him with strange eyes.

"Good-bye, mister!"

"You are coming on my ship, Maryska."

"Not with that man," and she pointed to her father.

"Pouf!" said Louis. "I will flay you with the whip."

"And I will kill you with my knife," she said quickly, in Italian.

It was the customary exchange of their daily compliments. Louis rather liked it.

"Say," he exclaimed on the threshold, "and who may you be, anyway?"

"I? Why, my name's John Faber."

"Faber—Faber? I used to know a Faber in Paris in the 'seventies."

"His son, sir."

Louis turned his cigarette over in his mouth.

"How did you hear of me?" he asked.

"Oh, I got your name in Paris. The *New York Mitre* people gave it to me."

"That's odd; I used to know your mother forty years ago. Well, so long," and he turned on his heel.

CHAPTER III
THE DAMNABLE MOUNTAINS

This was a bitter winter on the Albanian frontier, and God alone knows how the party got to Ranovica at all.

None but a madman would have attempted the journey at such a moment in the story of the Balkans; but as John Faber remarked, it needed a double-barrelled charge of insanity to venture it in the winter. Yet he had told Maryska that he would go, and go he did.

What a country, and what a people! The Almighty seemed to have blasted the mountains and the mountaineers alike. Such a wilderness of grey rocks, of weirdly scarped precipices, of awful caverns and fearsome valleys is to be imagined by none who have not visited it.

Depict a range of mountains built up of the barren limestone into a myriad fearsome shapes of dome and turret, castle and battlement. In the valleys far below, put the gardens of the world, fertile beyond all dreams; where the grapes grow as long as the fingers on your hand, and every tropical plant luxuriates. Drive humanity from this scene and deliver it up to the world and the bear. Such is the frontier of Albania where it debouches upon Montenegro—such are the "damnable mountains," as every Christian in their vicinity has learned to call them.

A desert upon an altitude, and yet it is not wholly a desert. Here and there ensconced in nook and cranny you will come upon an oasis where a village harbours wild people and a scanty patch of fertile soil keeps body and soul together. Such a place was Ranovica, to which Louis de Paleologue led his guest on the sixth day afterwards. They came up to it at three o'clock upon that December afternoon when the sun was magnificent over the Western Adriatic, and even these desolate hills had been fired to warmth and colour.

An odd party—three upon cheeky little Hungarian horses; three upon mules. Frank, the American valet, had much to say about the habits and character of the mule, but he reserved it until they should be safely upon the yacht again. The other two servants were Austrians who had been heavily bribed for the venture—even they would have refused had they understood that it was for an expedition to Ranovica. This hole in the hill was full of savage Christians who hated the Montenegrins much, but the Moslem a good deal more. It was bound to be burned sooner or later.

Ranovica has a fine old gate built by Stephen of Bosnia, heaven knows how many years ago. The party rode through this just after three o'clock, and was challenged immediately by half-a-dozen warriors with the most wonderful white breeches the Western world has seen. Already, and when far down the valley, the outposts of the little force defending this wild place had put the travellers through a searching inquisition; but they had to face another ordeal at the gate, and lucky for them that Louis spoke Servian so fluently. The soldiers listened to him as though a brother was speaking. They looked at Maryska with wide black eyes. Why not?—she was good to look upon, surely, with her high boots and crimson breeches and little Greek cap. Faber himself had looked at her a great many times on the way up, but he was by no means pleased that she should become the cynosure of so many evil eyes.

"Well?" he said to her, while Louis played the millionaire among the wild men, "and what do you think of this, young lady?"

She was still upon her pretty little horse and her eyes were here, there and everywhere; but not with the curiosity an untravelled woman would have displayed. Maryska had seen too much of the world to be troubled by Ranovica. Besides, she was hungry.

"I think my father is a fool to come here, and you also, boss, that is what I think."

"Guess you've hit it first time. Are you hungry, Maryska?"

"Why, yes. Are you, boss?"

She imitated her father perfectly, and Faber laughed. They were in a street so narrow that his horse had a head in the window upon one side of the road and a tail in a window upon the other. A tremendous battlement of rock lifted a sheer precipice far up above this peopled gorge. In the shadows there moved a fierce people, savage, wild, hunted. They gathered round the strangers menacingly, and but for the old white-haired priest, even Louis' gift of tongues might not have saved them. The priest, however, liked the jingle of good Austrian crowns. Let the strangers come to his house, he said, the inn was not fit to harbour a dog.

So the party rode on a furlong—the men, the girl, the American valet and the Austrians. At every step the crowd pressed about them, black and scowling. It was good at last to enter an open courtyard and to see that none followed. Dark was coming down then and lights shining from the windows of the miserable houses. Faber remembered that he had communicated with the Turkish authorities before setting out and congratulated himself upon his prudence.

"They'll want my guns, and so they'll want me," he said.

But he was still mightily anxious about Maryska.

II

The priest's house was about as big as a cow-house and as filthy as a Spanish podesta. Of food there was little save coarse bread and villainous-looking brandy. Here the guests came to the rescue, for Louis had carried up victuals at Faber's expense, and now the good things were spread upon old "Pop's" table, to that worthy's exceeding satisfaction. None ate with better appetite than he; none smacked fine lips so loudly over the good white wine, unless it were Maryska.

Louis had christened him "Old Pop" immediately, and he talked to him in voluble Servian during the repast. Occasionally he interpreted at Maryska's request, and fragments of talk were tossed down to her as bones to a dog. They made the girl laugh, but Faber found them grim enough. He was asking "What does he say?" almost at every sentence. Louis picked out the tit-bits and passed them on.

"There were Turks nine miles from here the day before yesterday. They burned Nitzke, and killed the women; some of the Nitzke people are here now; one has lost his nose—yes, they always cut off the noses, and so do our fellows when they catch a Turk. This place would be easy to hold if there were troops, but, of course, Nicholas can't send any until war is declared. Pop hopes that Alussein Pasha won't find us. If he does, there'll be a massacre; yes, it will be in the next two or three days. You're not behind the times, sir; you'll see the fun if there is any."

Faber looked at Maryska, and discovered that she was looking at him. Evidently she shared her father's whim of exaggeration and her curiosity as to "the stranger's" behaviour was now awake. These odd terms: "boss," "stranger," "master," picked up from the backwoods of America twenty years ago, pleased the Southern ear, and were guarded tenaciously. Maryska wished to frighten this American, and would have been delighted had she succeeded.

"What shall you do if they come?" she asked him.

He said, as quickly: "I should go to bed," and at that she laughed again.

"And what will you do?" he asked her. She leered as she put a whole sardine into her capacious mouth.

"I shall see them fight. Men are for fighting—women to see them. In your country, you have no soldiers. All the Americans talk a heap about it, but none of them have seen anything at all. You will be a great good man after this, boss!"

He opened his eyes.

"Why a great good man?"

"Because you will have seen something that is great and good."

He was very much astonished.

"Do you mean that killing other men is great and good, Maryska?"

Her face wore a pensive attitude, but she still had one eye upon the comestibles.

"I think they are a brave people. I think it is great and good to fight for your country."

"Well, wouldn't the Americans fight for theirs?"

"Perhaps; I don't know. You are all too clever to think about anything but money. He says so."

"Isn't money a very good thing to think about?"

She looked at him with great contempt.

"I was not born a shopkeeper," she said, and then, "Ask poppa and hear what he will say."

He nodded his head.

"Why has poppa come to Ranovica?"

"To draw pictures for the papers, yes."

"Is it for money?"

"If he will receive it, yes; if he does not like the people he will not receive it."

"Then how will you live, Maryska?"

She tossed her head.

"We shall live very well, sir; my father is a noble in his own country. He will not be insulted by such people; he is very proud."

And then she said with a ridiculous want of gravity, "And so am I. Please to give me some of the chocolates, sir. The old Pop will eat them all."

He passed her the chocolates and helped himself to a cigar from one of his own boxes. The room was long and narrow, the walls wainscoted in oak and painted a dirty pink above. An ikon hung in a corner, for "Pop" was of the Greek Orthodox Church, and very devout—when he was not drunk. The latter appeared now to be his condition, and when they rose from the table, he insisted upon taking them out into the village that they might hear him harangue the people. Night had come down at this time, but no one thought of sleep in that oasis of the bleak mountains. Far up on the desolate hills were the sentries who would tell Ranovica of the Turks' approach. In the street itself moved a heterogeneous company of old and young men, and women and laughing girls, everyone carrying a revolver in the girdle and some armed to the very teeth. A babble of excited talk fell upon the night air as a hum of insects. What was in store for the people of this new citadel? Would the Turk come or pass them by? God and the morrow must answer.

III

It was a far cry to the great arsenals at Charleston, but Faber's mind crossed the seas when he walked alone that night in the street before the priest's house. What particular freak of a latent insanity had sent him to this place?

Was it curiosity or the girl? Just the passing fancy for the wildest little woman he had ever met or the desire to see his fellow men butchered? One or the other it must be, and he was too honest to deny it. Either Maryska or the Turkish butcher, scimitar in hand.

If it were the girl, his vain folly had met with a swift rebuke. Looking up to her bedroom window, he remembered her "good-night," and the manner of it. She had told him that he was an "old, old man," and the words struck him as a thunderclap. An "old, old man!" Good God! had so much of his life already run? No one had ever spoken such words before and his vanity bristled. Had the girl been serious, or did she speak in jest?

An "old, old man"—and he was not forty. In America, it is true, they have little use for forty unless forty can command allegiance. He, John Faber, had ruled a city in Charleston. His works employed more than five thousand men; he was the high priest of the temples of labour his own brain had built up. No one remembered his age there. They spoke of him as "the new Krupp," the young genius in steel who could make or mar the fortunes of empires. The women pursued him relentlessly, remembering his eleven millions. He could have led the life of an Oriental debauchee and no one criticise him. To read the papers—many of which he owned—you might have set him down for twenty-five. This chit of a wild girl had burst the bubble with a little pin prick of her candour. An old, old man! The words raked his self-assurance, he could have boxed her ears for them.

If not Maryska, what, then, had brought him to Ranovica?

Was it to see if he could witness something of that wild life of the Balkans which had stirred his imagination in the past? When quite a lad he had read of these villages and of what befell them when the Turk came in. One incident he had never forgotten; it was on the Macedonian frontier where a little town had been sacked, the men butchered or burned by naphtha, the women violated, the old priest flayed alive. He had the account of it in the *Illustrated London News* among his papers to that very day. Such a village as this might have been the scene of it!

He passed on, musing deeply, and presently met an Albanian posted at the head of the street. The soldier had an American rifle, and he discovered that it had come from his own factory at Charleston. He gave the man a couple of crowns, and the fellow grinned savagely, pointing at the same time up to the silent hills. There were Turks somewhere up there, and he would shoot them. The rifle was about to do that for which it was made. Faber would see the fruit of his own work.

He walked on a little way and met his valet, Frank. The young man spoke German fluently, and had learned a good deal from the Austrian porters. He was much alarmed by his situation, and did not hesitate to say so.

"They tell me an attack is expected, sir. We shall fare badly in this hole if it comes off. I don't think the authorities can do much for us; what's more, there ain't any."

Faber thrust his hands into his pockets—a habit of his—and walked a little way by his servant's side.

"Why," he said half reflectively, "it isn't exactly the Ritz Hotel to be sure. Who's been talking, Frank?"

"All of them, sir, all together. Turks are known to be five miles away and the young lieutenant expects them to ride in before morning. He says passports are a sure road to paradise—you can get to heaven quicker on an ambassador's signature than on any other. I'd do this block next time if I was you, Mr. Faber, to be sure I would. We may all have our throats cut before morning."

Faber chewed his cigar heavily.

"Mr. Paleologue doesn't think it; he's been among them before. He says the Turks like newspaper men; he's one of them. I advised our people in

Constantinople I was coming, and I don't suppose they've gone to sleep. Anyway, can you fire a gun, Frank?"

Frank turned a little pale.

"I'd sooner see others fire it, sir."

"True enough, and guns won't be much good if the knives get going. I think we'll move on to-morrow, Frank; we'll learn what happens from the newspapers."

"I wish you'd go to-night, sir."

Faber shook his head.

"There's the young lady to be thought of. I guess she's asleep. It's got to be the morning, anyway."

"At any particular hour, sir?"

"As early as you like, Frank, if mademoiselle is ready."

The young man went off more afraid than he would say, but glad of the crumb of comfort. His master, however, continued to walk up and down the narrow street before the house and to regard the cold mountains wistfully. What an odd scene! What a place for him to be in! The hole was full of the queerest people he had met in all his travels. Every hour added to the multitude of souls, while as for the inn or guest-house, it might have been a barracks. Albanians whose belts were full of knives and revolvers wrangled with refugees from the mountains who had fled before the Turks; there were travellers, police, wild women, soldiers, all boxed up together like sardines in a tin; and to add to the uproar a mechanical organ played the "Merry Widow" waltz without an interval. From time to time shrieks were to be heard and the sound of blows. A man would come reeling out into the street with bloody face or gashed limbs. One of them fell dead almost at the door of the priest's house, but no one took any notice of him. As for Louis de Paleologue and "old Pop" they were far too busy getting drunk together to observe such a trifle.

Faber assured himself that the man was quite dead, and chancing upon two immense Albanians who were coming down the narrow street, he told them as much of the story as gestures would permit. They shrugged their shoulders and entered the guest-house, whence two or three tipsy fellows emerged presently to drag the dead man away as though the body were a sack. Following them to the lower end of the village, Faber perceived them disappear upon a narrow path by the side of the gorge he had climbed that afternoon, and he had no doubt that they would throw the dead man into the ravine, and leave the wolves to perform the last obsequies. He followed them no further, but stood a little while breathing the cool air and looking over toward Scutari. There lay Antivari and his own yacht. His voyage had been successful enough, and he had found the Emperor complaisant, but this estimate of his success was attended by another thought, and it concerned a woman. Sir Jules Achon would be at Ragusa by this time. Had Sir Jules seen the Emperor, and if so, to what end?

Here was a memory of Gabrielle Silvester speaking to him, and in some way moving him to an exaltation of success, not wholly chivalrous.

Had he not wagered that he would obtain an audience of the Kaiser, while the ridiculous ambassadors of a silly sentimentalism were still dreaming of their projects? And what he had promised, he had performed. The new Faber rifle would go to Germany—manufactured in part by Krupps, in part at Charleston. Meanwhile, universal peace remained a pretty topic for public platforms, and for certain distinguished old gentlemen whose philanthropy all the world admired. He, John Faber, owed something to it for it had introduced him to one of the cleverest women he had met in all his life, and this could be said despite their dramatic farewell. The latter troubled him, to be sure, but he did not despair of her when he remembered that the ugly business in Paris could yet be set straight. Claudine d'Arny must have a husband bought for her as other women have jewels or toy dogs. It should not be beyond his resources to contrive as much.

He lighted a new cigar upon this pleasant realisation of power—a gratification which his busy life made rare—and turning about, he retraced his steps toward Ranovica. The contrast between the lonely mountains which guarded the valley and the hive of armed men within was sharp enough, but it interested him at the moment less than other omens which a quick ear detected. The stillness seemed to him almost unnatural. He could have sworn at one place that a face peered down at him from a cranny of the precipice above, and, upon that, there came from afar the echo of a rifle shot. He was sure of it, faint as was the report and difficult to locate. A rifle shot over there beyond the great mountain which protected Ranovica from the northern winds! Long he listened for any repetition of the firing, but hearing none, returned at last to the priest's house. His nerves were playing tricks with him, he said. It was time to have done with it. There was a light in Maryska's room and a shadow upon the blind said that she was not yet in bed. Faber smiled as he looked up and remembered her words.

"An old, old man."

What had put it into the little cat's head to call him that?

CHAPTER IV
THE BURNING OF RANOVICA

There were two beds in the room, and one was occupied already by Louis de Paleologue, who lay in a heavy stupor, but was not properly asleep. Faber had slept in such rooms before—in the old wild days when he had travelled in Western America to sell revolvers to a Christian people, who were set upon shooting other Christians. This room impressed chiefly by its omnipresent suggestions of profound filthiness. He feared to touch anything in it—the chairs, the walls, the very coverlet on the bed. His own rugs were his armament. He wrapped himself in them from head to foot, and fell asleep at last, still wondering in his dreams why, in God's name, he had come to Ranovica.

When he awoke, it was at a touch of the hand of his valet Frank. He felt heavy and drowsy, and knew that he had missed a good night's rest—indispensable to men whose brains are dominant. It was already light, and the curtains were drawn back from the window. He sat up to listen and became aware of a strange hubbub in the street without.

"Why, what are you saying, Frank; what's that you're telling me?"

The valet was ghastly pale; he walked upon tip-toe as though afraid of being heard; his voice was hardly more than the whisper of polite servitude.

"The soldiers are in, sir—it's all up with Ranovica."

"You don't say so! When did they come in?"

"Five minutes ago, sir. Don't you hear that—my God, don't you hear it, sir?"

There is no mistaking the cry of a man who is being butchered by knives, and Faber could not mistake it then. He sprang out of bed at a bound and ran to the window. The street below was full of Turks—the red fez, the baggy blue breeches were everywhere. Leaning out to get a better view, he saw a huge Albanian held down by four assassins who had the faces of the devils in the pictures. Another, like to them, had a broad butcher's knife in his hand, and was deliberately hacking the prone man's head from his shoulders. It was clumsily done and the wretch shrieked horribly at every cut upon the bare flesh. His blood already ran in the gutters, where it mingled with the blood of fifty others.

A sense of utter helplessness—of a sickness and horror he had not yet experienced, held Faber to the window for some minutes. He could look at nothing else but the outstretched figure and the clumsy knife. When head and body at length were torn apart, and the former held up on the end of a scimitar, a loud shout of fury escaped him, and he ran across the room for his revolver. The uproar had awakened Paleologue, who sat bolt upright watching his friend. When he perceived the revolver in his hand, he sprang out of bed and caught him in powerful arms.

"What are you doing, boss—what d—d nonsense is this?"

"I tell you they're hacking men to pieces in the street out yonder. Let me go—by God, I can't stand it."

"Say, don't be a fool. Do you think you can shoot a regiment? Keep that pistol out of sight, and hold your tongue. We'll have them up here if you butt in like that! Don't you understand it isn't our business? Why, you're more d—d nuisance than any woman—and you talk as much. Now, be quiet, and hear me out. You've got to sit this through and say nothing. I'll do the talking for myself and the girl. You look on and remember why you're here. Haven't you sense enough at your age?"

The irony of it stung Faber, and he put the pistol down. The frightened valet still looked out of the window and howled at intervals, as though he himself were already in the hands of the Turks. They could hear rifle shots, sometimes a volley, then a few straggling reports, which spoke of fugitives, who were making a dash for the mountains. In the street itself, it seemed that men scurried hither and thither as rats from their holes. Shouts of triumph were followed by sharp cries of pain, often by groans and the shrill screams of women. The air came pungent with the odour of gunpowder. In the room itself there was now silence save for the servant's bellowing. Paleologue dressed himself without any fuss whatever, and he did not utter a single word. When he was quite ready, he went out into the street immediately—Faber at his heels. No one had asked for Maryska.

Paleologue was wearing a ridiculous suit of yellow tweed at this time, and a green Homburg hat with a feather in it. He carried no other weapons than a cigarette case and a box of matches. The Turks round about eyed him with amazement not untempered by curiosity; but before any of them could make a movement he shouted out in their own tongue that he was an English newspaper correspondent, and their rifles were lowered. Doffing his cap to a man upon a little grey horse, who appeared to be their officer, the artist crossed the street and offered him a cigarette, speaking rapidly in the careless way he could command, whatever the language. Faber listened open mouthed. He thought that he was as near to death as ever he had been in his nine and thirty years, and he made no poor guess.

"What does he say, Frank?" the question was hurled up at the window where the valet's white face could be seen. He might as well have asked the fellow a question in Chinese.

"I don't know, sir. I think he is mad."

"I guess we were all mad to come here. My God! what a slaughter-house!"

No truer description of the scene could have been uttered by any man. The streets of Ravonica had become a shambles. Turks ran in and out of the distant houses like dogs at a warren. There were twenty headless bodies within ten yards of the captain in command. From the door of the inn or guest-house a broad eddy of blood was oozing away to the gutter; they could hear the troops within looting and ravaging at their pleasure, while the wretched organ still played some trumpery waltz in irony most wonderful. So dreadful it was that Faber, who believed that he knew the whole story of war, staggered back in a revolt of nausea and would have re-entered the priest's house but for Paleologue's imperative summons. The artist had never been more at home. He wore his hat jauntily and smoked with gusto while he talked to the captain.

"Say, boss, come and report yourself. This is Alussein Pasha. He has had word of you from headquarters; just shake and look as pleased as you can."

Faber shook hands with the man, while Louis offered him a cigarette and struck matches for them all. The concomitants of the ghastly scene were wholly out of place and singularly at variance with the truth. These three men might have met by accident in this outlandish village and have been discussing the best road back to civilization. The bloody struggle, still proceeding in the miserable hovels round about, moved Alussein Pasha no more than did the howling of dogs in an Eastern street. And Paleologue was just as indifferent until some of the ruffians fetched out "old Pop" by the hair of his head and held a scimitar at his throat. Then, to be fair to him, he woke up to the truth and began to argue excitedly with the Pasha—at which moment also Maryska appeared at a window above and spoke to her father in Italian. He answered with a wave of his hand, bidding her disappear; but not before a Turkish subaltern had seen her and thrown her a kiss in the Western fashion. This was too much for Louis, who knocked him down out of hand.

Undoubtedly it was a mad act, and went near to costing the lives of the party. Alussein Pasha uttered a roar like a stricken bull when his officer was floored; the Turks about him drew their knives and pressed upon Faber with fierce shouts. He had as good as given it up, and thought that this was the end of the business, when a young man at the Pasha's side said something to his chief in an earnest note and appeared to bring that savage worthy to his senses. He roared an order to the hawking pack, and they fell back from the prey they had marked down. An excited exchange of doubtful compliments between Louis and the grand Turk was followed by a compromise, Alussein stipulating for an immediate return to the shelter of the priest's house until the affair was over. So, in they went, the soldiers half pushing them with the butts of their rifles and barring the door behind them. "Old Pop" was the only prisoner now. They had forgotten him in the excitement of that very critical moment through which they had passed.

"Have a drink?" said Louis, throwing himself into a chair by the window and his hat into another; he seemed quite unconcerned, even unaware that there had been an instant of peril. John Faber, on the other hand, was talking to himself in decided terms. "John, my boy, you're a d—d fool to be here," he was saying—and that was very true. When he had drunk a tumbler of white wine and mineral water he found the sweat running off him like rain.

"Hot weather for the time of year. Where's your girl, Louis?"

"Oh! I guess she's all right—better where she is. Will you pass over that drawing pad? I can see a picture here."

Faber passed him the pad, and he settled deep in the arm-chair and began to make a rapid sketch of the crowded street. At the same moment Maryska entered the room and closed the door firmly behind her.

II

"Where is the priest?" she asked them in a strange tone. The men looked at her together, then at each other.

"Why, isn't he in the house?"

"They are killing him," she said. And then, "What are you doing here?"

Louis put down his pencil, and leaning out of the window, which was on a level with the street, he watched the scene a little while in silence.

"By God!" he cried at last; "they're singeing the old man's beard. Listen to that."

They listened and heard a harrowing sound, neither cry nor scream, but the wail as of a cat mewing. Twenty Turks had "Old Pop" in their midst; they had torn his clothes from his back and cut off his nose. Now some of them brought naphtha and poured it on his head, and instantly he became a vomit of flame. [1] Every feature of the wretched man could be seen with horrid distinctness, clarified by the fire. The flesh withered up before their eyes. He stood for a long minute plucking at his own flesh with hands of which but the bones were left. Then, all his cries ceased, and he fell forward in a ghastly heap, while the Turks howled derisively and thrust scimitars into the fire. They had burned many a priest these latter days, but this fellow was famous, and had fought many a good fight for Ranovica. His death stimulated a frenzy of lust and madness, and they rushed away to enter the houses and drive out the women. All the make-believe of a military occupation had been put aside by this time. Alussein had led them across the mountains to teach these Christians a lesson, and they were good masters.

[1] The incident here described is taken almost unchanged from the recent story of Macedonia.

Maryska heard the priest's cries, but she did not see the manner of his death. Had it not happened so swiftly and with such dramatic finality, the men would have made some stir to save him; but, as though guessing their intention, a group of soldiers with rifles across their arms pressed about the window, and made it very clear that they would shoot upon next to no provocation at all. Alussein Pasha had ridden on at this time to the lower road overlooking Scutari, and would return when the good work was done. He would declare that the villagers had brought it all on themselves, and his report would be a model of tearful orthodoxy. Meanwhile, there were very few of the male inhabitants to bring anything upon anybody; the women alone remained, and they were dragged from their houses, some by the hair of their heads, some forced by thrust of swords, a few going without protest, as though they dreamed. Of the latter were the younger girls, mere children of fourteen or fifteen years, who stood in a little group before the priest's house, and looked at the soldiers, uncertain—nay, ignorant—of their meaning. Maryska saw these anon; and Louis also. He had been chewing his cigarette very busily since the priest died, and there were few lines upon the paper. As for Faber, he merely stood motionless by the window. The scene held him spellbound with an influence he knew to be evil.

"What have they done with the priest? Why do you not answer me, Mr. Faber?"

She touched him upon the arm, and he looked down upon a child's face from which a woman's eyes stared up at him wonderingly. What answer could he make to her?

"You must just run away and think nothing about it, Maryska," he said quietly. "We can none of us do anything. I wish to God we could."

"Are you not going to speak for the children, then?"

"The children! Oh, they're all right; they won't hurt the children."

"That is not true," she said, for the instinct of the woman guided her surely. "Someone must speak for the children. Will not you, father?"

The appeal touched Paleologue, and he threw away the stump of his cigarette and leaned out of the window. They heard him talking rapidly with the Turks upon the side-walk, and presently shouting something to an officer before the guest-house opposite. Whatever he said moved the soldiers to derision and the children themselves to hope. They knew that he was their friend, and their round eyes watched his every gesture.

"What's the man saying?" Faber asked. Louis hardly seemed to know.

"I guess it's a bad business, boss, a d—d bad business."

"You don't mean to say—"

"I do every word of it."

"We must see this thing through, Paleologue. I'm going out."

"You can't go out. What's the good of doing stunts? They'll shoot, sure."

He tried to hold back the impetuous man, appealing and swearing in a breath. From below, the children watched the scene with a look of bewilderment and despair. The unknown strangers were quarrelling, then! What hope of mercy had they if this went on? This must have been in their minds when Maryska, climbing nimbly as a cat, slipped by her father and leaped down among the Turks. She was kissing and hugging some of the children and telling them in a tongue they understood that all would be well with them; doing this, and defying the snarling troopers before a man could have counted ten. Then the men at the window lost sight of her, the throng closing about her as water filling the vortex of a falling stone.

"Good God, man, aren't you going now?"

Paleologue licked his lips, a little astonished, perhaps, not to find a cigarette between them. He caught up a great planter's hat and clapped it on the side of his head; then, without a word, he clambered over the casement and pushed his way among the soldiers. Of course, Faber was upon his heels, treading so close on his tracks that they stumbled into the press together and were instantly swallowed up by it. Instructed to deal patiently with the strangers, none of the sentries fired upon them, but all swarmed about them and tried to pull them back. The village itself had by this time become a Golgotha, from whose wretched houses came the groans of butchered men and the screams of women in an agony of fear and shame. Their terrible cries were echoed up and down the streets from many a group which stooped about an infamy; while at the far end near the church, flames spurted from an isolated house, and the wood burned with a detonation heard closely upon the still air. The outposts of the legions of hell had begun their work; they would do it thoroughly enough before their chief returned to call them off.

"Where's my daughter? What have you done with her?" Paleologue's voice rose to a shrill pitch as he pushed and fought his way into the crowd and was thrust forward and still forward by the wiry American at his heels. Faber had never imagined such a scene as this, nor could he have believed it possible. The heat and clamour of the street, the sweat of the fighting men; here and there a girl caught in a man's arms and held firmly as a wild beast holds its prey; smoke of the burning house coming down upon the wind—the crazy organ still rolling out its dirge-like waltzes. All this and the fierce oaths of the maladroitly butchered—the horrid, gashed corpses in the gutters—the rearing, terrified horses of Alussein's lieutenants; and, above it all, the serene sky and the desolate mountains lifting their scarred summits in savage menace. What an inferno, what a hell of human creation! And into this the girl Maryska had plunged, headlong as a bold swimmer into a raging sea which has engulfed a child.

He found himself imitating Paleologue by and by, and calling her name aloud. The attempts of the sentries to get the pair of them back to the house were met by thrust upon thrust; a good square push from the shoulder here and a dive into an opening there. Gradually they won their way up the street, but could not find her; and upon that a sense of desperation drove them to some imprudence, and they began to deal in blows. Such madness might have brought a swift penalty but for the fire which the priest's death had kindled. The God of Ranovica, designing that these people should perish to bear witness to their faith, willed also that Ranovica should fall with them, and that the priest should be the instrument. From his body the flames had run to the crazy house; from the house to the church, and thence to the narrow street, which instantly became aglow. Faber found himself pressing forward amid showers of sparks, and still crying "Maryska—Maryska!" as though the child's voice could be heard amid the din. Turks pressed about him shielding their faces with sun-browned arms and cursing the "spawn of dogs" by which the visitation had come upon them. He was driven in and out of courtyards, tossed hither and thither by the human wave, whose crest was the whirling scimitars of the destroyers. In the end he found himself out upon the hillside, flaming Ravonica below him, and the still air alive with the cries of its people. Paleologue had disappeared; there was no trace of Maryska, and he himself had hardly a rag upon his back.

He sat down upon a great boulder, and presently heard a familiar voice. It was that of his valet, Frank.

"Mr. Faber, is that you, sir?"

"I guess it is, Frank."

"Thank God for that, sir! Our baggage is done for, sure and certain. The house is afire from top to bottom, sir."

"Never mind the baggage, Frank. Have you seen Mr. Paleologue?"

"He was down among the soldiers five minutes ago, sir."

"And the young lady?"

Frank could not answer.

"She went away with some of the young women—I think toward the church, sir."

"Was that long ago?"

"About five minutes before they fired it; I'm sure it wasn't more."

"Well, look at the church now, anyway. This is an awful business, Frank."

"I suppose in their way it's what they call war, sir. But it's a terrible business."

"Ah!" said Faber. "I suppose it would be. You don't happen to have a cigar on you, Frank?"

"I've got a few cigarettes, sir."

"Then pass one up. We'll go and look for Mr. Paleologue presently; I guess he's taken the lower road. We should find both of them there."

"I hope we shall do so, sir."

He passed the cigarettes and the matches, and his master lighted one and sat and smoked in silence. It may be that he asked himself what he, John Faber, was doing out there upon this bleak hillside when he might have been on board his yacht in the harbour of Antivari. Such reflections had occurred to him on several occasions when some absurd venture had brought him very near to that haven where millions are the poorest credentials; but they were unduly ironical to-day, and not a little persistent. Why had he come to Ranovica? Because that little wide-eyed woman, who made such a curious appeal to him, had insisted upon his coming. It was very true, and he would not fence with it. He might lose his life for Maryska even yet; and that would be a grotesque finale enough. Meanwhile, a certain doubt about her remained and troubled him with a graver thought. Why had he not discovered her in the village? No man could venture into that inferno now, for the whole place was just a flame upon the hillside; but he had been up and down the street with Paleologue, and they had seen nothing of her. He thought it curious if nothing more. They should have discovered her immediately when the fire broke out.

Alussein Pasha rode up presently and his little staff with him. He had treated Faber with some deference from the beginning, and now that the fury of the sack was over he became almost grotesquely polite, gabbling in appalling German and expressing as well as he could his regret for the state in which he discovered the stranger. In return, Faber asked him of his friend—gesture serving where names failed—and the matter being understood, the Pasha told off a lieutenant and two men who invited the "infidel" to follow them. Ranovica had burned itself to a cinder by this time, and if it was not possible to pass down the narrow street, at least the precincts of the houses might be searched. Faber trudged after the men and came to the ruined church, now but a shell and a few blackened beams. A young Turkish soldier walked to and fro here; but the gulley of the road before the church was blocked by corpses, and near by them lay the figure of Louis de Paleologue. He had been shot through the head just as he reached the porch, and he lay face downwards, an unlighted cigarette between his lips and his kindly eyes wide open.

Faber knelt and turned the dead man over. He felt his pulse, and even laid his head upon his chest to listen for the beating of his heart. There had been horrors enough in Ranovica this day; but they had to do with a strange and savage people, of whom he knew nothing. He remembered that this man had taken his mother to America when she had no other friend in the world. Had he not come to Europe to reward him for what he had done as few have been rewarded, whatever the service? And this was the end of it—this prone figure, still and fearful—this, and the Turks who looked down upon the scene with Oriental indifference—this, and the sentry who leered behind their backs and made no attempt to hide his satisfaction. Faber caught the fellow grinning, and recognized him for one of the men who had turned on him earlier in the day when Paleologue floored the officer. The rifle in his hand had come from the arsenal at Charleston. Surely destiny spoke loudly enough here.

He borrowed a burned and tattered cloak from one of the dead in the gutter, and covered his friend's face reverently. Where to go, what to do next, he knew not; nor in what manner he should seek Maryska. The truth had gripped him with fingers of iron.

This was war—and of war was he not the disciple?

III

The Turks left the village about three in the after-noon. It was understood that they had other work of the kind, but more to the northward, and removed from the observant eye of their neighbours, the Montenegrins, who would surely avenge this day. Before they left, they were able to restore to Faber the mules which had brought his party to Ranovica. The beasts had been taken up the hillside during the conflagration, and would have been led much further afield but for the Pasha's desire to curry favour with the American. He knew that this was the man who made the rifles with which the infidel dogs must be destroyed; urgent messages from Constantinople had warned him to show deference to so useful an ally, and he obeyed his instructions with a display of manners quite pleasing. It was otherwise when the dead artist and his daughter were mentioned. Constantinople had said nothing about them, and it really seemed to Faber that the flat-faced, good-humoured Alussein could be a genius of understanding or the dullest blockhead at his pleasure.

So away the Turk went, just when the sun was beginning to dip down over the Adriatic and all the wilderness to glow beneath the shimmer of its deepening rays. A hillside, normally grey and cold, shone rose-pink and purple in the waxing splendour of the hour. The burned village became but the blacker for the gift, a charred log lying in a cup of the burnished rocks. Out of it, when every ruin had been twice searched, every heap of ashes turned for possible plunder, out of it went the baggy breeches and the little white horses and the fierce and bristling men, as cool and laconic as though this were but an episode and to-morrow would furnish another. Romancers' tales of troops drunk with lust and slaughter could not be told of them. All that passed, women's fearful struggles to escape their embraces, the shrieks of men whose hearts were being torn out, the gasps of the dying and the livid faces of the dead—all this was already forgotten, and would hardly be remembered when a week had gone. Had not the Prophet commanded them so to do, and was not he a discerning person withal?

Faber had taken a meal with Alussein upon the hillside about midday, and after that he had patrolled the village with Frank at his side, waiting and hoping for the coming of Maryska. To return to Ragusa without her would have been an infamy he could not contemplate; and yet he feared to meet her or to tell her the truth which must be told. When at last he did discover her, some hours had passed, and it was quite dark. The hillside with its savage boulders had given up the most part of the refugees then, and they had come down to the village to wander amid the ruins of their poor homes and to fill the street with their wailing. It was at this time also that another band of Albanians came up the valley to their comrades' rescue; alas, so many hours too late, but yet in time to help the desperate refugees and to bring them food and succour. Fires were now lighted by the valley road, and the women and children grouped about them. The most timid crept down from the rocks above; girls dishevelled and weeping, men who had fled with gashed limbs to the harbourage of caves, children whose parents lay dead beneath the ashes—all came at the summons of the shrill goat's horn. Meanwhile, none thought of burying the dead—none except Faber, who would not leave the body of Louis de Paleologue where it was, and returned with two lusty Albanians at his heels to do what could be done in the matter.

It was then that he found Maryska.

One of the Albanians carried a lantern, and the rays of it discovered her, kneeling against the broken railings of the church porch, but with face averted from the dead. She did not appear to have been weeping. Her eyes were big and round; her head bare, her hair dishevelled. What she had suffered at the soldiers' hands might not be imagined; but its memories had been obliterated by this sudden realization of the greater loss. All that humanity had been to her lay still and ghastly in that fearsome gutter. Father, brother, friend—he who had gone hand in hand with her through the wild wilderness of the world, he would lead her no more. The night had dropped a black curtain between her and the eternal hope of youth. Womanhood had revealed itself, its secrets thrust upon her by the bloody hands of monsters; but the drugged soul of the child could find no place in her mind for that. He was dead. Why, then, did she live?

She shrank from the light, but did not cover her eyes. Discerning Faber, she leaped toward him as an animal unchained, and bared her breast with frenzied fingers. "Shoot me, stranger—shoot me through the heart!" she cried. He caught her outstretched hand, and she fell almost lifeless into his arms. Oblivion, the greater mercy, saved her reason in the critical hour. She was in a delirium when they made a rude palanquin and carried her down to Antivari. She awoke therefrom upon the afternoon of the second day after in a cabin upon Faber's yacht; and then, for the first time, they believed that she would live.

CHAPTER V
A STRANGE VOYAGE

I

The *Wanderer*, carrying Sir Jules Achon and his party, lay in Ragusa harbour when the fugitives came down from the hills. The two boats were moored almost side by side in the offing, and hardly had Faber set foot aboard when he sent a message to Gabrielle, begging her help in an emergency. Half an hour later she met him at the head of the gangway ladder, and he led her at once into the gorgeous saloon of the *Savannah*, as his own boat was named.

"Is this the emergency?" she asked laughingly, as she pointed to the wonderful decoration of the cabin. He told her as bluntly that it was not.

"I've got a patient on board," he said. "Will you help me?"

"You know that I will—very gladly. Is he here now?"

"It's not he—it's she. That's why I sent for one of her own sex. God help a foreign woman in this part of the world! This is a mere baby. She calls me an 'old, old man.' So I guess she's interesting."

He betrayed no emotion of any kind. His anxiety concerning the child, his perception of the irony of fate directing his footsteps into such strange paths, the baser curiosity which had sent him into the hills, were masked successfully by that clear-cut face. Gabrielle imagined that his act was an impulse of charity, and she was pleased that he had made her the instrument of it.

"Where is this precious derelict, and what has happened to her?"

"She's in the pink saloon. Don't speak of it lightly. She's lost her father, and has not a friend in the world. I knew she would find her way to your heart. Shall we go and see her? The doctor's there now, I guess. We'll have to get our orders."

He led the way to the cabin, and they went in. It was a beautiful room, and his servants already had smothered it in flowers. A young Austrian doctor from Ragusa was trying to give the head stewardess his instructions, and failing as dismally. He turned with relief to Gabrielle, whose German was pretty if not eloquent. The cabin was to be kept as quiet as possible; the patient must be watched zealously in case of sudden collapse. He understood that this was a case of shock, and could know nothing until consciousness returned. His suggestion that a nurse should be fetched from one of the military hospitals was refused almost ungraciously by the English girl he so plainly admired. Gabrielle would play the part herself. She had already removed her furs, and was busy about the cabin where artistic fingers could do so much. It was quite needless for the doctor to repeat his instructions as he was prepared to; she dismissed both him and her host with a wave of the hand which said "begone" as no tongue could have uttered the word.

It was nine o'clock at night before Faber saw her again. His dinghy had gone across to the *Wanderer* with a message explaining the circumstances, but he himself remained on deck, waiting for news that might be a new echo of this pitiful tragedy. But a few days ago he had entered that beautiful place and discovered the little nomad whose life now hung upon a thread. He had wished to bring happiness to her father and herself, but had failed beyond repair. Money did not help him in the wilds of Albania, nor could money buy one jot or tittle of content for the child of the man he had discovered in the cavern. Had not he himself paid for the journey to Ranovica—a whim which cost the life of a man to whom he owed his very existence? And now the child was his legacy. He stood at the taffrail wondering what unnameable secret she had carried down from the hills.

Perhaps he remembered the multitude of women who had so suffered since God Almighty created a battlefield; but understanding had never come in that way hitherto. Little Maryska—he would have given a good deal of his lavish fortune to have saved her life that night. His heart bounded when Gabrielle came out of the cabin at last to bring him better news of the invalid.

"She is conscious and would see you. I think you had better go down."

"Do you approve my going?"

She looked at him in a curious way.

"She has asked for you, Mr. Faber."

"Why, then, I'll go right now. Have you eaten that dinner yet?"

"As much as I want. I must go now and get my things from the yacht."

"But you'll come back, sure?"

"I think I must—there's no one else."

"That's right down fine of you. I knew you'd do it when you understood."

She looked him full in the face and smiled.

"There are some things no woman can misunderstand. I shall not be very long. Please let her talk as little as possible."

"Ah!" he said, fallen to a grave manner. "I fear this is a bad business altogether."

She did not ask him why, nor had she any clue to his meaning. The whole affair was a mystery which could have but a human solution. She made light of the romantic story concerning Louis de Paleologue, and believed, with a feminine instinct for the obvious, that vulgar flirtation had been the impulse of Faber's journey. All this hurt her pride, but could not be the just subject of complaint. Tenaciously she clung to the idea that she might yet use this master intellect for the schemes which had lifted her father and herself from the slough of monotony to a little place in the story of the world. This very accident, this revelation of a man's weakness, might be a precious opportunity, however deeply her vanity suffered. If she succeeded, her triumph must be the greater; if she failed—But failure was a word which Gabrielle Silvester refused to add to her vocabulary.

So she went over to the *Wanderer* to tell her father of the sick girl, and to add, almost in a whisper, "I believe there's a good deal in it." To which Silvester replied that he was sorry to hear it, "for," said he, "there is no man alive who could do so great a work if he would come over to us."

II

Faber went straight down to Maryska's cabin and found her crouching upon a pillow. The long, jet black hair had been taken down, and lay in a tangled skein about her; she was very pale, and her eyes glowed as with a fever. Evidently she had been listening for his footsteps, for she turned instantly when he came in and fixed her eyes upon him.

"It's Mr. Faber," she said, but without satisfaction.

He took a chair and drew it to her bedside.

"Well, Maryska, are you feeling better, my dear?"

She paid not the slightest heed to the question. Sitting up in bed, she closed her gown about her chest and breathed a little heavily. Then she said, without warning:

"Where is my father?"

He bent his head, fearing to meet her gaze.

"My dear little girl, you'll remember all about that presently."

There was a long pause upon this.

"Yes," she said at last, and still apparently unmoved; "I do remember. Why did you let him die, Mr. Faber?"

"I, Maryska? I had nothing to do with it. If he had taken my advice he would not have left the Pasha's side. I was quite a long way off when it happened."

She insisted, looking at him with pathetic eyes.

"If you had not come to Ragusa, he would not have left me. I am sorry you came. Shall I be kept here long?"

"Do you mean in this ship?"

"Yes, of course. Is it your ship, then?"

"It's my ship—at least, I've hired it. Don't you like it, my dear?"

She looked round about her critically.

"You are not very rich," she said at last. "We came from America in a much larger ship than this. He was with me then."

Her eyes filled suddenly with tears, and she saw no longer either the cabin or the man. Faber covered the outstretched hand, and stroked it softly.

"My poor little girl! You must make your home with me now."

She shook her head.

"You are not rich; it would be different with you," she said; and then, in just the childish tone she had used at the Cantina, she exclaimed, "I don't believe you have much money."

He laughed, and reassured her.

"I've a great deal more than you or I will ever want, Maryska."

It was evident that the wolf-child was suspicious. The gipsy instincts were awake.

"Will you give me some money if I want any?"

"I'll give you as much as you ask me for."

"Five crowns, say—would you give me five crowns?"

"Of course I would."

"Here and now?" and she held out her hand.

He was nonplussed for the moment, but he took a bank-note from his pocket, and thrust it into her tiny fist.

"There, I guess there are fifty crowns and more there, Maryska. You shall have another when you want it."

The hand closed upon the bank-note like a vise. None the less, her thoughts were not wholly of the money.

"If my father had been here he would have been very glad of this. He will never know now."

"I don't believe that. He'll know that you've become my little daughter, Maryska. He'll understand that all right. My home's yours now. I want you to understand that right here."

She shook her head, the long hair smoothed back from her forehead.

"He will never know. I cannot speak to him. I have tried so hard and he does not hear me."

"Believe no such thing, my dear. He hears every word you say. He knows that you will be happy with me."

She looked up inquiringly.

"With you, Mr. Faber? Why should I stay with you?"

"Because I mean to make a home for you."

"Will you make it upon this ship?"

"Why, you couldn't live always upon a ship."

She became practical.

"I would sooner live in Ragusa; but not in the Cantina, because he would not be there with us. It is very cheap, and if you had the money we could live very well upon a crown a day and the wine. I have had no wine since I came away; the lady would not give me any. If you have any money left and would send for some wine—" She looked up beseechingly, with a look which reminded him of the little wild wolf who had run to the wine-shop the night he discovered her father. He hardly knew how to satisfy her.

"I'll send down anything the doctor orders for you. If he says wine—"

"Oh!" she cried, flown into a passion in an instant. "I could kill you—I could kill you for that!" And without another word she turned her face to the wall and still clutching her money tenaciously, she made it plain that she had done with him.

"All right, Maryska," he said, rising, "you shall have the wine all right. I don't care that for the doctors; I'll see to it myself."

She did not answer him, and lay so still that she might have been dead.

III

Gabrielle returned immediately after the interview was terminated, and with her Harry Lassett, who by no means liked the circumstances of her visit, and had come to verify them. She went at once to Maryska's cabin, but Lassett remained on deck to sample the green cigars, and incidentally to cross-question their owner. He talked upon a number of subjects with the assurance of twenty-three years and the experience of ten.

"I've heard a lot of things about you from Gabrielle. Of course, you know I'm engaged to her."

Faber finished the operation of striking a match and then lighted his cigar.

"Why, is that so? My congratulations. When is it to be?"

"Oh, I dunno; marriage is a considerable proposition. Besides, I'm going out to Australia next winter—cricket, you know."

"Ah! you play ball, then? Is there much to it?"

Harry grinned.

"Nothing. I'm an amateur, you know—that is, if you know anything about the game at all. We can't take any money for our services, so we have to charge expenses. And jolly well we're worth it—some of us," he added with conviction.

Faber nodded, as though he understood perfectly.

"I guess you deliver the goods. There's something of that sort in my country, only we don't call 'em amateurs. Anyway, the name doesn't hurt. You'll be married when you come back, I suppose?"

"Ah! there you *cherchez la femme*. Gabrielle isn't struck with marriage—not very much. She's full of this tomfool business about peace on earth and goodwill toward Wilhelm. It makes me sick to listen to it. The yacht loaded up with cranks, and every one of them trying to get something out of Sir Jules. It's almost as good a game as Throgmorton Street, if you can find the mugs, chiefly those with handles. I tell you, I'm just fed up with it."

"You don't get thin on it, sure. How long does Sir Jules propose to stop here? Has he said that?"

"He'll stop on the off chance of another interview with the Emperor on his return from Corfu."

"The first one wasn't satisfactory, then?"

"Oh, lots of pats on the back and that sort of thing—plenty of butter, but not much bread. By the way, do you think there's anything in the business, or is it just fancy?"

"I think there's a great deal. Sir Jules Achon is about the deepest thinker in this line I've yet struck. But he wants a man with him—he wants a hustler. Europe listens when you beat the drum, but it's got to be a mighty big drum nowadays. He's merely playing with fiddle-sticks."

"That's because his drummer is on the sick list. I hear he's a regular roarer—Rupert Trevelle, who hustled Balfour into the Blue Ensign Club. He was to have been here, but he's down with neuritis or something. They say that's why we're all drifting about the Adriatic doing nothing but patting each other's back. It will be different when Trevelle gets going."

"Then set him going right quick. Does Miss Silvester take to it kindly? Is she dead earnest?"

"That's just what I want to know. I'll tell you what, though—she won't be when she's married to me. No peace at any price in my house, I'm d—d if there is."

"Don't believe in it, eh?"

"Does any good Britisher really believe in it? Wars made us what we are. Would Nelson have gone to a law court? And what price would Drake receive in a county court action for singeing the Spanish King's beard? I tell you it's all d—d nonsense, and some of 'em must know it to be so. When I am married to Gabrielle—But here she comes, my boy, so mum's the word. There's time enough for arguments—eh, what?"

Faber smiled and stood up to get another chair. Gabrielle was very serious, and looked gracious in her perplexity. She had a strange tale to tell of her patient, and recited it in a kind of astonished despair which amused her host very much.

"Do you know," she exclaimed, "the child drinks wine like an alderman. Whatever am I to do?"

"What?" cried Harry. "You're rotting, Gabrielle, you're not serious."

"It's true, every word of it. She says that she is doing it by your orders, Mr. Faber. Is it really so?"

"How much has she taken? I sent a bottle down. It's only the light stuff they drink hereabouts. You can hardly call it wine."

"She has drunk the whole bottle. I was never more astonished in my life."

"We shall have to humour her a bit. Of course, it must be stopped. And that reminds me—I want a home for her in England. Will you and your father give her one?"

"She'll do for the 'horrid' example at your temperance meetings, Gabrielle. Better take her."

"I think," said Gabrielle, "you had better see my father. You know that he is undecided about this call to Yonkers."

"He won't be undecided about it when I've had my say. Is the patient all right now? Do you think well of her?"

"I think she is terribly distressed, and is hiding it from all of us."

"A brave little girl! I guessed as much. We must get her away from this place as soon as possible. When does Sir Jules propose to sail?"

"Not until the Emperor leaves Corfu. He said so at lunch."

"He'll weigh before then; the Emperor doesn't mean to see him a second time. Anyway, you won't leave her, Miss Silvester, I go pat on that."

She averted her eyes from both of them, and looked away to the other yacht.

"I don't think I ought to leave her. The better way will be for you to see my father. She's sleeping now. We might go over to the *Wanderer* at once, if you liked—"

"And make it an excuse for a jolly little supper on deck," said Harry voraciously. He had done little but eat and sleep since they left London.

IV

Gordon Silvester was as astonished as Gabrielle by the proposition which Faber made to him, but he listened sympathetically none the less.

"This would mean a definite refusal to Yonkers," he said, and Faber agreed that it was so.

"I'll tell you what, Mr. Silvester. This affair has cut pretty deep down into some of my old-fashioned notions, and is costing me more than I care to tell any man. I came across to Europe to pay a debt I owed to one who was my mother's friend. I meant to reward him pretty liberally. And what have I succeeded in doing after all? You know the story. Paleologue lies dead up at Ranovica—the child's on my yacht to judge me for what I've done. Henceforth, she is going to stand to me as my own daughter. I shall spare no expense to educate and train her. She'll have the best that money can buy; all that gives a woman a chance in the world. If you will, you and your daughter shall be my agents in this. Live where you please, take the best house the agents can find for you, spend all the money you can spend on making her what I would wish her to be. You say the pastorate has tired you out, and that you would like to devote yourself to literature. Here's the chance of your life time! Don't tell me that you will let it go begging."

Silvester knocked out the ashes of his pipe with some deliberation. He was very much excited by the offer, but at some pains to conceal his surprise at it. Many schemes ran through his head—alas! none of them had to do with Maryska de Paleologue.

"Of course," he said, "I could devote myself entirely then to the I.A.L. It would be a great opportunity. I can imagine no finer."

"There is one finer, Mr. Silvester."

"Of what are you thinking?"

"Of a woman's soul—just the heart and the soul of a little waif from the hills. She's a finer opportunity, for she's flesh and blood. Your geese are all swans, Mr. Silvester. You'll know as much when they fly."

"I fear you are as hostile to us as ever. Yet it seems to me—I say it with all reserve—that these days should have done something for us."

Faber thrust his hand deep into his pocket, and bit into his cigar.

"They've taught me nothing, except to say 'kismet.' Who knows truly how a man's destiny works? I shall make Maryska de Paleologue one of the richest women in Europe—well, there I come in. Money's stronger than most things, and it's going to be stronger than a man's death on this occasion. Wait until the story is written, then we'll draw the moral."

"Do you wish me to go to England at once?"

"To-morrow, in my yacht, if you can. I go to Berlin to sign up a contract for rifles, but I expect to be in London in a fortnight's time. You should have your house then. There'll be no difficulty when you show them the money. I leave all that to you and to Miss Gabrielle. She's got to be the good angel in this affair. I'm counting on her right through."

"You may well do that. She is a wonderful organizer; no talk, no fuss. I am sure they would have liked her in America if we had gone to Yonkers. As it is, I really don't know what to say to those people."

"Oh, tell them to go to hell!" said Faber, while he struck a match sharply and relighted his cigar.

V

The *Savannah* weighed at dawn, and all that day they steamed by the glorious isles of the matchless Adriatic. Their destination was Venice, whence Faber would go via Munich to Berlin. The others were to travel direct by the Simplon to London—all but Harry Lassett, who meant to put in a few days at Montana before he returned.

They carried a young doctor from Ragusa, but he soon discovered that he had little to do save to take a fee, a performance which he accomplished with truly professional grace. Maryska had a heart of iron, it appeared, and a constitution to match it. Whatever the unnameable night had taught her of life or of men, she held the damnable secret with the tenacity of a race born to such acts and schooled in the creeds of ferocity. Very silent, suspicious of all, agitated and given to fits of trembling when alone, those with her could not read that riddle of a child's dreams aright. To Gabrielle she remained an enigma, seemingly wanting in gratitude and anxious to escape every occasion for it. Gordon Silvester she treated as though he did not exist; Harry Lassett was a problem in manhood to awake distrust and find her eyes furtive. John Faber she trusted wholly.

They had allowed her to come on deck during the heat of the day, and she lay there in a hammock swung between hatches. An untamed restlessness found her starting at every sound. She would sit up and watch the passers-by as though afraid of them; or stare at the crew with deeply black eyes, as though seeking a friend among them. Her requests that Faber should be sent to her were unceasing. In his turn, he liked to hear her talk. He would watch those eloquent eyes, and forget that she had called him "an old, old man" in the early days of their acquaintance.

"Will you come and sit beside me, Mr. Faber, just a little while? I do not want the others to come. I will not have them near me."

"But, Maryska, my dear, they just want to be kind to you, that's all. Don't you like Miss Gabrielle, now?"

She thought about it. Then she said: "Is she your wife, Mr. Faber?"

"My!—what an idea! I haven't got a wife. She's engaged to the young man over there."

"Not the one with the wolf's whiskers and the teeth."

"Of course not; he's her father. The other one who's playing with the quoits."

She watched Harry Lassett a little while; her face became grave.

"*He* used to play that when last he came from America. He played with me, and then I won money for him from the others. We can't do that here; is that right, Mr. Faber?"

He laughed and took her hand.

"Let me tell you about this money, Maryska. Do you know I'm very rich, my dear? They call me one of the richest men in the world. You mustn't think about money any more. I've got more than you and I will ever spend if we live to be as old as Methuselah. So just change the subject, little lady, and find another."

She made nothing of it, the years of the human chase pursued her. Was she not alone now? *He* could never help her again, and he had been so great a part of her life.

"What is the good of telling me this? It is not my money, Mr. Faber. I must go and get some for myself when the ship stops. You had no right to take me away from Ragusa—my home was there. Why have you done it?"

He tried to tell her, but it was very difficult. In some moods she was little better than a waif of the streets, who had learned to beg like a mendicant at a church door; in others her birthright gave her a wonderful dignity before which the plebeian in John Faber was dumb.

"I want you to have a new home, Maryska, one that you'll be glad to call your own. That's why I'm taking you to England. Miss Gabrielle there is going to live with you and so's her father. But it will be your own house and everything that's in it yours. You'll like it, sure, when you see it, my dear. I don't think you'll want to go back to Ragusa again."

She listened pensively.

"Will that boy be there?"

"The one who's playing games?"

"Yes, the boy who laughs."

"Oh, I dare say he'll come sometimes. Do you like him, then?"

"I don't know; he is very young, is he not?"

"I haven't asked his age, but I dare say he'll tell you."

"I should not ask him. Men do not like to tell their age. He never would. Why are you paying for this house you speak of? You have no right to pay for anything for me. You know that very well."

The question gave him his opportunity, and he told her as much of the story as she could comprehend. Her father had been the best friend he had ever known. He had taken his mother to America at the crisis of her fortunes. It was an obligation he could never forget. He had meant to do so much in return, but fate was against them both. They must act together henceforth and make the best of their lives they could. She must help him to honour his mother's name. In her turn Maryska replied but vaguely. He had thought that she was not listening, but when he had finished, and following a little interval of silence, she threw herself back upon her cushions and cried wildly, "Jesus Christ! I never had a mother to honour." And that surely was as lamentable a confession as any he had heard from her lips.

VI

They were off Venice upon the following night, and so favoured by fortune that the waxing moon gave them a vista of the hundred isles, beautiful beyond compare.

A still sea hardly stirred a ripple upon the sandy shores of the Lido. Venice herself stood up in a haze of soft light, her spires and domes rising above the vast lagoon of untroubled waters, dim, mysterious, entrancing. Seen from afar, she might have been a great house of dreams; her windows so many stars above a silent lake; her palaces but the dark clouds of a vision. As phantoms about them, ships drifted upon a reluctant tide; sails took shape and glided away, spectres of an instant, into the deeper shadows. There were musical voices crying out of the darkness; notes of song most pleasing; the dwelling reverberations of ancient bells to tell of hours which should have been unnumbered. As they drew nearer still and the Dogana took shape with the vast dome of the Maria della Salute beyond it, then it was as though the centuries spoke with one voice, and all the lustre and the achievement of a thousand years were revealed in a splendid instant. So is it ever for those who approach Venice from the sea and obliterate the black modernity which wrestles with her story. Such is the vision of her which Turner beheld.

Faber watched the spectacle from the boat deck, and was far from displeased to find Gabrielle at his side. There had been few opportunities for confidential talk since they sailed from Ragusa, and she herself had said no word to lead him to believe that the course of her life was about to be changed. Very stately in mien this night, her height accentuated by the place where she stood, her hair a little wild beneath her wrap, eyes very bright and searching, her manner restful, he wondered whence came the "aristocrat" in her lineage, and how a mere manse had sent forth such a missioner. Let the assembly be what it might, Gabrielle Silvester would take a proud place. Intellectually she was far above him in education and artistic perception, but he suffered a sense of inferiority with patience, and admired her the more because she could awaken it. Bertie Morris had said that she was "cold and Saxon." Faber doubted the truth of that.

They discussed many things in an ordinary way. She spoke of the story of Venice and found him skilfully parrying his own ignorance. He knew little of the history of the place—had heard of St. Mark's and of the "Three." The lion's mouth struck him as a fine idea. There ought to be one in every city for cranks and faddists, he said, and a special box for politicians and newspaper men. When she asked him if the vision of the city suggested nothing more, he thrust his hands into his pockets and said that it reminded him of New York Bay.

"Which is to say that all this talk of fine buildings is so much flute blowing. I guess our people wouldn't give New York second best if they spoke the whole truth. You'll never admit as much yourself just because you're full of Eastern prejudices. That's to be expected. A thing which has stood a thousand years has got the moss of the world's approval pretty thick upon it. I take off my hat to Venice, but I'm thinking of New York all the time."

"Of the temples of a mighty industry? Isn't that in the advertisement line? I don't think you can be quite serious, though. It must mean more to you than that."

"Why should it mean more to me. I guess it's brick and marble anyway, and not so very much better because it's old. What we are seeing to-night comes out of heaven—light and atmosphere and the sea for a setting. I could show you a night in New York Bay which is up to anything hereabouts. Why should I spread myself when conviction isn't there? Yonder's a beautiful city—is it worse because there are others?"

Convention bade her smile, but she would yet try to teach him.

"You have no true inspiration," she said; "there will never be another great building in the world until we find the key to the old. If a man's faith could move mountains, he might build such a city as that. But the faith must be there, I am sure of that."

"Meanwhile the world gets along very well on stucco fronts. No one believes very much in anything but money. You yourself are but half convinced, and you want to make a convert of me. Now, isn't that the truth, Miss Gabrielle?"

She was very angry with him.

"You rich men have no ideals. You discredit the ideals of others. If I had your money, I would build such a temple to peace as would compel the world to come in. Oh! think what one might do, the name one might leave, the homes one might save. It is money that hides all this from you, money that hides even the purpose of life itself. You grub in the valleys when imagination should lead you to the hill-top. Your eyes look downwards—how shall anyone teach you to see?"

He smoked on patiently. Presently, he said:

"There's something in the Bible about the blind leading the blind. I'll tell you what. You are trying to convince yourself about this peace nonsense, and in the end you may succeed. When you do, I'll build your temple for you; it's a promise between us, and shall be kept. The heretic building the church for the faithful; I like the idea of that, don't you?"

"You will never build it," she said. "I have come to know that now. You have not the imagination to build; nothing teaches you in spirit."

And then she exclaimed with very real conviction:

"You are a man without pity for humanity—all your story is told in that."

He accepted the savage assault with a smile that was unchanging. Candour in women pleased him; as his wife, this woman would carry him far upon an unfamiliar road his ambition had often sought. In the vulgar phrase, she would bring culture.

"I may be without pity for humanity," he said, "but humanity's had a good many dollars out of my pocket. Do you know how much humanity I employ at Charleston, I wonder? Well, all told, I dare say there are some nine thousand hands, all eating and drinking at the expense of the man whom nothing touches in spirit. When I'm dead, maybe I'll write as good an epitaph as your friends who blow other people's trumpets and give their money for the archangels who don't exist. Anyway, I'll let the record stand, and as to this temple of yours, I'll build it all right, and you shall have it as a wedding present. Can I say fairer than that?"

She looked up quickly, her face flushed.

"Why do you speak of a wedding present?"

"Because I must make haste to do what I ought to have done long ago, and congratulate you—of course, I did not know."

She laughed rather hardly. Very wonderful castles were falling all about her, and a woman's chagrin did not help her.

"We were both very ignorant," she said helplessly.

He watched her closely. "A very old friend, Mr. Lassett, isn't he?"

"I have known him all my life."

"Ah, that is the sure way of knowing him better. Did I hear he was a cricketer? I thought he said something of the kind."

"He is one of the greatest cricketers England has had. Anything else?"

"Why, no; well, I congratulate you. You'll be married, I suppose, before we meet again."

She was surprised at this.

"Are you not coming to see Maryska?"

"When she asks for me, yes; but I know the sex. She'll have forgotten my name in a month's time; it is the privilege of women."

"And in that case—"

"Oh," he said, "I shall be in America building my temple. It's steel mostly, and butters a good deal of humanity's bread."

She was very much perplexed.

"Maryska will never like that. I am sure she will be very unhappy without you."

"I don't agree," he said, and bade her listen.

The sound of young voices came up to them from the cabin. Harry Lassett was talking to Maryska, and when she answered him, there was a little ripple of girlish laughter, which seemed to say that she had found a friend.

"I don't agree," Faber repeated, and then with some sternness, he added: "Mr. Lassett is teaching her cricket, I suppose. Well, that's a game I'd rather she didn't learn!"

CHAPTER VI
GOODWILL TOWARD MEN

I

Faber arrived in Berlin three days after the yacht had put into Venice. The cordiality of his reception in the German capital surprised him. Known both as the inventor and the manufacturer of the famous "Faber" magazine rifle, the greatest instrument of war the twentieth century had yet seen, he found himself a celebrity most welcome to the Germans. Rarely had there been so much "hoching" for a comparatively private individual. Remarkable personages in remarkable uniforms overwhelmed him by their hospitality; he was made familiar with superb "vons" in accoutrement more superb. The gay city—by far the gayest in Europe at the present time—delighted him by its capacity for enjoyment and its freedom from social cant. The women flirted with him outrageously. He had never been made so much of since fortune first smiled upon him.

Bertie Morris came from Paris on the fourth day, and brought him all the news in exchange for his own. Bertie was not surprised that Faber's first question should be about little Claudine d'Arny, and what had happened to her since the tragedy of her father's death. He had come to Berlin prepared to give a good account of his stewardship in that affair, and he was very proud of what he had done. They were at dinner when the narration took place, and the restaurant of the Metropole Hotel glowed with light and colour, and the glitter of fine uniforms. There were officers everywhere; women whose gowns neither Paris nor Vienna might shame. They moved in an atmosphere of soft tints; the warmth of crimson carpets and the spotless white of polished walls setting off their "creations" to perfection. The air was heavy with the scent of crimson roses, which were on every table, despite the season.

Faber had a table in the corner of the room, and he allowed *hors-d'œuvre* and soup to be served before he interrupted the journalist in his occupation of criticising the company with that running and often ironical commentary in which writing people delight. When the prettiest women had been "sized-up," famous people reduced to pulp, and the European situation dismissed in twenty words, Bertie was ready to speak of Claudine. He was too good an actor to bring her on the scene before.

"She arrived at Cannes yesterday," he said at last. "I chose the Riviera Palace because it's the kind of hotel where she'll meet the most people, and forget the quickest. Of course, Issy-Ferrault is going. It was difficult enough to do your business, but I did it bluntly in a business way. 'Marry Claudine d'Arny,' I said, 'and she'll have a guaranteed income of one hundred and twenty-five thousand francs a year.' His own douceur was to be another hundred and twenty-five thousand paid on the day the contract was signed. I put it to him as plainly as if I had a picture to sell. In the end, he bought her with no more scruple than if she had been a horse."

"Blustering first; I suppose, and talking of his ancestry."

"I don't think—there was about an hour and a half of it. Issy-Ferrault came out of the history box like pepper out of a pot. You'd have thought they made France and that Charlemagne was a bagman. When he was through with his talking, I just put the cinch on him with the remark that he wasn't writing history books but contracts. He pumped me like a tax-gatherer to learn the why and wherefore of it all; but the most I could tell him was that an old friend of Claudine's was determined to see her through and that good hard dollars expressed the measure of his determination. There I left it, and that's what he signed upon. He'll go to Cannes and marry her directly public opinion will let him do it. They are to live in London, I understand. He's a good sportsman and is out after the English shooting and fishing, so I told him to get a house in the shires, and he promised to do so. Claudine's money will tie him up all right—and as for that, I should think a girl with those eyes could hold most men. You may take it, Faber, that the matter is settled—as, of course, it was bound to be—after your generosity."

Faber brushed the suggestion aside as one which hardly concerned him. He was pleased by the news and his pride stirred at the suggestion of power, the reality of which he began to understand. Who but a man of vast fortune could have repaired such a tragedy as that? He looked Destiny full in the face and laughed at its omens.

"I've bought most things," he said, "but this is my first deal in husbands. Well, I'm glad the little girl is on the road again. Isn't this Issy-Ferrault rather a hustler in his way? I heard him well spoken of when I was in Paris; they say he's an aeroplane on the road or in the air. Do you know of it?"

"Oh, there's some talk. He was with Blériot a month or two back. The French army does not sleep much nowadays—a pretty wide-awake lot without any whiskers on their ideas. Issy-Ferrault is one of the aviation detachment. I suppose he'll be flying on his own account now if he can keep out of the arms of that black-eyed little girl. But he won't, if I'm any judge of women. She'll stick like the best glue; she's just the sort."

"Then you haven't altered your opinion of her since we left Paris?"

"Guess not; nor of your flaxen-haired Venus either. You don't tell me, by the way, what's become of her."

"She's gone to London to get married."

Bertie opened his eyes very wide.

"To get married! Who's the man?"

"He's a boy—knocks balls about and considers himself famous. Just one of these British boys, nice voice and manners, and legs like the Moses in the pictures. I don't think you would have named him for her choice in twenty guesses, but there it is. They've been billing and cooing on the Adriatic for a week, and now they've gone to do it in London. They're a difficult proposition, Bertie."

Bertie, watching him shrewdly, guessed the same.

"Is she in love with him—real?"

"Ask me something else. She's a woman, and being a woman, many sided. One side likes being kissed on the lips by twenty-two, who must be big-limbed and masculine. The other sides are turned toward various objects—ambition, money, and a woman's common vanities. She's at an age when they turn like a wind vane, and as often. If he catches her in a calm, he'll marry her."

"But if he doesn't—well, that's in the air. You were speaking of Rupert Trevelle a while back. He's over there in the corner yonder. Shall I introduce him?"

Faber looked up and saw a man of about his own age, faultlessly dressed, and accompanied by two pretty women in the smartest gowns. Trevelle, by his looks, should either have been a major of a smart cavalry regiment, or in "the diplomatic." He had jet black hair and a fierce moustache, large manners and a habit of authority. His party, like their own, had just finished dinner, and presently they all found themselves in the lounge where mutual introductions were made.

"My friend, Mr. John Faber, of Charleston, the Baroness von Hartmann, Lady Florentine. This is Mr. Rupert Trevelle, of whom Sir Jules Achon has spoken. So now we all know each other and may get down to business."

Bertie placed chairs for the party, and with one of his characteristic "Shall we's," he ordered coffee and liqueurs. Faber found himself between

Trevelle and the baroness—a woman with a milk-white skin she was at no pains to conceal, and a method of crushing her handkerchief in a fat hand which was quite deadly with young men. She spoke little English, but that was sufficient to convey to the somewhat reserved American an intimation of possible weakness under pleasant conditions and of her own indifference to the absurdities of some modern conventions. Trevelle, on the other hand, had great news, and he bestowed it as gracious manna upon a field of fertile flirtation.

"They are talking of you at the Embassy to-night," he said.

Faber merely retorted, "Why, is that so?" and edged a little farther from the baroness.

"Indeed, it was very much so. You know that you are to have the White Cross of Prussia?"

"That's fine news. Has Sir Jules got anything?"

"Nothing whatever. They don't give white crosses for ideas, more's the pity. Jules Achon is a great man—the world will find it out some day."

"The sooner the better for its credit. What you have to do, Mr. Trevelle, is to educate the people; but I'm telling you nothing new. You know that as well as I do."

"Most certainly I do; I have told Sir Jules so some ten thousand times. He has a great idea, but he must have public opinion behind it. The people make war to-day, not the princes."

"But princes have a say in it, sure."

"They do when the people are willing that they should. At present the popular mind is pretty well where it was fifty years ago. Look at the reputation you bear in Berlin. Why? Because you have made an instrument which allows the German to kill his enemies as he has never been killing them before."

"You are saying, vat?" asked the baroness, impatient of neglect. "You are telling Mister Faber to kill ze enemies?"

"Of his own sex, madame," retorted Trevelle immediately.

"Then he is not like ze Spanish king, who do not kill his enemy because he have killed him already. I should be afraid of this friend of yours; he have nothing but killing in his mind—he live to kill, is it not so?"

"Oh!" said Trevelle, "you must ask the ladies about that."

The baroness shook her head.

"We was all to go to the Alcazar to see the Russian dancers. Why do we stay? I am all hot. I would get far from here—all hot, and yet they say dat in England is joost one good big cold, so cold dat ze nose is freeze off the face. Shall we go to dance, Mr. Trevelle?"

Trevelle said, "Certainly." He had heard of the terrible winter they were having in England, and was glad not to be in London.

"The Thames will be frozen right over," he told them, "the first time since the beginning of the nineteenth century. I suppose there is something in this story of the weakening of the Gulf Stream after two years of drought over yonder. Anyway, it's extraordinary. I wonder what would happen if the Channel froze—?"

"Ah!" said Faber, "a good many people would wonder then, and some of them would be in Berlin. I don't think Sir Jules's stock would stand very high if that happened, Mr. Trevelle."

"But you think it quite impossible?"

"Which is to say that I dictate to Nature. Well, I don't think I should do that at my time of life."

They all laughed, and went off to the Alcazar, where a Russian woman danced divinely, and was followed by a red-nosed man, who broke plates to the great delight of an immense audience. Faber was not displeased to find himself with these two pretty women in a box, where all the world could see him; and it occurred to him before he had been there very long that the house had recognised him, and that he was being pointed out to other pretty women in the seats below. Certainly, this visit to Berlin was becoming a famous thing in its way. It compelled him to understand the meaning of that fame he had won for himself and the homage paid both to him and to his house. A glamour of life, unknown hitherto, but very dazzling, could influence even so balanced a judgment and so cynical a student of humanity. Hardly one of the women, rustling in silks and velvets, bedizened in jewels—hardly one of them to whom he might not have thrown the handkerchief, if he would. The knowledge flattered his pride, and set him thinking of Gabrielle Silvester. Well dressed and wonderful as these women were, Gabrielle would have held her own among them all. He thought of her as destined to rule amid a glitter of jewels and an incense of roses. There was no house in all Europe she could not grace, he said.

A vain thought. She was engaged to a fool of a boy, who could play cricket; and that very night upon his return to the hotel, he found a letter from her in which she confessed to the folly without excuse. Harry wished for an early day. He had altered his plans, and thought now that he would not go to Australia.

II

Faber read the letter in a deep chair by the fireside—in his private room at the Metropole. Bertie Morris, meanwhile, had the English newspaper and a very large whisky and soda. Both men had caught the Berlin habit, and lived rather by night than by day. The hotel itself was then, at a quarter to one in the morning, beginning to amuse itself seriously.

Gabrielle wrote a pretty hand, round as her own limbs, precise as her own habits, with here and there a fine flourish to denote a certain want of stability. It was to be expected that she would make early mention of her charge; but she dwelt so insistently upon what Maryska de Paleologue had done that she must have presupposed an interest beyond the common. And then there was the postscript—a word of real alarm or of deep design. Faber readily granted the former, and would have nothing to do with the latter. Gabrielle was transparently honest in all that she said and wrote.

> "We arrived in London after a bitter journey," the letter ran, "the frost has returned, and the cold is dreadful. I am afraid Maryska feels it very much after Ragusa, and is not grateful to us for bringing her to such an inhospitable country. The streets of London shone like rivers of ice as we drove through, and even my father now admits that there is something in a taxi. What Maryska does not understand is your threatened journey to America, and your unkindness in leaving us all with so brief a farewell. She is very strange here, and she is entirely without friends—though Harry has done his best to cheer her up, and has really developed surprising powers as a private entertainer. Perhaps the cold and the fog have affected her spirits unduly—I would not make too much of it, but she is undoubtedly changed since we left Venice, and the change is not for the better! This much you ought to know.
>
> "Of course, it is much too early yet to speak of the house. We are all at Hampstead in the old home, and it seems difficult to believe that so much has happened in so short a time. I refuse to allow that Christmas Day falls next week, and that in twelve days we shall be ringing the old year out. If anything could convince me it is this bitter

cold, this biting cruel weather, which is like nothing England has seen before, and I hope will be like nothing that is to come after. Here at Hampstead, they say the ice is inches thick upon the ponds—I can hear the whir of the skates from my windows, and everyone who passes is dressed like a grizzly bear. Maryska has seen a severe winter in America, and suffered terribly there because of the cold. So you will understand how anxious we are about her, and how very watchful it is necessary to be.

"My father says she is the strangest compound of oddities he has ever encountered. It is a description which does less than justice to an original character. Of religion she has none. Her god is an oath—nothing more: and yet to say that she is without a deep capacity of feeling would be untrue. Some of her ideas are fantastic—I suppose the orthodox would call them barbarous. She has a locket about her throat with a miniature of the Crucifixion after Francesco. I know that she has painted out the face of Christ, and made a crude likeness of her father in its place. Her trunk is full of his drawings—there are hardly any clothes, poor child, and we shall have to fit her out directly she is well enough. By that time we should know where we are to live, if I can persuade my father to see the house agents. He has a morbid idea that he will commit some great mistake, and I should not be surprised if he took a good many houses before the New Year.

"The only other news is that Harry does not now think that he will go to Australia. He appears to be capricious in his new ideas, and is ready to insist upon a crisis in our affairs. This is so wholly unexpected, that I do not know what to say about it. The foundations of the Temple are not laid, and it would be terrible if the building fell. I suppose it is all very serious, and I should consider it in that light, but I remain an enigma to myself, and am content to let the future speak for itself.

"Oh, how cold it is—how cruelly cold! I can write no more, even by a warm fireside. Perhaps Maryska will write herself soon—horrible thought, I have yet to learn if the child can write at all. When she reads, she terrifies me with the possibilities. Her acquaintance with the most dreadful words is a daily fright to me! She speaks Italian and French quite fluently, and another language which my father does not recognise, but thinks may be Roumanian. He brought a professor of Oriental languages from one of the Universities here yesterday, but the poor man was utterly at sea. I am sure he did not understand a single word of what she said—none knew that better than clever Maryska!

"She is asking for you every day, and I must tell her that you are going to America. It is a heavy burden upon my poor shoulders. Yesterday she said, 'Even *his* friend has gone away.' So, you see, she knows that you were his friend, and I am sure that will not be unwelcome to you.

"Believe me, with all our kindest regards,

"Dear Mr. Faber, yours sincerely,

"Gabrielle Silvester."

"P.S.—The news is not so well to-night. We have had another day of the damp cold, and I am seriously alarmed for her. Have we done right to bring such a hot-house plant to England at all? She is asking for you again even as I write, for she knows that it is written. 'Tell him,' she says, 'that *he* would have wished it. Then he will come to me.' I am doing my duty even if it be done without hope."

III

Bertie Morris drained his glass and then folded the paper he had been reading with great nicety. The journalistic habit inspired a restless curiosity which would probe even the intimate affairs of his friends. He knew that the letter was of great importance, and was almost indignant that his great friend did not speak of its contents.

"Well," he said, with a pretence of a yawn, "I suppose it's time for me to be trotting. See you to-morrow, anyhow."

Faber thrust the letter into his breast coat pocket and lighted a new cigar.

"If I am here, why, yes; maybe I'll not be here."

"You'll not be here! But haven't you an appointment with General Heinstein, to say nothing of the Count?"

"An excellent pair; they can amuse my man of business. I guess I'm going to England."

Bertie whistled.

"You don't toe the mark for any ceremony, Faber. What about this White Cross?"

"Let them hang it round the neck of the little girl at the Alcazar. I've seen the Emperor, the one big man in this country, perhaps the one big man in Europe, unless you care to name Kitchener. The others are no good to me."

"Then you'll be going sure?"

"Not sure at all. See me in the morning, and I'll write the bulletin. Just at the moment I'm thinking about it."

"Well, I hope you won't go, anyway. If you do, so long."

He put on his hat slowly as though still hoping to hear the reason why. That the "flaxen-haired Venus" had something to do with it Bertie Morris was convinced; and being a mere man, conviction amused him. Had Faber said a word to invite his confidence, he would have spoken freely enough. What was this multi-millionaire, who might marry where he pleased in any famous family in Europe, what was he doing in the company of a mere parson's daughter? Here, in Berlin, Bertie could have named half a dozen high and mighty personages, beautiful women with wonderful swan-like necks and the blood of bountiful barons in their delicate veins, who would have packed their traps like one o'clock had John Faber but dropped a handkerchief in their path. And here he was, restless and uneasy and stark indifferent to his social opportunities in the German capital, just because a tall girl with flaxen hair had preached sermons upon peace to him, and rubbed in the moral with some meaning glances from far from inexpressive eyes. Bertie could not make head or tail of such primitive passions, and he gave up the business as incomprehensible.

He had left Faber upon a note of interrogation, and to the man chiefly concerned it was a perplexing note enough. Should he go to England because this little waif of the world had called him, or should he leave her to forget, as forget she must before many weeks had run? If he went, he would recreate for himself all those difficulties he experienced when in the presence of Gabrielle and of her sometimes inexplicable charm. That she was drifting, drifting into the marriage with Harry Lassett, he would not deny. The tragedy of her life might be the consummation of that marriage based upon the passion of an hour and doomed to perish as swiftly. Dimly he perceived the truth about himself and about her. Both had been tempted by a physical instinct—both were born to a destiny more spiritual. He himself had stood for an instant toward Maryska de Paleologue as Gabrielle towards this very human boy. And the child had called him "an old, old man," awakening realities with her words and opening his eyes as no other had dared to do.

Long he debated it, perplexed beyond experience. Should he go to England, and if he did, what then? Day did not help him, nor the early hours of a busy morning. It was not until he had lunched that they handed him a cable from Gabrielle, and he knew that the argument was ended.

"She is very much worse. I think you had better come."

So the cable ran. He caught the night mail, and was at Ostend upon the following morning.

BOOK III
AFTERMATH

CHAPTER I
THE MEMORABLE WINTER

I

The leap into the dark is made willy-nilly by every passenger who steps upon a mail boat at night and asks no preliminary question concerning the weather.

What a spectacle it is of ease buffeted by necessity at the harbour station; of luxury driven out howling to the rigour of a raw and relentless atmosphere; of gregarious humanity sent as sheep to the slaughter or the satiety of the elements. Here comes the train blazing with lights. The passengers wake from their unsettled slumbers to de-wrap and thrust anxious faces from the carriage windows. They call for porters in many tongues, and porters often enough are not vouchsafed to them. There is a dreadful confusion upon the platform—the strong pressing upon the weak, the helpless giving place to the cunning, the rich wondering that they cannot bribe the sea. So we go to the ship lying as a phantom at the wharf. She must laugh at all this humanity so suddenly uncoddled. It is little to her whether the night be fine or windy. She has no rugs to cast aside, and the porters can do nothing for her.

Faber was an expert traveller, and his man, Frank, a paragon. He found a cabin reserved for him upon the steamer *City of Berlin,* and was surprised when making his way below to rub shoulders with Rupert Trevelle, the last person he believed to be on the train from the capital. Trevelle, old hand that he was, admitted that he had been caught napping this time, and was without a berth. It was the most obvious thing to offer him one.

"Come right along with me—I always book a second bunk, and you're welcome to it. You didn't say last night you were going across?"

"I hadn't heard from Sir Jules then. It's his business which is taking me. He's thinking of going to St. Petersburg."

"A wonderful man, sir!—this appears to be our den. Come right in, and when the ship starts we'll get some cigars and some claret if they've any aboard. Ever try claret against sea-sickness? It's the finest thing in the world! I'll give you a dose just now."

Trevelle laughed, and began to dispose his things about the cabin. It was the best on the ship, and the beds looked inviting enough. He, however, had the Berlin habit, and would gladly make a dawn of it. It was a wonderful piece of good luck that he should have happened upon this amazing man, who went through the world on the magic carpet of luxury. Trevelle determined that John Faber was the man for him.

"I don't know about claret, but a little rye whisky would suit me very well. You're going through to London, of course?"

"As the crow does not fly this odd weather. Sit down and take your boots off. I'm Western enough to know the road to comfort, and boots don't carry you far along it. We'll make ourselves snug while Frank is putting the fear of God into the steward. Go right slick, my boy, and let us hear the sound of corks. We shall want all the warmth we can get before we make Dover harbour."

Trevelle assented to that. He had already lighted a cigar and was deep down in an unprotesting bed. Soon glasses rattled in the cabin, and the well-desired music of corks was to be heard. The steamer moved slowly from her moorings: they had sailed.

"So Sir Jules is going to St. Petersburg? Does it strike you as not a little extraordinary that this great man, who has the sanest ideas about the peace question of anyone alive, should be wandering about Europe in this way, knocking at every door like a weary evangelist? To me, it's a sad sight, sir. I wish I could do something to make it better."

"I, not less," said Trevelle. "Do you think, though, that the world is very much in love with sane ideas just now? I don't. You hit the multitude either with fact or fiction. The *via media* leads nowhere. Sir Jules says to these people, 'I can give you peace, but my scheme may take twenty years to mature.' So they think in a twenty years' measure!"

"Meanwhile the other man, who says 'Here is the millennium, take it!'—he is on the first floor. None the less, I would go on if I were Sir Jules. He's got a real good thing. When he's advertised it long enough, the public will know it's real good, and he'll get a hearing. I said and I repeat: 'Educate the people—the others wouldn't let you educate 'em, if you could.'"

Trevelle laughed at that.

"I wish you'd come in yourself," he said, falling suddenly to great earnestness. "By gad! that would be a coup for Sir Jules! Have you ever thought about it, Mr. Faber? You are one of the few who could really help him. Why not come and form an international committee? You could work the American end yourself—no one better! I'm sure it must be some interest to America to see a final settlement in Europe, even if she has to make sacrifices to obtain it. Now, won't you think of it?"

Faber seemed very much amused. He had expected this request from one or the other, but he recognised now that Sir Jules had been too shrewd to make it. Why, the very essence of his scheme was an assault upon American enterprise. It required this undaunted hustler to put the thing in plain terms—he liked Trevelle none the less for his effrontery.

"I'll think of it all right," he said, still smiling; "perhaps I can see myself upon an American platform telling my fellow countrymen that the only way to keep Europeans from cutting each other's throats is to tax our goods another twenty per cent. That's the pith of Sir Jules's proposal. Free trade in Europe as a federated state—no more internecine rivalry. All brothers, except when the United States are on hand. You save your war bills because you fight for commercial reasons nowadays, and there won't be any commercial rivalries there. Well, I don't think it would do on my side, great as it is here. Make a federated state of Europe, if you like, but my countrymen would sooner federate Christ and His disciples. That's an honest truth, sir. I do believe my country is averse to war, because Almighty God has taught her to be so. I am thankful that it should be so, and yet I don't put human nature on too high a pedestal, and I believe America would fight to-morrow if a slap in her face rang loud enough. That's why I go on making guns for a living. I don't want to see men shot any more than any other man; but I do hold that the fighting instinct is deep down in the heart of every man, and that you will require some centuries yet to root it out. My gospel's there in so many words—I'm too old to alter it, and some of you will say I make too much money out of it."

Trevelle expected nothing less, but he still persisted.

"What then of the others—of Carnegie and the arbitration movement, and all that? Do you turn your back on them also?"

"I never turn my back on brains wherever I find them. These earnest men, some of them men of genius, are educating the people of the whole world. I wish them God-speed! They are as truly defending their country as the man who holds a rifle. Their enemy is the brute beast, born in us from the beginning. They have to cast out devils—there's one in every man's story, but the best of us keep him under. It's just because there are others that men like myself are necessary. We bring brains into the argument—no country was yet saved without them, or ever will be."

"Which is as much as to say that you do your work in your own way. America first in your mind all the time."

"All the time, sir, except when I go to England, as now, to do what I can for those who may have need of me."

"Privately, of course, Mr. Faber—"

"Both privately and publicly, Mr. Trevelle, if the occasion should arise."

"Ah," said Trevelle, "you are thinking what might happen if this frost should bring a panic."

"I am thinking of nothing else, sir."

II

The *City of Berlin* slowed down very much as they drew near to Dover, and even those in the private cabins became aware that something unusual was happening. Loud cries were heard from the bridge, and then heavy blows upon the steel plates—repeated while the ship shivered and trembled, and the dullest intellect awakened. As it was not yet light, none of those who ventured from their beds to the decks could make much of the circumstance; but when dawn broke, the state of affairs was revealed, and surely it was significant.

Faber had not closed his eyes during the first four hours of the passage, and he and Trevelle went out to the upper deck together directly the light broke. They were off the Goodwins then, upon a sea so still that the rising sun made of it one vast and silvered mirror. From an almost cloudless sky above a powder of snow fell, as showers in summer from the blue ether. Not a breath of wind appeared to be stirring; the air was like ice upon the cheek; the whole atmosphere ominously still.

The men had lighted cigars, and they walked aft to peer down into the white water and learn what secrets it had to yield. An old salt, round-barrelled and full of wise saws, a man who had spent a long life upon that narrow sea which girds the silver isle, edged up to them, and for once in a way uttered sentiments which had not possible half-crowns behind them. He was genuinely astonished; "took all aback," and not ashamed to say so.

"It's ice, gentlemen, that's wot it were. I seed it with these eyes, and I've been looking down into that waterway nigh four and forty year. Ice off the Goodwins: d—n me, who'd believe it?"

"I guess some of them will have to believe it," said Faber dryly, "unless the weather keeps them out. You don't see any sign of a break, eh, my friend?"

"I don't see no sign at all, sir, not as big as a man's hand. The wind's from north by east, and little to speak of. Who's to change it? Would you kindly tell me that?"

"Oh, don't look at me," exclaimed Trevelle with a laugh. "I'm not a bagman in weather. So far as my memory goes, there was a good deal of ice in the English Channel somewhere about 1820, and a very little in the year 1887—I've read it somewhere. You don't remember that, my man?"

The old fellow spat into the sea with some contempt.

"As much ice as you could put down a woman's back. I remember 1887 well enough. The Thames was nigh froze, and there was a fringe of summat they called 'ice' right round by Herne Bay and all the way to Dover. But this here's more than a bucketful, gentlemen—by gosh! it is."

He jumped involuntarily as a floe, some yards wide, struck the steamer and set the metal reverberating. All on deck ran to the side and watched the dirty ice bobbing like a human thing in the vessel's wash, and then drifting upon the tide over toward Cape Grisnez. Hardly had it passed when the captain rang an order from the bridge, and the ship went to dead slow. Another floe had been sighted ahead, and it was large enough to provoke greater wonder; a mass of black ice as though coming down from a considerable field over yonder towards the land. The ship passed by this and began to swing round to make Dover Harbour. The cold seemed to be increasing with every knot they made. Such an experience upon the English shore was within the knowledge of no living man.

"I've been up to the ice-blink twice, and I was in Alaska three years ago," said Trevelle. "This beats anything I have seen, easily. What would you say the temperature was, Mr. Faber?—phenomenal without doubt."

"About as many degrees below zero as you can get into a common swear word. Look yonder on the shore. Is that ice or am I dreaming it?"

"It's ice right enough! Hi, my man, that's ice by the harbour wall, isn't it? Good God, what a sight! In the English Channel, too!"

The sailor enjoyed this spontaneous tribute to the eccentricities of nature. He thought he would catch them upon an exclamation sooner or later, and he did so triumphantly.

"The harbour's going to be froze," he said sardonically; "they'll be cutting of it with sardine-openers—at least they were a-talking about it. You could walk as far as the bathing machines gin'rilly git out. I dare say you'll see some of 'em a-doing it now if your eyes are good enough. They tell me it's the Gulf Stream what's responsible. Well, d—n the Gulf Stream! say I, and that's all about it."

His peculiarities produced no other effect than the *sotto voce* of a chaplain's lady, who thought that he was a very wicked man. The others were far too much interested in the unusual appearance of Dover Harbour and the environs to take any notice of such emphasis. Early as it was, groups of boys and lads sported with hard ice which ran right round the seawall, and even floated in great lumps in the mouths of the basins. Rills of waves ran, not upon a beach of shingle, but over the frozen waters, spreading as molten silver and often freezing as they ran. There were effects of the frost most bizarre—buoys covered with the hoar, ropes of ice where ladders stood, vast stalactites as of pure crystal from the roof of every walled bay into which the sea ran. The cold, still air breathed upon all as with the breath of the Arctic wastes. The town of Dover was frozen out from the heights of the Castle Hill to the very depths of its meanest streets.

They went ashore over a gangway dusted with sand that they might obtain a foothold upon it. They had thought that it would be warmer off the sea, but when the train moved away and they crossed the frozen fields of Kent, a new rigour penetrated the ill-warmed carriages and seemed to search their very bones. At Dover newsboys had cried the morning papers with the latest news of the phenomenal frost and of the rumours of a great strike of transport workers following upon it. It seemed to be the one topic of conversation in the train and out of it. Great experts in meteorology had been interviewed in London, in Vienna, in New York. They agreed that England was suffering this abnormal spell because of the reduced flow of her old friend, the Gulf Stream. There could be no other logical conclusion, and the best that could be said was that the severity of the visitation was the soundest argument for its speedy disappearance.

Trevelle read all this out to his companion in the reserved compartment which carried them to Victoria. He seemed willing to be impressed by such authorities and was amazed to find that his companion differed from him absolutely. Faber confessed that he had looked for such a winter in England and would have been surprised at any other. His manner had become a little restless again, and he was very anxious for the journey to terminate.

"We are going to have a lively time in London," he said. "I guess I'll be caught in this pit after all, and pretty warm it will be for some of them. Do you know how much wheat your country wants every week to feed its people, Mr. Trevelle? I've figured it out, and it seems to me it's somewhere about five million bushels; that's wheat alone, to say nothing of an Englishman's roast beef and what goes with it. Well, I suppose you've food enough in the country for three weeks at a press. Perhaps you have and perhaps you haven't. Let this frost hold and the strike continue in my country, which I hear is likely, and you're going to see the biggest panic in London you ever saw in all your life. I had a notion of it when I was last here and I mentioned it to some of them. Professor Geikie, of St. Louis, first put it into my head as long ago as last October, when he was taking observations of the Gulf Stream for the Shippers' Institute of the southern ports; he noticed this check in the flow. 'Let it go on,' he said, 'and they'll have a winter in Britain which will be memorable.' I knew the professor and put my money behind him. You've got the winter, and you're only at the beginning of it. God knows when it will end or how, but I'd be glad to be out of this country if I could, and that's sure. It's too late to think of that, now, however."

"Do you seriously believe then that the wheat supply from your side will fail?"

"It's failing already—the cables tell me so. Great extremities of temperature are as sure a call to discontented labour as the spring to the cuckoo. Let this go on a week and there'll be something like a national panic. Then you'll see who believes in universal peace, and I guess you'll see it quick. For my part, if I were a free agent, I'd pack and be off to-night. But I'm not a free agent, and there's work for me to do; mighty serious work, I know. Perhaps I'll ask you to help me. You're just the man for the job. You step quick, and don't talk on the road."

"It doesn't concern the weather, of course?"

"It concerns the people, Mr. Trevelle. I'll tell you when the time comes. We are in London now, I think. My address is the Savoy Hotel. Send me yours there. To-night I'm off to Hampstead to see a little girl. She's just out of Ragusa, and it's to be imagined what this means to her. The north is merciless to the south in that respect. I'm afraid of the news I shall hear; more afraid than I can say."

He fell to silence suddenly as the train crossed Cannon Street bridge and the face of the river was disclosed. A drizzle of snow had begun to fall again, and many hummocks of block ice floated beneath the bridges. Such a night had not been seen since Victoria was Queen and Melbourne her Minister. They entered the station to the raucous shouts of the newsboys, crying the latest tidings of the frost.

III

In the suburbs, there was little real understanding of the momentous truth.

Kensington, Paddington, and Hampstead were frozen out, but their young people enjoyed the predicament. Weary water-men plugged the mains and wondered if Christmas half-crowns would compensate them for the trouble. Plumbers left footprints on the silks of time and had become great personages. The roads were like iron; the wood pavement impossible but for the sand which covered it. Even the meanest wore some kind of shabby furs, while the well-to-do were so many bundles of fine skins, from which rubicund jowls peeped out.

Faber went to the Savoy Hotel and rested a few hours in his room before going on to Hampstead. There were a few of his own countrymen there and they, oddly enough, spoke of a mild winter in Eastern America and a general absence of severity throughout the States. He learned with some surprise that his meeting with the Emperor had been made known to New York and was considered a triumph of a personal kind—though it had given offence in some religious circles and was supposed to be antagonistic to the peace idea. He determined to confute this without loss of time, holding, as he did, the firm faith that the Kaiser was the one great instrument of peace in the western world, and had the sanest ideas upon the subject. For the first time in his life, there was a trouble of the conscience concerning his own business and the mission upon which it had sent him. Was he, in truth, an obstacle to a gospel which had begun to obsess the minds of the Anglo-Saxon race? He knew that the charge was false and his pride resented it warmly. He desired peace absolutely—what forbade him to prepare the nations for war?

It was growing dark when he set out for Hampstead, and there were many lights in the little house in Well Walk when he arrived there. A very ancient parlourmaid, who would have served Rembrandt for "a head," opened the door and told him that Mr. Silvester was at home. She added also that she had supposed he was the doctor, and plainly conveyed her disappointment that he was not.

"Ah!" he said, "the young lady is no better, then? Well, I'm sorry for that!"

"Indeed, and ye may be, sir. We think it's new-monica."

He shook the powdered snow from his boots and went into the hall. Gabrielle, hearing footsteps, ran out on the landing above and looked over the banister.

"Is that you, Mr. Faber—how good of you—how glad she will be!"—and saying all this in a breath, she came down the stairs and held out her hand.

"So, there's no great danger after all," he rejoined.

She looked surprised. "Why no danger?"

"Because you come to me smiling. Well, I'm anxious, anyway. Shall I be able to see her?"

"Of course, you will. She is asking for you always. Please come right up at once. Oh! there I am, speaking your language—how ridiculous it must sound to you?"

"I guess it makes me feel at home. Is this the room—will she be ready, do you think?"

"She heard you at once. She has been counting the hours."

Her soft fingers knocked twice and they went in. The room was small, but it had been furnished with a great elegance. He was glad to see some beautiful white flowers on a little table by the bedside, and a basket of fine grapes with them. The note of it all was pure white, with rich red curtains and pictures in gilt frames. The bed had dimity hangings with great red roses for a pattern. A fire of logs roared up the chimney and a thermometer was hung upon the wall by the mantelpiece.

"Hallo! Maryska, my dear!" he said, going to the bed and pressing her thin fingers with his own. He thought her terribly changed: the black eyes shone as those of a famished animal; the face was very white; the breathing laboured; the hands hot to the touch. But she smiled at him nevertheless and tried to sit up.

"I've got the marsh fever," she said, as though satisfied by her own diagnosis, "it's your ship that did it. Why did you leave me in this damnable country when I was ill? Don't you hate it as much as my father did? Oh! I think you must, you really must."

He was a little taken aback, and sat at the bedside before he answered her. Gabrielle nodded as who should say, "Now, you would like to talk to each other." Then she slipped away, and closed the door softly. The crackling of the logs and the ticking of the clock were loud sounds in the cheery room.

"Why!" he exclaimed at last, "you surprise me, Maryska. I thought your father liked England?"

She shook her head almost fiercely.

"I'd tell you what *he* said if she would let me! She says it's wrong. Why should it be, when my father said it? He called England—but there, it hurts me, boss. Oh! it hurts me so much!"—and with that she flung herself back on the pillow, warm tears of the memory in her eyes.

He perceived that she had no business to be talking, and for some time he sat there, holding her hand and watching her. What a child she was, and with what justice had she called him from the platform of her age, an "old, old man." The tragic irony of his attempt to bring happiness into the life of the man who had befriended him struck him anew and would not be silenced. How little money could achieve when destiny opposed! He reflected that brains were the greater instrument and fell to wondering if brains had helped him in his dealings with Maryska.

"Feeling any better, my dear?" he asked her by and by. She turned upon her side and looked at him with eyes pathetically round.

"I should be all right if I could get away from England, Mr. Faber. Do you think that you can take me?"

"Of course, I'll take you, Maryska. Where would you like to go to, my dear?"

She thought upon it, biting the sheet with fine white teeth. Her white cheeks flushed with the effort.

"I would like to live in a city where there are many lights—in Paris, I think. *He* liked Paris. He said it was a bit of a hell, and he liked it. I told the wolf man with the whiskers that, and he said, 'Oh, hush, hush!' Why did he say that, Mr. Faber?"

"Because, my dear, he's a clergyman, and your father was what we call a Bohemian. They don't say such words amongst our people. You mustn't be offended with them, Maryska; you must try to do what Gabrielle tells you."

She looked up, her suspicion on an edge.

"Are you going to marry Gabrielle?"

"Why, how can you ask me that?"

"Because I think that you are."

"What would she want with 'an old, old man' like me?"

Maryska reasoned it out.

"You are not so old when you are with her. Besides, I am getting used to you. It is your looks which I don't like. You are not really so old, are you?"

"I'm not forty yet, my dear."

"And how old is Harry Lassett?"

It was a surprising question, and he turned sharply when he heard it.

"Don't you know that Harry Lassett is going to marry Gabrielle?"

She bit her lips and half sat up in bed again.

"I don't believe that. They say so, but it's wrong. You can't make any mistake in those things. *He* used to beat me when I asked him; he wouldn't let me talk about it, but I know. It's something which changes your life. It is not that awful thing I saw in the streets of Ranovica. God Almighty! none of those girls will ever have a lover now, will they, Mr. Faber?"

The child's eyes were staring into vacancy as though she saw a vision beyond all words terrifying. Here in this silent house remote from London's heart, the unnameable hours of war were lived again both by the man and the girl. John Faber's soul shivered at the hidden meaning of these words of woe. Had not his act carried Louis de Paleologue's daughter to the hills? Was he not responsible for what had been? And he was a servant of such a nation's instruments—a servant of war in its lesser aspect as in its greater. He did not dare to look the truth in the face. The judgment of God seemed to be here.

"We won't speak of the things which are dead, Maryska," he said at length. "The men you name are like the beasts; it is well to leave them in their kennels. Your life begins again with me. I'll take you to Paris directly you are able to bear the journey. Can I say more?"

"Will you, Mr. Faber? I could bear the journey any time—now, this minute, if you would take me."

"My dear child, you are not fit to go. We must nurse you many days yet."

"That's what the doctor says. *He* never liked doctors. They were all—yes, knaves, he said, and the other word which Mr. Silvester hates. Why should I be kept here for these men?"

"Because this time they are right, my dear. It's too cold for anyone to go out of doors. What's more, the sailors are on strike, and so we couldn't go if we wished. You'll be well when the thaw comes, and then I'll take you."

"Will Harry Lassett come too?"

It troubled him to hear the reiteration of this idea. The anxiety with which she regarded him, her eyes so big and round, her breathing so laboured, her cheeks so flushed—this anxiety added not a little to his own.

"Why do you bring that young gentleman into it?" he asked her. "How can he go with us? Hasn't he got his duties to do here, my dear? What would Gabrielle say if she heard it? Wouldn't she be put out, don't you think?"

The round, dark face assumed an air almost of cunning. It was evident that she knew just what Gabrielle would say, but was unmoved nevertheless.

"What does 'engaged' mean in England? When *he* and I were in Paris, a lot of them came to the studio. They would be engaged for a little while, and then there would be others. Jeannette Arrn had three lovers while I was there—Henri Courtans was the last. Was she engaged to him?"

It was very earnestly put, and it embarrassed him. What a life the child had lived; what an education had been hers! And now he feared that the inevitable had come to be. Thrown into the society of the big-limbed boy, she had immediately fallen in love with him. This should have been looked for, and it would have been if he had realised a little earlier the nature of her birthright and its consequences. She was born in a land where passion is often uncurbed and the blood runs hot in the veins. Religion had done nothing for her; those who would educate her must begin at the very beginning. He himself felt totally unfit for the task. And she had refused already to live with the Silvesters, at any rate in England.

"Has Harry Lassett spoken to you about going to Paris?" he asked upon an impulse. She shook her head.

"I wish he would. I wish he would ask me to go away from her."

"Don't you think it would be very unkind to Gabrielle to go with him even if there were no other reason?"

"I don't think that. She wouldn't care."

"She is going to be his wife."

"Yes, and that is why I hate her."

No further question could be asked or answered, for Gabrielle entered the room at the moment, and immediately the child hid herself in the bedclothes and would not speak another word.

CHAPTER II
OF LOVE BUT NOT OF MARRIAGE

I

"You'll stay to dinner?" she asked, as they went down to the drawing-room together a little later on. It was very warm and snug there, and the deep red shades upon the lamps appeared to him particularly English. They had few such suggestions of home in his country.

"Why," he rejoined, "if it will not be putting you out."

"We have some pea soup and a sole. My father is Popish enough to eat little meat, but that is for his stomach's sake—as Timothy was to drink wine. Of course, the baby cannot eat anything at all. Did you think very badly of her, I wonder? Is she really as ill as the doctors make out?"

"Tell me how ill the doctors make her out, and I'll say what I think. Anyway, it isn't pneumonia yet. I've seen too much of it to be scared by that particular spook. She's a bit of congestion of the lungs, and she's worrying herself into a fever. The rest's doctor's talk—what they take a fee to say."

She smiled, and went on busying herself about the room. The fire light showed all her height and the fine contour of well-developed limbs. Every movement was full of grace, he said. Gabrielle Silvester could have taken her place in any society in Europe. For an instant, he thought of her as the bejewelled hostess of a Fifth Avenue mansion, and that thought returned later on.

"It is good to hear you," she said with a light laugh. "Everyone who comes to a sick house seems to think it necessary to speak in a morbid whisper. They expect to look sorrow in the face on the doorstep. Of course, she has been very ill—dangerously ill, I think. Our bringing her to England was a very great mistake; even father knows that now."

"Then she isn't very happy here?"

"Very far from it. Did she say anything of it to you?"

"Why, yes; she asked me to take her away by the next train."

"I thought she would; was it back to Italy?"

"No; to Paris—and what's more, she wants Harry Lassett to be of the party."

He thought it necessary to tell her this: he had debated it while sitting there and watching her graceful movements about the room. His own act had committed Maryska to her charge; his own words must warn her of a possible danger. Upon her part, however, the whole thing was treated without concern, merely as the odd whim of a capricious child who was sick. She surprised him very much by her attitude.

"Harry amuses her," she said without turning, "he can be so atrociously vulgar. An accomplishment, is it not, when it brings a little sunshine? They have been the best of friends, and he comes here every day with some present or other for her. It is all quite pretty, and I am very grateful to him."

"Then you would approve of his coming on my yacht?"

"If he could go, yes; but I know that it is quite impossible. He has developed a surprising interest in his business; he is in town every day. It's really most wonderful!"

"May I ask what his business is, by the way?"

She looked a little pained.

"He gets money from the people who sell stocks and shares—the jobbers, don't you call them?"

"That's the name, to be sure. So he goes down to the city to watch them making money for him. It's a joyous employment, sure; it won't make him bald!"

Gabrielle did not like the tone of this at all, she bridled instantly.

"I dare say that Mr. Lassett is very well content with it. Don't you think that we might be?"

"Why, certainly, I do. That's just what was in my thoughts just now. If he's so well occupied in London, he won't mind your taking a little holiday with me—!"

"With you! How odd it sounds!"

"Odd, or even; I mean every word of it. Will you come to Florida on the *Savannah*?"

She hesitated and flushed. There are some tones of a man's voice a woman never mistakes. Let him lie to her, and she may be wholly convinced; deceive her by vain promises, and she will believe him—but let him touch the tonic of a lover's chord, and her instinct is immediately attuned. Gabrielle knew that John Faber was about to make love to her. It came as a bolt from the blue.

"Why should I go to Florida in your yacht? Do you propose to take Maryska there?"

"I do indeed—and you also!"

"As her nurse, I suppose?"

"No, as my wife!"

He bent forward and watched her closely. She had been standing by the piano, the aureole of the lamp about her flaxen hair, making pure gold of its silken threads. For an instant she trembled as though some strange chord of her nature had been touched. Then, very slowly, she crossed the room and sat in the chair upon the other side of the fireplace. A warm light played upon her young face now; she was, indeed, a beautiful woman.

"Why do you ask me to be your wife when you know I am engaged to Harry Lassett?"

"Because I believe it is necessary to your happiness and mine."

"Just a guess at reasons then. If I believed it, I would say it is a want of compliment to me. But I don't believe it. You are masterful and would brush aside all obstacles. If I were not a woman with some faith in things, you would do so. I happen to be that—perhaps to my sorrow. No, indeed, I could never be your wife while I believe in the reality of my own life, and the good of what I work for. You must know how very far apart we are."

"In what are we apart? In causes which politicians quarrel upon. I guess that's no reason. Does a man love a woman the less because she believes the earth is flat? If he's a fool—yes. A wise man says, she is only a woman, and loves her the more. Gabrielle, I don't care a cent for your opinions, but I want you very badly."

She sighed heavily, and raised herself in her chair.

"My opinions are my life," she said quietly. "I have built a temple to them in my dreams. How it would come crashing down if I married you!"

"I'll build it, anyway—it's a promise. You shall have your temple if it costs half a million. They won't miss me there if I find the money. I shall be proud enough of my wife the day it is opened!"

"Caring nothing that she could only speak of money. Oh, don't pursue it; don't, don't! All my years have been a schooling against such things as are dear to you. There are a hundred interests in my life I have never dared even to mention to you. This home, my father's work—do they not say 'no' for me? I should be a burden to you every day; you would have nothing but contempt for me."

"If a man were fool enough to base his unhappiness on his wife's goodness—why, yes. Don't you see that I may admire all this, and yet differ altogether? Isn't it one of the reasons why I ask you to be my wife, that I know how much reality and honest faith lies behind all you do? You haven't considered that—you'll have to before it's done with. I've a habit of getting my way; you'll discover it before I am through!"

The taunt turned her patience to defiance.

"No," she said, standing up as if impatient of it all, "I shall discover nothing, Mr. Faber. I intend to marry Harry Lassett in February!"

"Ah! then I'll have to begin upon that temple at once. Have you thought about the plans of it?"

She shrugged her shoulders.

"Do not spoil my dreams—there is the bell. I think it must be Harry, for my father has a key."

She went toward the door, he watching every step she took. Was it the face of a woman going to meet her lover, the face of an ecstasy, or of a painter's dream? The prosaic man deemed it to be neither.

And yet he believed that she would marry the boy.

II

Gabrielle believed that also, but it was a vague thought, floating amid a medley of reproaches and vain longings.

She had gone to her bedroom at eleven o'clock, when the night-nurse came on duty, and the quiet house was hushed to sleep; and there she sat before a great fire listening to the footsteps of the skaters who passed by, or the chime of bells upon the still air.

What momentous thing was this which had happened to her to-day—what flood of fortune which had swept by and left her to a woman's reckoning? Was it not the thing which she had conceived in dreams most sweet—the hope which her father had not been ashamed to utter, the golden shore to which her eyes had been turned in hours of vain imagining? In a twinkling the gates of great promise had been opened for her, and she had refused to enter in. A word, and all the power and place of money would have been at her command. She had been silent—the coach of opportunity had rolled by and left her alone.

She would have been less than a woman if some blunt truths had not emerged from this labyrinth of changing ideas. It is true that Faber had offered to make her Maryska's guardian, an obligation she was to share with her father to their mutual benefit. No money was to have been spared. They were to take a great house in London, and furnish it regardless of cost. The gates of that narrow social enclosure which money can open were no longer to be barred to them. Luxury of every kind was to be at their command—but all as recipients of a comparative stranger's benevolence, and as the servant of his whims. It would be different as his wife, for these things would have come to her then as a right.

She was but a minister's daughter, but these are democratic days, when money builds altars whereat even the ancient houses worship. Men are made peers because they have so much money to put on the political counter, or were famous as makers of jam and vendors of good provisions. All sorts of vulgar personages crowd the royal precincts and wear a William the Conqueror air, most ridiculous to see. The old titles of birth and breeding are hardly recognised; unrecognised absolutely where women are concerned. Gabrielle looked at herself in the glass, and knew that she would have gone far in this latter-day hurly-burly they call society. She had all the gifts, youth, beauty, wit; she was found sympathetic by men and they were her slaves whenever she appeared among them. She could have built a social temple, and there would have been many worshippers.

And for what had all this been put aside? For the love of a man, or for the trick of an imagined sentiment? Harry Lassett made a purely physical appeal, but she was hardly aware of the fact. Faber had said that she was drifting into the marriage, and this idea occurred to her when she sat alone in the silence of the night. The years had conspired to bring this impasse, from which there was no escape but by marriage. She believed that the opportunities of the day would not recur, or if they did recur, that she must give the same answer.

He would build her temple and lay the first stone, perhaps upon the day she became Harry Lassett's wife.

III

John Faber himself had thought very little of this wonderful building when she had first mentioned it to him; but the idea began to obsess his mind as he returned to his hotel.

To say that he was greatly impressed by Gabrielle's refusal of his offer is to express his feelings upon that matter somewhat crudely. There are women's moods which hurt a man's pride, but heal it as quickly. His early astonishment gave place anon to a warm admiration for her principles. They must be something more than mere professions, after all, and were so real that she had refused one of the biggest fortunes in the world because of them. This of itself was a considerable fact which dwelt in his mind. He had discovered few great characters in the course of his busy life, and was tempted to believe that Gabrielle Silvester was one of them.

Her passion for Harry Lassett, if it existed, was a more difficult matter. The man of forty, who has never married, is prone to some sentimentality where calf love is concerned. Well as he may disguise it from the world, there is a bias towards a lover's Arcady; a tenderness for the secret groves which he will never confess. The mere man goes out to the witching hour of the young life. He has mad moments when he rages against his lost youth, and would regain it, even at the cost of his fortune. One such moment Faber himself had known when he went out with Maryska to the hills. It would never recur; he had mastered it wholly even before they returned to Ragusa; but he could credit Gabrielle with a similar weakness, and wonder how far it would wreck her story. Let her marry Harry Lassett, and the first chapters of a pitiful tragedy surely were written. He was quite certain of that.

With this was some new estimate of his own position. He could be no hero in the eyes of such a woman. From that standpoint his appeal to her must be quite hopeless. There had been nothing of the dashing cavalier in his record, nothing but the mere amassing of money; no glamour, no public applause. Women like all that and forget much else when it is there. He had not done the "great good thing" which Maryska, the untutored child, had promised him he might do. Was it too late even yet? This temple he would build at Gabrielle's bidding, must it stand as the perpetual witness to the futility of his own attainments?

And so, finally, and merging into the one great thought was his own awakening love for a beautiful woman. He no longer doubted this. Admiration was becoming a passion of desire, which might lead him to strange ends. He saw her as she sat by the fireside, the warm light upon her eloquent face—he heard her sympathetic voice, watched the play of gesture, the changing but ever-winning expression. He would have given her every penny he had in the world that night to have called her his wife. It came to him as an obsession that he could not live without her.

For thus do men of forty love, and in such a passion do the years often mock them!

CHAPTER III
AFTER TEN DAYS

I

Bertie Morris was a man who rarely knocked upon any doors, and certainly, had he stooped to such a weakness, it would not have been upon the door of his very democratic patron, John Faber, who was never surprised to see him whatever the hour or the place.

"So it's you, my boy! I thought no one else would butt in at this time in the morning. Well, and what brings you now? I thought you were in Portugal!"

Bertie Morris, who smoked a cigarette which had the obliging quality of rarely being alight, sat down by his friend's bedside and thrust his felt hat still farther upon the back of his head.

"Guess I came over last night—the hotel clerk said you were visiting. Say, I must have a talk with you. Benjamin has cabled Paris for the news, and he's got to have it. You know Benjamin, sure! Well, then, you know what you've got to do."

Faber knew Benjamin Barnett of the *New York Mitre* very well, but the process of "doing it" seemed to amuse him. He sat up in bed and called for his man, Frank, who had been brushing his clothes in the bathroom.

"What time is it, Frank?"

"A quarter past nine, sir."

"Then go and order half a dozen Bass's ale for Mr. Morris, and bring me my coffee."

The journalist offered no objection whatever to this drastic prescription, and when the beer was brought, and coffee, with hot-house grapes and other fine fruit, had been set at the bedside, he drained a glass to the dregs and then spoke up.

"Benjamin says the strike on their side is going to keep wheat out of England for a month. You're the man most concerned in that, for a word from you could end it. It's because your Charleston people went out that the others followed. What I'm thinking is that you're hoist with your own petard. You must tell me if it's true or false?"

Faber was out of bed by this time, dressed in a wonderful Japanese kimono which gave him the appearance of a theatrical mandarin. He was always amused by Bertie Morris, and generally ready to help him. Now, however, he seemed at a loss, and he walked to the window and looked out before he gave him any answer whatsoever.

What an unfamiliar spectacle he beheld from these high windows of the Savoy Hotel! The River gave promise of soon being frozen from bank to bank. Great lumps of shining ice protruded from its black face, and thousands of idlers were ready to play in the arena this memorable winter would create for them. Far away, to Westminster and beyond, the scene suffered no change, the river of ice flashed in the wan sunlight of the bitter day. He had heard yesterday of a pageant the city would prepare, and here this morning were the outposts; jovial men who waited to prepare the theatre, hew down the hummocks, and make many a broken path straight. An ox would be roasted whole upon the Thames to-morrow, and many a keg of good beer broached. The citizens themselves watched the strange scene from the banks and the bridges, thousands of them in black lines—well-to-do and ill-to-do; men and women about whose glowing bodies fortune had put fair furs; wretched out-of-works who shivered in the cold and had hardly a rag to cover them. Stress of weather could break many a barrier; there would be little caste in England when a few weeks had run.

Faber regarded the scene for a little while in silence; then he took up the conversation at the exact point where Morris had left it.

"Does Benjamin name me in this?"

"Be sure he does; you're the marrow of it. What's Faber going to do with the wheat he's cornered? That's what he asks. I don't suppose you'll tell him, and so I ask also. What are you doing in corn?"

"I'm buying it, Bertie. I began about a month ago when the weather first did stunts. Of course, you don't say that. For Benjamin the news is that I happen to hold a number of steamers at Liverpool and in the Thames, and that the men on strike there won't unload them. Say I'm a d—d unlucky man, and leave it there."

"I'll do that, sure. The British public won't, though. Guess you're out for a big scoop this time, John. I'm d—d if you're not the quickest flier I ever saw at any game you like. Selling it, I suppose to the philanthropic agencies?

Is that the line? They pay a hundred per cent. to feed the hungry, and you look on and bless 'em! What a story for Benjamin! How he would put the ginger in!"

"Dare say he would. I know Benjamin. The philanthropic agency business is in his line. He met Miss Silvester, I think, when she was over. Does he know that she's at the head of this good Samaritan flare? Has he heard of the national committee with her name among the four hundred? I'd say something about that if I were you; it's the 'homes of the people' lay, and goes down every time."

"I don't think—a committee for feeding the people and a minister's daughter at the head of it. Shall I tell 'em they must buy the corn from you in the end at a forty per cent. rise? By gosh! that laugh would be on time, anyway."

"Why, it would, certainly. But you may leave my name out there. Say I take a serious view of the situation, and if the frost holds, I look for something like a panic."

"Then you don't think the government can feed them?"

"I have no doubt about it whatever. If you'll come with me by and by, I'll show you such scenes in London as you may not see again if you lived the lives of your great-great-grandchildren. It's war and no war. When some fool gets up and cries that the Germans are sailing from Kiel you'll have pandemonium. There's sure to be one before the week is out. I open my papers every morning and expect to read the news. I tell you we are going to see something and see it quick. Let Benjamin understand that. I don't suppose you'll forget to point out to him the advantage of having such a brilliant man upon the spot. You won't be backward in coming forward, my boy."

Bertie assumed a meek look which served him very well upon these critical occasions when he interviewed a great personage for the purpose of taking away his character. A pleasant "I don't think" was his only comment upon the impertinence of the observation; but for the rest even his conventional imagination was impressed. John Faber was not the man to be wasting his time upon mere speculations. When he indulged in the luxury of a guess, a fortune usually lay at the back of it.

"Are you meaning to say that there is any real danger of this same invasion?" he asked rather timidly. "Benjamin would like to hear you about that; you're the first man he'd send to if he thought the game was on. Do you think it yourself, now?"

"I think nothing of the kind. The Germans are not madmen. They've got the sanest man in Europe at their head, and he is not likely to do stunts with the Gulf Stream holding the stakes. What the Britisher has got to fear is the consequence of war without its actuality. He's had that to fear any time these ten years. Now that wheat is cornered, and the shipping trade has fallen foul of the sailors, there is a flesh and blood bogey behind it. By gosh! he's frightened. I know it, and so do the newspapers. The Cabinet met last night and the King sent for Kitchener afterwards. They know there where the shoe pinches, and they see other bogeys. Let this frost hold, let hunger get a grip on the people over yonder, and there isn't an institution in Great Britain which will last a week. You can tell Benjamin as much, though there's no need to say I said it."

He had become unusually serious, pacing the room while he talked, and often looking out at the frozen river. Shrewd interviewer that Morris was and blessed with an excellent memory, nevertheless these things were big enough to be made a note of on the spot, and he took paper and pen for the purpose. That was the moment, however, when a servant came in to announce Mr. Rupert Trevelle, and immediately afterwards Faber fell to earnest talk with this famous diplomatist who was Sir Jules's right hand. There was nothing left for the journalist to do but to drink up the beer—a task he performed with alacrity.

To be sure, his curiosity was provoked not a little by the vivacity of the talk to which he listened, and when a little later on Faber apologised for taking his guest into the adjoining room to discuss some private business, the journalist prevailed against the man, and stooped without hesitation to the methods of Mary Jane. Bertie's ear fitted the keyhole very well, and he did not mind the draught overmuch. What he heard seemed to interest him very much. And the greater merit of it was that it had not been told him in confidence.

II

The three men left the hotel in a private car some hour and a half later, and told the driver to go past Aldgate to Commercial Road East. They all wore heavy fur coats and were put in good spirits by the vigour of the day and the stillness of the frosty air. London looked her best that morning. The whiteness of her roofs, the iron hardness of her roads, blue sky above and a kindly sunshine to make a rare spectacle of the gathered snow—never had she worn a fairer aspect. Even the Americans felt at home and needed but a blizzard to deceive them utterly.

The cheerful aspect of London chiefly impressed the imagination of the people in the West End at this time and they had got little beyond it at this stage. They talked in the clubs of the newspaper canards and pooh-poohed them. It was true that the rivers were frozen, but it was ridiculous to suppose that the severity of the frost would endure. As to the food-supply, what did it matter to men who could order a sole à la Victoria or a *tournedo* without causing the club steward to lift an eyelid? The frost was phenomenal, but it would in due course be followed by a thaw. Meanwhile, those d—d bakers were charging a shilling a loaf, and making a fortune by other people's necessities. It was a scandal with which any but an incompetent Radical government would have known how to deal.

Such a pleasant way of regarding things was universal through the West End, where business went on much as usual, and only the newspapers displayed the vulgarity of agitation. It is true that the cold caused a seeming bustle upon the pavements; but this was merely the cold, and the old gentlemen, who trotted vigorously where yesterday they walked, were not driven to such antics by the bakers, but by the bitterness of the weather. Not until the car had carried the three men past Aldgate Station to the junction of the Commercial Road, was there any evidence whatever of that menacing spectre the wise men had dreaded. Then it came upon them without warning—a procession of the social derelicts with a red flag for their banner.

"Hallo, now!—and what do you call this?" Faber asked, as the car came to a standstill and the mob pressed about it. "Is this a dime show, and do we get you?"

Trevelle, a little shaken by the attentions of his neighbours, who had climbed upon the footboard to look at him, declared that they were the "out-of-works."

"Just one of the usual January processions—I expect we shall see a good many before we are through."

"I guess they look ugly, anyway—see that fellow with the lantern jaw and the club? It will want a pretty big baker to stop him if he's hungry!"

"We are stopping him by food—the government must help us."

"And buy Faber's corn?" chimed in Morris, "he's about two or three hundred cargoes to sell—at a price," and he laughed as though it were the finest of jokes. Trevelle, however, was too busy with his neighbour on the footboard to say anything at all. A swarthy ruffian with a ragged crimson tie had grabbed at his watch and chain, and discovered a fifteen shilling enamelled timepiece, which annoyed him.

"A — fine gentleman, you are—I don't fink!" and he went off, rattling the money-box, which he had dropped for the purpose of this assault.

It was an aggressive procession—long, disorganized, revolting in aspect. Men of all ages had set out upon the long march to Trafalgar Square, where they would demand of the government work or bread. You may see the same any winter; but this winter of surpassing cold had given the wolf's jowl to many who were pleasant-faced without it, and the fire of hunger shone from many eyes. A few girls of brazen mien walked by the ragged coats and occasionally danced a few steps to keep themselves warm. With them went grandfathers and grandsons; old men, whose backs were bent by the labours of distant years; mere lads looking for a row with the "coppers."

"What do those fellows think they will do?" Faber asked of Trevelle. He had seen the same kind of thing in his own country—but there, as he put it, the club of the policeman was more powerful than the brotherhood of man. Trevelle admitted that it was so. He had been three days in New York. Therefore, he knew it must be so.

"If the frost holds, they will loot the shops. They've done it before with an embryo Cabinet Minister to lead them. I tell my journalistic friends that they are going to do a finer thing than they have ever done before—they are going to help the mob to loot Bond Street. We are on the top of a volcano; we have been really, for twenty years. The wonder is that we have never discovered it before."

"Meaning to say that the volcano is now about to take a hand in it! Well, Bertie here will be on the spot if there's any looting to be done. I guess the side-track won't see much of him."

Morris was rather flattered.

"I was up among the lakes one winter," he said, "and I saw the wolves pull down a buck. He came out of the woods like a race-horse on the straight. There were twenty snarling devils at his heels, and they had eyes like live coals. Presently one jumped at the buck's throat, and you could not have struck a match before the others had fixed their teeth in him. He bleated for about two minutes; then he was so many gnawed bones on the ice. Well, that's what I think of the social system sometimes. Let the cold get a cinch on those particular wolves, and you'll count some bones! It has got to be—hunger is going to make it so!"

No one contradicted him, for the scenes on the side-walk were too engrossing. All Whitechapel appeared to be abroad that day as though curiosity drove it out of the mean houses. Wan women stood at their doors seeking vainly for some tidings which should be carried to the famished children within. Hulking labourers took their leisure with their broad backs supported by friendly posts. Paradoxical as the thing seemed, the public-houses were beset by fierce mobs of ruffians, both sexes being fairly represented in the mêlée. By here and there some anxious philanthropist in a black coat moved amid the throngs, and spoke words of good cheer to all. There were ministers of religion whose faith knew nothing of new theology but much of bread.

Through this press, by many a filthy street, the car conveyed the strangers to their destination. This lay some way down the Commercial Road and was officially in Stepney. Long before they reached it, the increasing throngs spoke of its whereabouts. A vast mob of the hungry, the homeless, and the desperate strove to reach a square-fronted building over whose doors were written in golden letters the words "The Temple." A shabby structure of dull red brick, this day it had become a house of salvation to the multitude. And high above them, upon the topmost step of a stairway which led to its unadorned halls, stood Gabrielle Silvester speaking to the people.

She was dressed from head to foot in grey furs, and her flaxen hair showed golden beneath the round cap of silver-fox which crowned it. The excitement of her task had brought a rich flood of colour to her round girlish cheeks, and her eyes were wonderfully bright. The nation's tragedy had dowered her with a rare part, and finely she played it. All this publicity, this movement, this notoriety of charity was life to her. She worked with a method and an energy which surprised even her most intimate friends. In Stepney they had come to call her "Princess Charming"—a title taken from their halfpenny stories and apt for them. Whenever she drove, men doffed their caps, while the eyes of the women filled with tears. This very day she was feeding the people even as Christ, her Master, had fed them. And, looking on with new wonder and pleasure, was the man who knew that she was necessary to him—she and none other.

The car came within a hundred yards of the Temple and then was held up by the press. Faber called a sergeant of police, and slipped a sovereign into his hand.

"Get us up to the door and there's another," he said, and immediately five sturdy policemen drove a way through the hungry throngs with shoulders hardened by such tasks. The car followed them slowly, and as it went Faber threw silver among the people. It was a mad act, for they fell upon it like wolves, and when the police had quelled the riot, two of those who had come to the Temple for bread lay stark dead upon the pavement.

III

There were two long counters running down the centre of the Temple, and between them lay piles of new crisp loaves. Many servers handed them out to whoever asked for them, and continued so to do until the day's supply was exhausted. It was a study to watch the faces of those who came for relief—cunning faces, pitiful faces, the faces of mean desire. Some of these people would go out with their bread and return immediately for more, trusting to the press to remain undiscovered. Others were given to wild words of thanks; but these were few, and in the main it would seem that natural greed dominated other thoughts.

Gabrielle shook hands with Faber a little coldly; her manner toward Trevelle was cordial; she hardly noticed Bertie Morris. A habit of authority is easily assumed by some women, and it sat upon her gracefully. With unfailing dignity, she moved amid her assistants, directing, criticising, applauding them. When the mere man ventured a word of suggestion, he perceived very plainly that he was no hero in her eyes.

"Why," Faber remarked, "have you nothing in the ticket line? Do they all come in here on the nod?"

"Absolutely. Why should we have tickets?"

"Well, I've seen one old woman stow away five loaves since I came in. Is that your idea of it?"

"Oh, we can't stoop to trifles. And we have so much to give away. Mr. Trevelle is so wonderful. He has done a beautiful thing."

"A good collector, eh? So he's doing it all?"

"Indeed, and he is. It would not last a day without him. We are coming to a time when the others will have no bread to give away. He says that we can go on for weeks and weeks."

"I shouldn't wonder. Trevelle is a bit of a hustler, anyway. I suppose you've no time to tell me the news?"

She shrugged her shoulders, almost impatient of the mere cynic who could watch all this and say nothing in its favour.

"She is much better—of course, you are thinking of Maryska? I don't think she wishes to go to Italy now."

"Then you will take that house we spoke of?"

"I will talk to you about it when all this is over. If you could only live a few weeks among these people! And they say it is but the beginning. There will be downright starvation soon. Thousands dying in the very streets."

"Just because God Almighty has sent an extra turn of winter. Well, you are doing fine things, anyway. This is better than the Temple we spoke of."

"Why is it better?"

"Because there are brains behind it. They are the only things which count in the story of great causes—brains and money. I put them in their proper order."

"Ah!" she exclaimed; "of course you think of the money."

"How can I help it? What is feeding these people? Bread! But you don't buy bread with a stone."

She smiled.

"There will be always money for those who really suffer. I count upon Mr. Trevelle for all that. He is a miracle."

And then she said:

"I suppose he has begged of you?"

He brushed the question aside.

"Trevelle knows me better. You don't come to rich men unless you have a proposition. What are all these people to me? I didn't starve them, anyway. Why should I give them money?"

She thought him quite brutal, and went away presently to speak to some of "her guests," who had nearly fallen to blows on the far side of the hall. The heaps of bread were vanishing at an alarming rate, and the sea of faces beyond the doors of the building declared its tragedies of want and hope. In many a street in Stepney and Whitechapel that day the bakers had no bread to sell. Men told you that the government were at grips with the affair, but could any government compel men to work when they had the mind to be idle? A panic of threatened starvation drove the women to frenzy—the men to oaths. There is always hope in the meanest house; but there could be no hope if this frost endured and England were paralysed by strikes. So they fought for the gifts of the Temple, the strong triumphant, the weak to the wall.

"Guess you will have to lay on those tickets," Faber said to her when next she came round to his side of the room. She listened, now impressed by the reason of it.

"We could feed ten times the number," she said—"it is awful to turn them away!"

"Why not take your Temple across the road? I saw an empty factory as I came along; rent that, and see that each man and woman comes but once a day. Trevelle will do it for you."

She said that it must be done, and went away to speak to the unwearying aide-de-camp about it. Later on, with hardly another word to him, Faber saw her enter a plain hired carriage and drive off through the streets, followed by a howling mob whose moods were twain: gratitude on the part of some, rage and disappointment of others. She was going down to Leman Street to the children's institute there, Trevelle said; but he did not suggest that they should follow her.

"By the lord Harry! you've let me in for something!" he protested, mopping a perspiring face when Gabrielle had gone. Faber replied that he would let him in for a good deal more yet. "Anyway, you're a hero in her eyes," he said—and as he said it, he reflected once more upon the meaning of that quality to women, and how far he seemed, from its possession where they were concerned.

CHAPTER IV
CINDERELLA

I

Gordon Silvester's mission to the East, as he would call his work beyond Aldgate, was really a charity of ten years' standing, and one that often proved a thorn in the flesh to Gabrielle, who, at heart, had no great love for poor people.

When the memorable winter came, it was a natural thing to use the resources of this mission for the purposes of that undiscriminating charity the season required; and so we had the Temple (suggested by Rupert Trevelle and other organizations not less useful). Silvester himself went into this work with the ardour of a man of twenty. His sermons at Hampstead were masterpieces of eloquence; his labours at Stepney would have wearied a giant. The national necessity demanded heroism—there will always be many in England to answer such a call when it comes.

Gabrielle herself had been handicapped somewhat by Maryska's illness; but the child responded quickly to the devoted care bestowed upon her, and youth emerged triumphant. Her every whim gratified, as Faber dictated, she was nevertheless often alone in the little house now, and many were the solitary hours she spent there. Harry Lassett alone saved her from despair; and so much did she come to rely upon him, that she would send a note round by hook or by crook whenever Gabrielle went out, and sometimes when she was at home.

One of these letters went up the fifth morning after Faber's visit to the Temple. Silvester was to address a big meeting at the Mansion House upon that day, and Gabrielle to open the factory as a second centre for the distribution of bread. Maryska, who heard with impatience all this talk of things she failed utterly to understand, sulked for an hour in the lonely house, and then dispatched a letter by a friendly butcher to Harry's rooms, near the Holly Bush Inn. To her great joy, he came at once, wrapped in a monstrous fur coat and evidently amiable. This little waif from the unknown was already growing into his life, though he would have been angry had his oldest friend told him as much.

"Hallo, little Gipsy!—and what's up this morning?" he asked, as he came like a great bear into Silvester's puny dining-room. "Gipsy" was his favourite name for her, and she liked it well enough.

"Oh!" she said, "they've all gone praying again, Harry—they're not fed up with it, even yet! I'm sick of this house! Oh! I'm d—d sick of it, Harry. Won't you take me out?"

He always laughed at this trick of strong expression, caught by the child from a Bohemian father; an anathema to Gabrielle and the Reverend Gordon. Harry rather liked it, for it seemed to him somehow that he was talking to a man when he and Maryska were alone together.

"Why, Gipsy!" he cried, taking both her hands, "you do look blue, upon my word! Where do you want to go to now? Where shall I take you if we have a spree?"

She thought upon it with a quick and serious glance aside.

"To a café!" she said at length. "Let us go and eat bouillabaisse at a café! *He* always did when the drawing had tired him. Let us melt the old pot, and drink it—that's what he used to say!"

"But, Maryska! If I haven't got any money?"

She laughed at that.

"Oh!" she cried, "I've got lots! Here's a whole bank-note. Cannot we buy bouillabaisse with that, Harry?"

Harry took the bank-note and perceived with astonishment that it was for no less a sum than one hundred pounds.

"Guess Papa Faber gave you this, now, didn't he? Generous old daddy, too. Have you seen him lately, Gipsy?"

She was a little troubled by his question.

"He came—it would be many days ago. He is going to take me back to Italy. Why do you say he is generous? Was he not *his* friend?"

"Do you mean your father's? Well, but we don't always give a lot of money to the daughters of our friends—not in this country, anyway! You ought to think yourself very lucky, Maryska!"

She did not understand that.

"He is very old," she said. "Once I thought that he looked at me as other men do—as you do sometimes, Harry! It was when I first saw him at Ragusa.

Then it became different! He took us to Ranovica, and I saw dreadful things. Jesus Christ, what things I saw! Oh! if you had known—but I try to forget them now. *He* would wish that—he never let me speak of yesterday."

Her eyes were very wide open and shining; the expressive face spoke of woe most piteous. And this memory of suffering affected the boy also, destitute of sentiment as he was in a general way. He stooped suddenly and kissed her warm lips.

"Never mind, Gipsy dear! You've got some jolly good friends, and old Papa Faber will see you through. I know he means to, for Gabrielle told me so. Just think of it!; one of the richest men in the world your godfather! Aren't you in luck?"

She smiled. Money, by hook or by crook, had been Louis de Paleologue's gospel; how could she forget it?

"He's in love with Gabrielle," she said, making no shadow of a resistance to his kisses, but rather lifting her lips to his, "I know it, and so does she! Why aren't you angry with them, Harry—don't you care? Doesn't it make any difference to you?"

"Oh," he said with just a touch of hardness in his voice, "I'm not going to be jealous of an old bounder like that. He's old enough to be her father. Let's go and spend some of your money, Maryska. Does the doctor say you may go?"

She made a wry grimace.

"*He* used to say doctors were—But no, I mustn't tell you. I hate them! How can they know what's inside us and why we feel it? Of course I shall go! Why are you such a fool?"

He gave way with a shrug, and she went up to get her furs. It was a clear day with little wind and a fine red sun. The frost had not broken, and these two went down toward a city over which loomed the menace of a peril terrible beyond imagination. But of this the suburbs said nothing. Here and there a baker would have a flaring bill in his window; there were advertisements and appeals upon some of the hoardings, but few stopped to read them. Such idlers as gathered at the street corners had long exhausted the only topic of conversation and smoked in silence when they did not beg in companies. "Bread, for the love of God!" was the chant of gangs of impostors whose corduroys were no ornament to streets of red brick.

'Buses, trams and taxis seemed quite unaware of a crisis. The newspapers alone were hysterical. They were covered with flaring black headlines.

Harry had engaged a taxi, and he took her for a drive round Hyde Park before going on to the Savoy Café for luncheon. There were a few horsemen in the Row, but they looked cold enough, and Maryska, who had seen the Italian cavalry ride, thought but little of their performance. For the most part, the big houses in the West End were left to Jeames and his humours. It would have been unfair to the owners of these to say that panic had driven them away. They were just wintering at Cannes or Monte or Aix as they always did. Out there, the news from England seemed very dubious; it was almost impossible to believe that such consequences had attended the severity of the winter. Here in Western London, the intensity of the cold, the relentless winds, the bitter weather taught men to incline an ear to every rumour. Perhaps even the sanest critic experienced a new sensation when he stood apart and asked himself if it were true that the sea might freeze from Calais to Dover. A menace of an unknown peril troubled all; the East End alone gave tongue to it.

They went down St. James' Street and turned into Pall Mall. Here their taxi was held up by a howling mob, indulging in the ancient and amusing pastime of breaking the windows of the clubs. Did a politician as much as show a nose at a window-pane and a shower of stones rewarded long years of salaried labour or unfeed eloquence. Was he not one of those who pocketed the profits the bakers were making?—and if he did not, was he not, at any rate, "capital in a black coat"; and where would you have a better target? The hulking youths, who rattled their money-boxes offensively in every face, cared much about beer and little about bread, but that little had become rather a grim reality these later days. They saw men, and, women, too, dying, down East of absolute starvation—the ghosts of the "might be" stood at their elbow and whispered "Better the jewellers' shops than the mortuaries." And to Bond Street they went, adding to their numbers quickly and uttering bolder threats. "Bread or death!" An odour of beer was the incense to this prayer.

Maryska regarded these gangs of loafers with inquiring eyes. She had seen nothing of the kind in any country, and they excited her contempt. When she asked Harry why none of them carried guns, his laughter seemed to her quite silly.

"The police would never let them do that in Austria," she said emphatically. "Each side would have guns and they would kill each other.

The English are afraid, I think. They should not let such people be in London."

"But, Gipsy, don't you know this winter is killing them by thousands? Haven't you read it in the newspapers?"

"Oh!" she said. "He would never believe what was in the newspapers. He said it was—but you would be angry. Are we going to have bouillabaisse soon? I am dreadfully hungry; I could eat a man, truly I could."

"Then I mustn't take you where any man is. This is the Strand, the place a lot of your people come to. Do you see that sign over yonder? We are going to eat there."

"But, Harry, it's a tailor shop! Oh, you little beast! You would not take me to a tailor's shop? You can't mean to take me there!"

"Cheer up!" he said, squeezing her arm, "they cut very well," and so they drove into the courtyard, and seeing the actresses in weird furs at the door of the café, Maryska leaped down from the taxi and laughed with pleasure.

"I could kiss you if it were English," she said.

Evidently she was of the opinion that it was not English, and so no more on that point was said.

II

Her idea was still a café chantant, and the Savoy met it badly.

She had seen a number of well-dressed women in Berlin, in Madrid, and in Paris; but these, apparently, had belonged to the undesirable classes, and she could hardly believe that any showy creature in the neighbourhood of the ancient hospice of the Fratres de Monte Jovis—a fraternity unknown, may be, to the courtly Gustave—could be of any other kidney. Twenty times during the elegant repast must Harry say, "Do shut up, Gipsy!" and as often must her eyes express wonder. What had she done?

There were odd moments when the mere girl in her came out with a bang, and the boy blushed up to his ears. She laughed uproariously at two waiters who cannoned each other off the soup, and when a clumsy fellow dropped her box of chocolates on the floor, she was after it in a twinkling and down on her paws like a cat. This was a depressing interlude which alarmed her conventional cavalier. Harry hated "scenes" with the distaste habitual to the Englishman of strait laced manners.

He forbade her to smoke, moreover, and that was a grievance. She had smoked cigarettes since she could remember anything at all, and were not other women, especially the daughter-in-law of a personage famous in great circles, were not they smoking? Maryska knew nothing about palaces, but much about tobacco, and this was a question which nearly led to the resignation of the Cabinet.

"I shall tell the waiter to bring me a cigar," she exclaimed at last, resting her pretty face upon her clasped hands and dealing him out a look which was feline in its intensity. Harry gave up the contest at that and ordered her a little box of Russian cigarettes upon the spot.

"What would Mr. Silvester say?" he asked her. He might as well have talked of the weather.

"I don't care a —, and if you provoke me, I will say it. Am I a little, little child that the priests shall beat me? Give me a liqueur, and I will call you a good boy. If you do not, I will go away."

He did not wish her to go away, and he gave her the liqueur. When, at length, he escaped, she besought him to take her to "the café chantant," and for very importunity they went over to the Coliseum. Here both the *Connaisseuse* and the child were in evidence. She called the echo of a tenor "a beast," was dreadfully bored by a comic sketch, but enraptured by the "plate-breakers." When a Russian *danseuse* appeared, her eyes sparkled, and all her body swayed to the rhythm of the graceful movements. She would like to be a dancer—she said so.

"When I leave the Silvesters, I will come to the man who owns this theatre, and ask him to let me dance. How much will he give me for that, Harry?"

He was watching the Russian when she spoke, and hardly noticed it—but she persisted, and would be heard.

"I used to dance for *him*, sometimes—after we had been to the cafés together. He played the fiddle—oh, so badly!—and he said I was born to it. Why should I not dance when those Silvester people are tired of me?"

The man said, "Oh, rot!"—but chancing to look at her presently, he was startled to see the expression upon her face, and the evidences of an ecstasy she could not conceal. The music had entered into her very soul. She bent to it; seemed to suffer a trance because of it, while her eyes watched the scene as though this were a house of visions. Harry Lassett wondered; she was, indeed, an extraordinary child. When the ballet was over, and they were in the cab again, he told her so.

"What about this dancing nonsense? Did you say your father put it into your head?"

"I used to dance for him—very well, *he* said. I would like to be that woman, Harry! The Russian one, with the diamonds in her hair."

"Don't be a fool, Maryska! She's been dancing ever since she was four, I suppose. I expect she's got a husband who drinks champagne and thrashes her with a horse-whip. If you tried that game, they'd laugh at you."

She leaned back upon the cushions of the cab, and looked straight before her.

"No one laughs when I try to do things. I know what I am saying. I could dance as well as the Russian woman, and they would give me a lot of money. Why should I not do it? I have no one who cares for me! Mr. Faber is going to America—the Silvesters do not like me because I am tired of praying. There, I shall come to the theatre, and they will keep me."

Harry was not a sentimentalist, very far from it; but the restrained dolour of this confession made a curious appeal to him, while, at the same time, the childishness of it exasperated him. Was she not in reality one of the most fortunate women in London that day? Her failure to realise what John Faber's friendship meant was incomprehensible, and yet it could not be disputed that she did fail to realise it.

"Look here, Maryska!" he said emphatically, "you don't want me to be angry with you, do you, now?"

"No," she said very quickly, "not you, Harry." And she laid her hand in his. He did not repulse her, but went on with the argument.

"If you don't want me to be angry, talk sense! Faber has adopted you, and he is one of the richest men in the world. Very well, you'll never want for anything on this planet. You're going into life on a good pitch, and the bowling is bilge. I expect they'll speak of you as a famous heiress presently, and half the men in London be after you! What's the good of romancing, then, or pretending you don't understand? I'm sure you understand just as well as I do—and if it were me, I'd knock up a century, certain! Don't you think you're rather foolish, little Gipsy?"

She shook her head, and put her arms about him in a gesture she could not control.

"No," she said, "I am very lonely, Harry!"—and she spoke no other word until the cab drove up to the house in Well Walk.

III

These excursions were no secrets between a boy and a girl, and Maryska would recite every detail of them upon her return to Hampstead. She was spared the necessity upon this occasion by the appearance in the road of another taxi, bringing Silvester and Gabrielle from Stepney. The four met upon the pavement, and immediately fell to a narrative of events. So much had been done, Gabrielle said; it had been a day of triumphs, and they had been achieved by Rupert Trevelle in the face of great odds.

Harry looked at his fiancée while she was talking of her success, and he could not but realise that the recent days had changed her greatly. She had won dignity, he thought, and a new outlook upon life, which could not be a transient influence. There was in her manner towards him a sense of superiority, which the inferior intellect resented; while her good-natured badinage upon his "holiday" suggested anew his inability to play any serious part in the grave affairs which now occupied her. But, beyond this, was her utter indifference to his attempts to make her jealous, and he knew that she hardly listened to him when he spoke of Maryska and the theatre.

"She wants to be a dancer! Oh! every child wants to be that some time or other. Were you not going to be an engine-driver yourself when you were seven? You told me so."

"Yes, but she's a jolly lot more than seven, and if you don't look out, she'll catch and bowl the three of you."

"My dear Harry, that is nonsense. Are you going skating to-night?"

"Yes, if you are coming."

"I can't. Mr. Trevelle is going to dine with us."

"What! hasn't he done talking yet? Someone ought to take away the key. That man is wound up!"

"At any rate, he is the life and soul of things. He's got nearly twenty thousand pounds for us in five days."

"I'll have to borrow a monkey of him. Is your tame millionaire coming also? They say in the papers that he's been sent for by the Cabinet! Is he going to sell some of his wheat cheap, or what?"

Gabrielle froze perceptibly.

"I have seen very little of Mr. Faber. It is not to be supposed that he is interested in what we do. They say he is going to America from Queenstown. All the steamers are to sail from there next week."

"If the strike lets them! Is Maryska going with him?"

"I don't think so; we are to have charge of her. Won't you come in, or must you go? I am perishing here!"

"Oh!" he said with chagrin, "I must go, as usual"—and he lurched off down the street without even offering his hand to her.

The truth was that he was angry both with himself and with her. Brief as their odd engagement had been, he knew that it had been a great mistake. He felt vaguely that his brains were no match for hers, and that she was coming to understand the fact. And then there was his new attitude towards Maryska. How strangely the child could influence him! He remembered almost every word she had said since they set out for the Savoy together. The memory of the many *faux pas* she had made was so humorous that he stood upon the pavement to laugh at them again. There followed a recollection of the moment when she had put her arms about him, and he had kissed her. His whole soul had gone out into that kiss! The warm lips upon his own, the hands which thrilled him, the hair brushing his face lightly—all had moved him in a transport of desire he could not resist. And he was engaged to Gabrielle! His step quickened when he remembered it, and he tried to sweep the inevitable accusation aside. He was engaged to Gabrielle, who trusted him. A silent voice asked, was it cricket?—and he could make no answer.

In his own rooms, by the Holly Bush Inn, the hag who robbed him had stirred up a splendid fire in the grate and set the teacups for two, a suggestion which caused him some irritation. Here was his holy of holies, chiefly devoted to cricket bats and tennis rackets. The walls were decorated by a number of "groups" of the teams for which he had played, including two English elevens against Australia, and at least six which had opposed the Players. Elsewhere, and chiefly upon the writing table at which he rarely wrote, were smaller pictures, including one of Gabrielle which had been taken in New York, and another which he called "the Flapper" portrait. The latter showed a chubby-faced child of fourteen with her hair down her back, and legs of such ample proportions that she might have been in training as an athlete. The picture had been his ideal for many years, but he regarded it a little wistfully now. When he sat down to tea, he took with him a little book between whose leaves was a miniature of Maryska, done by her father some three years ago. Such an exquisite painting had never been in his possession before. It had been one of her few treasures, and yet she had given it to him.

Louis de Paleologue had painted this in Paris, intending to sell it; but Maryska stole it when he was at the café one day, and neither threats nor persuasion had robbed her of it subsequently. It showed her head and shoulders, a veil of gauze about her, and a Turkish cap upon her head. The note of it was the passionate intensity of the girl's eyes, glowing like jewels in the picture, but with a depth of human feeling art is rarely able to convey. For the rest it might have been a miniature of the Bologna School and it had all the virtues of colour of which those masters were capable. Harry understood its value, and he thought that he knew why Maryska had given it to him. He did not ask himself why the gift had been kept secret, or why he had no courage to speak of it to Gabrielle.

He was at the stage when he knew that something must be done, and yet would consent to drift upon the tide of circumstances. The inevitable had happened, and this boy and girl, thrown by the chance of confidence into each other's society, were lovers already. What the future had in store neither dared to ask. Vanity and John Faber were driving him into a speedy marriage with Gabrielle, and they had spoken already of the week previous to Lent. This was to say that in five weeks' time he would be her husband. It seemed impossible to contemplate. Harry drank his tea with his eyes still upon the picture of Maryska.

CHAPTER V
THE MAN OF THE MOMENT

I

It was quite true that Faber had been summoned to Downing Street; equally true to declare that not even the wit of that engaging Paul Pry, Master Bertie Morris, would have divined the nature of the interview.

Perhaps good common sense might have helped him had he trusted to such a cicerone rather than to his ears.

Here was the head of one of the most famous engineering firms in the world held prisoner in London during these days of national tribulation. The house of John Faber and Son had achieved colossal undertakings in all quarters of the globe. Its transport mechanism was beyond question the finest in existence. The genius of it was known to be the man who had recently sold some millions of rifles to Germany—a man accredited by rumour with such sagacity that he had cornered the wheat-market during the earliest days of this memorable winter. The latter proceeding did not help his popularity in England, though it was ignored by the politicians who invited him to Downing Street. In a word, they desired to know how he was going to bring his wheat into England.

Faber was some hours at the conference, and directly it was over he left London with Rupert Trevelle, and set off for Liverpool. Unusually quiet and obviously troubled by a "brain fit," he delved into a mass of newspapers while the train rolled on over the frozen fields, and it was not until they had passed Crewe that he laid the paper aside and addressed a remark to his ready friend.

"I guess London is pretty well like a rat pit just now; at least these newspaper men make it so. Hunger's a useful sort of dog when his dander is risen. I suppose Miss Silvester has found that out already?"

Trevelle, who smoked an immense cigar, and wore a fur coat with a wonderful collar of astrachan, rose to the occasion immediately.

"We are living on a volcano," he said. "The government knows it, and others must guess it. I am waiting every day to see the shell burst and the lava come out. We want imagination to understand just what is going on in England at the present time. That is where we are short. All the way down here, I have been looking at these cottages and asking myself in how many of them the children have no bread this night. My God! think of the women who are bearing the burden—but, of course, you are the man who has thought of it. I wonder sometimes how much you would have made but for certain things. You didn't buy corn to give it away in Stepney, Mr. Faber; that wasn't in your mind a month ago. I'll swear you had very different intentions."

"No need to swear at all. I'm not a philanthropist; I never was. I bought that wheat because the cleverest weather man in New York promised a winter which, anyway, would make the market sure. I went in as any other speculator. How I am coming out is a different proposition. They don't seem to think much of me in England—not by what these writers say. I guess if I were a prize fighter, I'd be doing better business in the popularity line."

Trevelle was a little upset about it.

"It can all be put right in a day if you wish it."

"But I don't wish it."

"I know you don't; you are wanting the girl to have the credit of it."

"Why not? It's a bagatelle to me. And the game will soon be up. I can feed a few thousands in London, but I can't feed a nation. Either I send a cable to Charleston surrendering to my men or I do not. If I do, it will cost me half my fortune; if I don't and this frost holds, you'll see red hell in England before twenty days have run."

"Then the rumours about the strike breaking at Liverpool are true? There is something in them?"

"There is everything in them. The government can deal with this side if I deal with the other. It's up to me in the end and I must say 'Yes,' or 'No.' If I say 'Yes,' all America will laugh at me—if I don't, well who's to charge me? That's the situation, that and your own people, who are going to give the politicians their day. I tell you, it's a considerable proposition and is going to make me older before I have done with it."

He was unusually earnest, and his manner forbade any inquiry as to what had happened in Downing Street, a matter Trevelle's curiosity would have probed if it could. To be candid, this polished gentleman, who indirectly had brought the fact of Faber's presence in England to the notice of the government, was immensely pleased by the part he had played in the stirring events of recent days. Not a lover of money, but a persistent seeker after social credit, when it could be gained by worthy ends, Trevelle had won distinction in twenty ways: as a founder of boys' camps, an officer of Territorials, and a promoter of some schemes which had become national. And here he was in these critical days by the side of the man whose genius might well be the salvation of his fellow-countrymen.

Then entered Liverpool a little late in the afternoon, and went at once to the scene of the strike. It was bitterly cold weather, but nothing to justify the fearsome stories which had delighted London for some days past. The strike itself appeared to be the result as much of lack of work as of any fundamental discontent; starvation had been busy here, and the fruits of starvation were now to be reaped. As in London, haggard gangs paraded the streets and clamoured for bread; there were turbulent scenes in the darker quarters of the city, and not a little of that unmeasured mischief which ever treads upon the heels of want. An interview with the men's leaders convinced Faber that America alone could unlock the doors of this compulsory idleness, and it set his own responsibility once more in a lurid light. Let him cable that message of surrender and the end would be at hand; but in that case his own people would call him a genius no more and Wall Street would deride him. He saw himself as the enemy of the British people, dominant in victory and yet upon the eve of a defeat which never could be retrieved. And if this befell him a woman must answer for it—an ancient story truly.

From Liverpool he journeyed to Fishguard, thence to the south coast. A greater rigour of the frost was here, and it was possible for the dreamer to understand some of those fears which had haunted the timorous during the eventful days. Perhaps a man of large imagination might have been justified in looking across the still seas and asking himself what would befall the island kingdom if the prophets were justified.

At Dover, even John Faber dreamed a dream and did not hesitate to speak of it to Trevelle. Sleeping lightly because of the bitter cold, he imagined that the Channel had become but a lake of black ice in which great ships were embedded, and that far and wide over the unbroken surface went the sledges of the adventurous. Driven to imitate the leaders in this fair emprise, he himself embarked also upon an ice-ship presently, and went out into the night over that very silver streak which had been the salvation of England during the centuries. The white cliffs behind him disappeared anon in the mist; a great silence fell all about; he passed an ice-yacht moving before the lightest breeze, and she was but a shadow picture. Ultima Thule and the frozen wastes were here.

It was a dream of the darkness, and it carried him many miles from the English shore; he perceived that the coastwise lights blazed out as usual, and he could discern in the far distance the magnificent beams from Cape Grisnez and nearer to them the splendid message of the Forelands. A phantom light upon his own ship was powerful enough to cut a golden path over the frozen sea and show him its wonders and its solitudes. Here where great steamers went westward to the Americas, eastward to the city's ports; here where many thousands crossed daily at the bidding of many interests; here a man might stand alone and hear no other sounds than that of the freshening winds of eventide or the groaning of the ice when the sea refuses its harbourage. A weird, wild scene, stupendous in its suggestion, an hour of Nature's transcendent victory. And yet but a dream of his sleep, after all.

II

Such was the vision which reality supported but ill.

There was ice in the southern harbours, but there had been ice there before, and nothing but the imagination of discerning journalists had bridged the peaceful seas and put upon the frozen way the armies of the invader. Faber perceived immediately that a few of his ice-dredges from Charleston could undo any mischief that Nature had done, and he sent a cable to America there and then, as a sop to the fears of the timorous rather than a measure of real necessity.

It was odd how, through it all, this man whose name was known to so few Englishmen had become the arbiter of the nation's destiny. He held the bulk of the wheat which could be shipped from the West if the men who loaded the ships were willing; with him lay that "Yes" or "No" which should unlock the gates and bid a starving population enter the granaries. Once in his younger days he had heard a preacher who took for his text the words, "Sell that thou hast," and he remembered how that this man had declared the need of an all-embracing sacrifice once in the course of every life. The words haunted him, and could not be stilled. He had become as a King or Emperor of old time who could make war or end it by a word. Irony reminded him that he was an apostle of war, and that a sentiment which would deride it had no place in his creed. Why, and for whom, should he beggar himself to serve this people? His financial empire would come down with a crash if he surrendered now—he believed that he would never surrender, and yet he sent a compromising cable to America that day.

This was just before Trevelle and he returned to London through a country which seemed to have no other thoughts than the pleasures of the frost. Everywhere the villages kept carnival upon the ice with merriment and music and the pageantry of snows.

To Faber this seemed a wonderful trait in the national character, and not to be met by Trevelle's cheery reminiscence of the gladiatorial salute.

These people had not saluted the frost because they believed that they were about to die, but because they thought that the national intellect would enable them to live. It had been the same during the Boer War and far back during the Crimea. Beneath the veil of tribulation lay the enduring faith that the nation would emerge, purified by the ordeal and greater for the knowledge of its own strength.

"You see yourselves worrying through, and that's all you care about," he said, as the morning train carried them to London, and the daily papers were strewn about him like the monstrous leaves of an unhealthy plant: "the skin of this nation is the thickest on the globe, and perhaps its most wonderful asset. When you do get into a panic, you show it chiefly in the smoking-room or over the dinner-table. This time you've the biggest chunk to chew I can remember, and yet you are only beginning to see how big it is. The mob is teaching you something, and you'll learn more."

He took up a journal from the seat, and passing it over to Trevelle, indicated some immense headlines.

"See, here! the crowd has burned down your Temple, and is asking for another to keep 'em warm. That's British right through, I guess, and something to go on with. It's just what a man should expect when he turns philanthropist on his own account. You give them what they want, and they are mad because they want it. It's a pretty story, and you should read it. It will certainly interest you."

Trevelle took up the paper and read the report to the last line. Yesterday at five o'clock, an enormous rabble had surrounded the factory by Leman Street, and there being no one in charge who could deal with them, the hooligans had set the place on fire and burned it to the ground. From that they had gone on to other pleasantries, chiefly connected with the philanthropic agencies in the East End. A mission had been burned at Stepney; a boys' institute at Bethnal Green. There was hardly a baker's shop in the locality which had not been looted, while some of the larger stores were but shattered ruins. The report added that a vast horde of ruffians, numbering at least two hundred thousand men, was then marching upon Pall Mall, and that troops were being hurried to London. It was altogether the most sensational affair since the beginning of the frost.

"Poor little Gabrielle!" said Trevelle, thinking first of the woman. "I'm glad she wasn't there. This will be an awful blow to her!"

"Not if she's got the common sense I credit her with. Women's ideals are not readily shaken, and Miss Silvester has some big ones, which are permanent. I'll see her to-day, and we'll know what's to be done. Tell her as much when we get to London."

"If there is any London left to get to—"

"Oh! there'll be a nook and corner somewhere. Your fellows have a genius for dealing with mobs. I would back the police in London against all the riff-raff east of St. Paul's. But they'll do some mischief, none the less—and even this may not help us for the moment. Do you guess what's in that cable, Mr. Trevelle—why, how should you? And yet it might mean more to your people to-day than ten million sovereigns, counted out on the floor of Westminster Hall!"

He held up the familiar dirty paper upon which the Post Office writes the most momentous of messages, and then showed his companion that it had come from Queenstown.

"The men on my side have given in," he said, adding nothing of his own act in that great matter, "the steamers will be sailing inside twenty-four hours. It's a race, sir, between me and the worst side of your nation. And I guess I'll win."

"If you do," said Trevelle earnestly, "there is nothing our government can do to repay the debt."

"Unless they teach the people the lesson of it; do you think it is nothing to an American to see this great country at the mercy of the first food panic which overtakes her? I tell you, it is as much to my countrymen as to yours. Teach them that they have a precious possession in this island kingdom, and you are doing a great work. I shall be a proud man to have a hand in it—"

"You certainly will have that. It's a lesson we all need. I don't think I could have repeated it myself, but for these weeks. Now, I know—and the man who knows can never forget."

He fell to silence upon it, and regarding the drear country from the blurred window, perceived a barren field and a drift of snow falling from a sullen sky. Yet sore afflicted as she was, he remembered that this was Mother England, and that he and countless others had been but ungrateful sons in the days of her glory.

Would it be otherwise when the shadows had passed?

Ah! who could tell?

BOOK IV
MERELY MEN AND WOMEN

CHAPTER I
AFTER THE DEBACLE

I

Gabrielle was at her club in Burlington Gardens when the news of the riot in Stepney was brought by her father. She determined to go back at once that she might know the worst.

"How can they say such things?" she protested while a footman helped her on with her furs, and her father watched her humbly, as latterly it was his wont to do. "Why! everything is going so well, father. I had a perfect ovation this morning; it was nearly half an hour before I could get away from the people. Why should they have done this?"

Silvester said that he could not tell her. All that he knew he had learned by the mouth of a messenger, who had been dispatched headlong from Stepney and came panting with the news.

"You should not have listened to Mr. Faber, my dear. He is an American, and he does not understand our people. The ticket idea was quite wrong. It led to many jealousies, and now to this. The people think there is a great store of bread in Leman Street, and that it is being given only to our friends. I am sorry the story got abroad, very sorry! Charity cannot discriminate in such times as these."

He would have gone on to preach quite a little sermon to the hall porter and the footmen, who told each other afterward that the young lady gave it to him "'ot"—but Gabrielle, amazed and chagrined beyond all experience, immediately ordered them to get a taxi and drive without any delay to Stepney. It was then about seven o'clock of the evening; a bitter cold night with a wraith of snow in the air. The West End seemed entirely deserted at such an hour—even the music-halls had no queues at their doors, while the theatrical managers complained dolefully of their financial sorrows. London had awakened to the truth of the situation at last, and London was frightened. Even the unobservant Silvester could realise the omens of menace, and say that the city was in peril.

"I don't know what it means," he told Gabrielle, as they drove, "but I passed a regiment of cavalry as I came here, and it was going toward Oxford Circus. Do you notice how many police there are about, and mounted police? There is hardly a shop in the West End which is not boarded up. Perhaps they are wise—this has taught them what lies on the other side of Aldgate, and it is a lesson they should have learned a long time ago. My own opinion is that we are upon the brink of a revolution; though, of course, I would not say as much to any of these newspaper people!"

"If you think it, father, why not say it? Surely the day has gone by for the old foolish ideas. The government has left the people to starve, and must take the consequences. We have done our best, but we are not policemen. I feel tempted to go back to Hampstead and having nothing more to do with it. Think of the ingratitude, the shame of it all—and we have worked so hard!"

"You should not have listened to Mr. Faber, my dear; I said as much at the beginning. He is very ignorant of English people; it was a mistake to listen to him."

"You didn't think that on the steamer, father, when we came over from America. You were his bravest advocate; you called him one of the world's geniuses, I remember it."

Silvester admitted it.

"I hoped much from him. If we could have won him, it would have been the greatest victory in the cause of peace we have ever achieved. I fear now he must be called our evil genius. He has undoubtedly sold all those rifles to Germany, and that is to say that we shall have the old foolish scares again and very soon. A man like that is a terrible instrument of mischief. I think we shall have to dissociate ourselves from him altogether when the little girl is well enough to leave us."

Gabrielle sighed as though all these things had become a burden on her mind. An innate sympathy for John Faber prevented her saying what otherwise it would have been a truth to say. How much he could have done for them had he chosen to do it! His money would have helped them so—an inconsequent thought, for her charities had never wanted money.

"He was certainly wrong about the tickets," she admitted. "I know Mr. Trevelle thought so, but he gave way. If it is really true that he is keeping bread from the people to serve his own ends, nothing bad enough can be said about it, but I want to know that it is true. It has been very unkind of him to do nothing for us when he might have done so much. My opinion of him is greatly changed; I do not think he is really our friend."

Silvester was quite of that opinion also.

"He made us such extravagant promises. A house in the West End, motors—every luxury. I really thought he was quite serious when I left Ragusa. Sir Jules Achon did not wish us to go. He knows these people; he thought I was ill-advised to give up Yonkers for such vague promises. I wish I had listened to him now; he is still on those delightful waters, far away from all this. We should have been with him but for our foolish generosity."

Gabrielle avoided the difficult subject. She must have been a little ashamed of it when she remembered the gifts John Faber had lavished upon them already and the concern he displayed for Maryska. The conversation, indeed, carried her back to a somewhat commonplace reality from which she had emerged to win this temporary triumph as a ministering angel in the East End. And now they had burned her Temple and the idol was cast down. Her father would send Maryska away, and they must return to the old humdrum life. John Faber and his riches would pass as a ship of the night. Harry Lassett and the dead leaves of a withered passion remained.

"Oh," she said at last, "how vain is all we do! How vain, how hopeless! We are just like ants crawling about the earth and trying to set ourselves up for gods. We talk of peace and war, of good and evil, of what we shall accomplish and what we have done, and then down comes the great flat foot of circumstance and out we go. I lose the power even to hope sometimes. Why should we not let things drift? Who is the better for our work?"

Her father would not agree to that.

"Every stone cast into the lake of the world's ills is an asset in humanity's balance sheet," he said. "You have cast many, Gabrielle, and will add to the number. Look out there at those poor people. Is it all vain when you remember how many of their kind you have succoured? This American hardness is no good influence; I wish we could shake it off forever. Indeed, it were better so."

"We shall do that," she said quietly. "Mr. Faber will not be many days in England when the frost will let him get away."

He remained silent. They had passed Charing Cross, and now their way was blocked by a vast torchlight procession of women, debouching upon the Strand from the neighbourhood of the Old Kent Road. It was a sorry spectacle, for here were young and old, white-haired women with their backs bent toward the earth which soon would receive them; drabs in rags who flaunted their tattered beauty in the face of every male; quiet workers whose children were starving in garrets; women from mean streets who had never begged in all their lives; children who wondered if the end of the world had come. Headed by a lank harridan who wore a crimson shawl and carried an immense torch, these miserables tramped stolidly toward the West End, seeking God knows what relief from the shuttered houses. And after them went a dozen mounted policemen, good-humoured, chubby-cheeked fellows, who had never wanted bread and were never out of patience with others less fortunate.

A thousand expressions were to be read upon the faces of this haggard crew, and not a little fine determination. Here would be a woman reeling in drink; yonder a young mother hardly strong enough to walk the streets. There were sluts and shapely girls, creatures of a shabby finery, and hopeless woebegone figures of an unchanging poverty. From time to time wistful glances would be cast up at the lighted windows of the houses as though succour might be cast down thence. All moved with rapid, shuffling steps, an orderly concourse which concealed the forces of disorder. By here and there, some of the younger members broke into a mournful song, which was checked at intervals to permit of the exchange of coarse wit with the passers-by on the pavements. The whole throng seemed driven relentlessly on toward a nameless goal which must break their hope when at last they reached it.

"Isn't it dreadful to see them?" said Gabrielle when the last of the procession had passed by and traffic in the Strand was resumed once more. "This sort of thing affects me terribly; it makes me feel sorry that there are women in the world at all. Think of the children of such creatures! What can we hope for them?"

"It is the children for whom we must work," rejoined the father. "I should think of England with despair if it were not for the children."

Worthy man! Despair had always been among the wares in his basket; and yet, how often had this unhappy British people gone laughing by with never a thought for him or his melancholy gospel?

II

The menace of the streets was not less when the women had passed by and the traffic flowed again.

London was full of wild mobs that night; of savage men and men made savage by hunger, and they were drifted to and fro upon the shifting seas of authority and stranded on many a relentless shore. There was riot, too, and upon riot, pillage and the incendiary. Now for the first time since the winter set in, hunger drove even the orderly to the West in the wild search for the food the East could not give them. Long through the dark hours, in Bond Street, in Piccadilly, by Hyde Park, away in the remotest suburbs, sleepers were awakened to listen fearfully to the tramp of feet and the hoarse voices of the multitudes. Those who had the curiosity to look from their windows beheld a sky quivering with light, a glorious iridescence above many a flaming building the rioters had fired. It was the beginning of the end, men said; a visitation of Almighty God against which all were impotent. Who shall wonder that those whose faith was sure prayed for the salvation of their country in that hour of her need?

There were enormous crowds about Aldgate, and the taxi containing Gabrielle and her father made but slow headway. When at last it entered Leman Street, they perceived in an instant the whole extent of the disaster; and so irreparable it seemed that the girl's pride broke down utterly, and she shed bitter tears of shame and grief. How she had worked for these people! What a heroine they had made of her! This very morning there had been a kind of triumphal procession from the old Temple to the new. She had been followed by a vast concourse of thankful people, who cheered her as she went; while the bishop had addressed the throngs from the doors of the mission, and spoken of the "noble lady," whose services to them had been priceless. This was just eight hours ago, and now there were but reddening ashes where the workers had stood to give the children bread.

The cab made its way to the doors of the wrecked building and an inspector of police received them. The few who had been admitted within the barriers were evidently ashamed of what had been done, but quite unable to apologise for it. The inspector put it down to the hooligans.

"We breed too many of them in these days, sir," he said, "the country finds it out when there's hard times, and God knows they're hard enough now. It must have been set afire after Mr. Gedding had locked it up for the day. There were flames as tall as chimneys coming out of the roof when I was called."

This was a man who took tragedy as a matter of course, and would have used the same words if St. Paul's had been burned. When asked if the incendiary were taken, he replied that he was not, but that acting upon "information received," he hoped to make an arrest before morning. His anxiety for the "young lady" was real, and he advised that she should return immediately to her home.

"Now that there's this spirit abroad, I'll answer for nothing at all," he said; "you'd be better the other side of Aldgate, and that's certain. There's nothing but a pack of foreign cut-throats in the streets to-night, and no man is safe. Just you take my advice, sir, and come back in the morning, when they've had time to cool awhile. This is no place for the young lady, whatever it may be for us."

Silvester agreed with him, but he found it impossible to influence Gabrielle. She seemed strangely moved by the melancholy glamour of the scene; by the savage figures shadowed in the after-glow; by the reddening skeleton of the Temple which stood up so proudly a few hours ago. To-morrow there would be but a pit of ashes, where to-day a sacrifice had been offered to the nation. She suffered profoundly when she surveyed this wreck of her handiwork, and it seemed to her that her work among the people was done.

"Let us go on to the old Temple," she said with what resignation she could command, "if they have burned that also, then I will return with you, father, for I can do nothing more."

Silvester disliked the idea of it. He would have been pleased enough to have been back in his little study at Hampstead, where he might have composed a sermon upon "ingratitude," as an obstacle; but he had long been schooled to obedience when his daughter commanded, and so they re-entered the cab and drove to the old Temple. A silent multitude watched them as they went, but none cheered. The bitter cold night either sent people to their houses, where they might shiver upon heaps of rags, or it drove them to the open street where many a huge fire had been kindled that the outcasts might warm themselves. Hereabouts you would often see a whole family lying upon a filthy pallet of straw, and so huddled together for warmth that it had the appearance of some fearsome animal which had crawled from the darkness to the light. The shadows gave pictures more terrible, husbanding the dying and the dead. Starvation abetted the rigour of the winter. Nature waged war here in these silent alleys, and no sound attended her stealthy victories, which were multitudinous.

In London beyond "the gate" there were other anxieties, but these poor people knew nothing of them. War and its menace: the chimera of fabled foes crossing the black ice in endless columns; cannon rumbling where ships had sailed; England no longer an island, her ramparts of blue waters gathered up; her gates thrown open to any who would affront her—if the West End discussed all this covertly and as though afraid, the East knew nothing of it. Here the danger was not of to-morrow, but of to-night! The peril, ever present, fell upon them now at the bidding of the natural law. For the first time since the outcasts of the world had found sanctuary beyond Aldgate, their city of refuge had been unable to feed them. And now hunger bade them go forth to the land of promise, so near, so rich in all they needed. Shall we wonder that starving mobs gathered in every square; that the courts were full of desperadoes with murder in their eyes; that even the honest would listen and admit that this or that might be done?

Upon the other side were the police and the soldiers, many thousands hidden prudently from the eyes of the mobs. If the Government could do little to feed these people, it could, at least, protect the people who were fed for the time being, at any rate. Commanded by the "man of iron," the cavalry were marched hither and thither, but always to form a cordon about the dangerous areas. Special drafts of constables came from the distant suburbs to overawe poor devils whose greatest crime was their hunger. Stepney was besieged by authority, fearful that men would go out to get the children bread, and ashamed that bread should be withheld. Here had Nature's war become one of a civil people, paying a debt they long had owed to their exacting creditors, "Want of Forethought and Economy." The sword of a foreign enemy would have been the lesser peril—it was evident enough now to everyone!

Through such scenes, by the dark and dangerous streets, went Gabrielle to the ancient Temple. She found it occupied by busy missionaries, who knew neither night nor day while the work of mercy must go on. In and out they went as they returned from some mean house, or set off for another. Dawn found them still at work, the terrible dawn when the country waited for the verdict in Nature's court, and even the dullest had come to know that this was an island kingdom.

III

Faber and Trevelle reached Stepney early on the morning of the following day. Gabrielle was still at the Temple and while she had expected the visit of the resistless "inspiration," as she had come to call Trevelle, John Faber's advent was unlooked for.

"We heard you were burned out, and came along at once," he said, in the best of humours. "I guess you'll want all the masons you've got, Miss Silvester, and want 'em on time. That old factory should take five days to put up if you go the right way about it. If it were me, I'd leave it where it is, and make 'em toe the line among the ashes. That would teach them to behave themselves next time. You can't burn the house that's been burned already, and if they want to warm themselves, coal is cheaper. Say, write that upon what's left of the door, and you'll have the laugh on them, sure!"

She was chagrined at the tone of it, but none the less, she seemed to understand that he wished her well.

"If we rebuild, where is the money to come from?" she asked him, helplessly. "And what is the good of it if there is no bread to give the people? My father says the end is coming. What have we to hope for if that is the case?"

"You have to hope for many things, my dear young lady—the weather for one of them. Your good father is a little premature, maybe, and is prone to believe what the newspapers tell him. The end is coming sure enough. It's not the end he looks for by a long way."

He glanced at Trevelle, and they smiled together. There had been great news from Queenstown that morning. Why should they withhold it from her?

"The fact is," said Trevelle, "the strike in America is over and the wheat ships are sailing. You read your evening paper to-night and see what it says. We have brains amongst us and they are busy. That's what we've been asking for all along, in peace or war, not the dreamers but the brains. And we've got 'em, Miss Silvester, we've got 'em!"

He snapped his fingers, an habitual gesture, and seemed thereby to imply that he, Rupert Trevelle, had laid down a doctrine which henceforth must be the salvation of the British people. Gabrielle, however, heard him a little coldly though she was full of wonder.

"I did not think you were so interested in this matter," she said. And then, "Will you, please, tell me why the men in Liverpool are striking still?" When the scientific exposition had left her more in doubt than ever, she asked of her work once more. "Then it is no good going on here if the wheat will come in," she said; "our task will be finished then, will it not, Mr. Faber?" He shook his head at that and told her of his fears.

"It will be a slow business. I advise you to stand by yet awhile. If we get the cargoes slowly, as we shall have to do, the price of wheat will still stand high, and that's no good to these people at all. Take my advice and go on with what you are doing. The country owes you something, sure, and it is just beginning to find that out. Did you see your pictures in the halfpenny illustrateds, this morning? I like those fine; I've got 'em here somewhere, and I mean to keep 'em."

Trevelle thought it wise to move away at this point, and they were left together in the great bare hall of the Temple, whither the people would soon be flocking for bread. A winter sun shone cold and clear through the wide window above them; then voices echoed strangely beneath the vault as though they were tricked by a mutual self-restraint to an artificiality of tone foreign to them. This man had come to love this woman passionately, and he was about to go to his own country, never to return.

"Oh!" she cried, surprised and delighted when she beheld the pictures, "what a dreadful guy they have made me! Now, don't you think this sort of thing ought to be stopped?" He shook his head as though she had disappointed him.

"I never knew a woman yet whose picture was in a newspaper who didn't say they had guyed her. The thing seems well enough to me, and I must keep it for a better. Say, now, you know, I'm going away the first mail that sails. Will you give me a better portrait or must I take this one?"

Her spirit fell though she did not dare to tell him why. He was going, and the building her hope had raised must come crashing down. With this was her feeling that in some way he had failed her in the critical hours. There were men who cried out upon his astuteness, made manifest in the hour of crisis, but she had never heeded them.

"If you really think that you will remember my name when you are in New York again—" Her hesitation was the complement of the obvious, and he smiled again.

"It will be a new name. Let's hear how it sounds. Mrs. Harry Lassett! Well, I don't like the sound of it overmuch, but I suppose it's not my say. The wedding, I think, is for next month, is it not?"

"For the week before Lent. You will not build me a Temple now; it would be a mockery!"

"Why, as to that, if it's a Temple for brains, I don't know that we mightn't build it after all. That's what your country needs, Miss Gabrielle. All the brains at work to educate the people. Sentiment will carry you a very little way upon the road. Let your Temple go up to the men with brains."

"Ah!" she said, "I think we are all beginning to understand that. Even my father says that universal peace will be won by the intellect not by the heart of the nation. You will see him before you go, of course?"

"I shall try to; it will be a misfortune for me if I do not."

"And Maryska?"

"Ah, there you get me into harbour at once. I've been thinking over what Mr. Trevelle has told me about your difficulties, and I guess I'd better see you out of them by taking Maryska to New York. Does that seem to you a wise thing to do?"

Her face became very pale, her thoughts seemed distant when she said:

"Quite wise; she will never be well in England."

"Or happy?"

"Ah, who can say just what happiness is?"

"True enough," he replied. "We look up and down the street for it, and sometimes it is on our own doorsteps all the time. We say that we were happy yesterday, and talk of happy days to come when to-day may be the happiest of our lives. Some of us are not born for that ticket, and it's human nature which shuts us out from it. Who knows, you and I may be among the number."

"An auspicious thing to say, remembering that I am to be married next month."

"Pardon me, I should not have said it. It's like one of your Lord Salisbury's 'blazing indiscretions.' You are taking the line which your welfare dictates that you shall take. You have thought this out for some years, I don't doubt, and you say, there is just one man in the whole world for you. Well, that's a bid for happiness any way. I'll put a motto to it when I cable you on your wedding day."

He held out his hand, and she took it. Their eyes met, and he knew that he read her story.

"The Temple," he said; "I guess you'll want me to help you open that. If you do, I'll come."

"Shall I write to Charleston?"

"Yes, to Maryska de Paleologue, who is going to keep house for me."

Her hand fell from his and she said no more. The doors of the Temple were already open that the hungry might enter in.

CHAPTER II
THE SHADOW IS LIFTED

I

When a woman has drifted into an engagement imposed upon her by years of friendship, it is rare that she has the courage to break the bonds, however irksome she may find them.

Gabrielle knew that she was drifting into this marriage with Harry Lassett, and yet her will was paralysed. The baser appeal had passed as a menacing wave upon a strange sea, and all that was left was the troubled waters of the seemingly inevitable. Her love-making had been so many hours of a dead passion, which no pretence could reanimate. She had posed as the fond mistress of a man whom her coldness gradually repelled until his pride revolted. Held in his arms, treated still as the child, kissed upon her lips, all her sentiment appealed to by his ardour, she tried to say that this was her destiny, beyond which she might not look. Hundreds had drifted as she into that desert of the waters where no tide of life emerges nor harbours of a man's love are to be found. She had been tricked by circumstance, and delusion must be paid for by the years.

Be it said that this was chiefly an aftermath of the busy weeks. While the shadow lay upon England, the fame of her work had blinded her to the true meaning of the promise Harry Lassett had won from her in an irresponsible hour. Swiftly, upon the tide of the national misfortune, she had risen to notoriety; been applauded in the public press and named as a heroine for her work at Stepney. When that work was ended; when England awoke one day to the thunders of a thanksgiving more real than any in her story, then she learned for the first time by what means her triumph had been won, and whose hand had guided her through the darkness.

The letter came from Paris, one of the very first the mails brought in. Well she remembered afterwards how that there had been a bruit of the passing of the frost many days before the deliverance came. Crowds who had learned to say that the American engineer, John Faber, had been the master mind during the terrible weeks; that his were the wheat ships now coming into the ports; that his genius and his money had accomplished miracles—these crowds heard with new hope of his promise that the weather was breaking, and the end at hand. Waiting patiently during the momentous hours, London slept one night through a bitter frost to awake next day to a warm south wind and a burning sunshine. Never shone sun so kindly upon a people which mourned its heritage. The oldest became as children in that hour of deliverance. The church bells rang for a peace, not with men, but with God.

The island home! God, what it had meant to them all in the past! And they had dwelt in ignorance; blind to their possession; regardless of the good sea which sheltered them; of the ramparts which were their salvation. Now, as in a flash, they perceived the truth: the gifts were returned to them; the meanest knew that he was free. In a frenzy which the circumstances may have justified, men took train for the seaports and watched the passing of the ice. They stood upon the high cliffs and beheld the sun shining upon the open waters; lakes of golden light at the heart of the ocean—a widening girdle of security their country had put on. The loftiest imagination could not soar to the true heights of this revelation, or embrace it wholly in the earlier hours. The dullest were dumb for very fear that the Almighty would but trick them after all.

In London, it was as though the whole people took one great breath together. Just as upon the conclusion of a peace, the church bells were rung and the City illuminated. Vast crowds poured from the houses, and gave themselves up to the most childish manifestations of joy. There were scenes to disgrace the story; scenes to lift it to great nobility. But yesterday, it had seemed to some of these revellers that they were no longer the inhabitants of an island which the strongest power would hesitate to assail. All the tradition and glory of the kingdom had gone out of it—to return in a twinkling at the passing of the frost.

Gabrielle could hear the church bells ringing in Hampstead, but the theme of their chime was less to her than the letter which Eva Achon had written to her from Paris—a girlish, gossiping letter, full of inconsequential chatter about absurd people, and ending ever upon the tonic chord of the masculine scale. Eva's Odyssey had been full of event, but she had returned to Paris as a maiden Helen, torn by imagination only from the phantom bridegroom of her dreams. Incidentally, and as though it had to do with a fair in a remote country, she spoke of the great strike and of the man whose name was upon every tongue.

"My father thinks very highly of Mr. John Faber," she wrote. "He would very much like to work with him. I wrote to Rupert Trevelle about it, but he seems too busy to remember me now. It was so like an American to spend all that money on charity and leave the people to think he was a scoundrel. The truth came out from Mr. Morris, who made what he called a 'great story' and sent it to America. I am sending you the cutting from the *New York Herald*—it has also been in the English *Times*, I think. All the English people here are gone mad to know Mr. Faber now—they say he is one of the cleverest men in the world, and one of the kindest. All the same, my father says his brains are better than his money, and when you come to think of it, I suppose that must always be the case. Even he, rich as he is, could do little for that poor artist, Louis de Paleologue, and now there comes the news from Montey that Claudine's *fiancé* has been terribly hurt at the aviation meeting there, and is hardly expected to live. So you see, dearest Gabrielle, his money seems to bring ill-luck to everyone; but when he works, there is no one like him. If only he would help father, how much he could do for the world! But, I suppose, he is going back to America, and we shall see him no more.

"And that reminds me. Isn't it provoking how many people we never see any more! I have had a delicious flirtation here with a fair man whose name I don't know. We passed each other on the stairs of the hotel nearly every morning, and one day I dropped my bag, and he picked it up and spoke to me. I was frightened to ask anyone who he was, and I never saw him in the *salle à manger*, but he used to pass me on the stairs—oh, quite six or seven times a day after that; and we had such a jolly time. Then, suddenly, he went away, never said a word to me or wrote any letter. I shall never see him any more—*mais tout bien ou rien*, if it were always to be on the stairs, I am glad that he is gone."

II

A tinkling gong called Gabrielle to lunch, and she found her father alone in the dining-room. A mutual question as to Maryska's whereabouts revealed the fact that she had not been seen since breakfast and that none of the servants had news of her. Once or twice before, when Harry Lassett had been cajoled into some wild excursion, Maryska had spent most of the day out of doors; but both Silvester and his daughter seemed to think that this was not such an occasion, and they were troubled accordingly.

"I really fear that it is time that Mr. Faber took charge of her," Silvester said, as he sat down wearily. "She is very self-willed, and we have no hold over her. Would Harry be responsible for this, do you think?"

"How can he be? Is he not at Brighton? I hardly think that even he would keep the child out without a word to us."

Silvester looked at her shrewdly. That "even he" suggested a train of thought which had been forced upon him more than once latterly.

"Do you think it is wise for Harry to take her out at all, Gabrielle?" he asked. "We treat her as a child, but is she one really? I hope our confidence is not misplaced. We should incur a very grave responsibility if it were."

Gabrielle did not like Maryska, and was hardly one to conceal her prejudices.

"We should never have consented to receive her, father. It was all done in such a hurry; I think we were the victims of our own good nature. Who is she? Where does she come from? A gipsy girl, perhaps, and one who dislikes our country, and us. It was sentiment upon Mr. Faber's part—altruism at our expense. Of course, he talks of taking her ultimately to New York. But is he likely to do that? Do you believe that?"

"I must believe it or say that he has not written the truth. There was a letter from him this morning—you will find it on my study table. He wishes us to keep her at least for a time and until he can make some provision for her in America. It will be possible for him to sail to-day, he thinks, if Sir Jules Achon arrives from Cherbourg. He appears to want to see Sir Jules very much before he goes."

"Then Maryska remains, father?"

"For the present, yes."

"And that is the last we are to see of our friend? Well, our castles come tumbling down, at any rate. We have been his builders, but he leaves us a wretched house. I think you would be wiser to go to Yonkers."

"I think so, too—when you and Harry are married."

"Need Harry and I enter into the matter? I am thinking all the time of the way these clever men make less clever people their dupes. Sometimes I say that what I need to make a success of my life is the help of a man of genius. I felt it every day when Mr. Faber was here. It was to stand upon a rock and laugh when the sea flowed all around. And you need it too, father. Think of all that good men might do in the world if they had brains such as his behind them. He preaches all his sermons from that text. Brains will save the people, the country, even religion. I am sick of sentiment; it accomplishes nothing. We have meetings and speakers, and conferences and discussions, and the world just goes laughing by, like a boy who passes the open door of a schoolroom. What have we done since we left America? How have we helped our great cause? You know what the answer must be. We have done less than nothing, while a stranger has made our people think and learn."

He was much taken aback by her outburst, and a little at a loss. A man of high ideals, he knew how hopeless was the task of uplifting the people, and yet hope and endeavour were the breath of life to him.

"Oh," he said, "I won't say that we have done nothing. This dreadful winter is just what has been needed to make the people think. A reaction will follow, and we shall go to them with a message of peace they cannot resist. I am sure the truth will come home to all now. It will be easy to say that God Almighty did not create mankind for the shambles. What astonishes me, Gabrielle, is that in this twentieth century it should be necessary to preach such a doctrine at all. When you consider what universal peace would mean in every home in the country, what it would do for the poorest, how it would help the children, I am altogether at a loss. The thing is an incredible anachronism giving the lie direct to Christ and His gospel. And we are powerless to cope with it; we seem to address those whose hearts are of stone."

"Then why do you address them? That is just what Mr. Faber asks. Why not turn to those who can lead the people? If the great names of Europe and America were behind you, the millennium would come. I myself would hope more from two such men as Sir Jules Achon and John Faber than from all the sermons in the world. But I have become a very practical person, father. I think sometimes I am growing terribly masculine."

"You always used to be, Gabrielle. I remember when you were the greatest tomboy in Hampstead. That, by the way, was before your engagement to Harry. Do you know, my dear girl, I wonder sometimes if marriage is your destiny at all."

"If not marriage, what then, father?"

"Public work. The practice of the ideas you have just been pleading to me."

Gabrielle shook her head. She spoke with little restraint, and in a way that astonished him altogether.

"I don't agree with you. I believe in my heart that I am destined to love and marriage. If it is not so, I may do something mad some day. Sometimes I long to get away from all this; but it must be with a man who can lead me. I shall never marry Harry—I wonder that I have not told him so before. Perhaps I should have done so had it not been for these awful weeks.

Do you know, father, that I find life in opposition to every convention you have taught me since I was a child? There are no fairy godmothers in the world. Our guardian angels might be gamblers who throw us headlong into the stream and make wagers about our condition when we come out. We have to decide the most momentous questions when we are still babies and understand nothing about them. In the end it comes just to what Mr. Faber says, our brains make or mar us; and neither you nor I have any brains to speak of. Let us leave it there, father. I am growing really anxious about the child, and must know the truth. If she is not with the Bensons, I don't know where she is."

He assented, moved to some real anxiety by her obvious alarm. They wrote a note and dispatched it to the house of their friends the Bensons, who had shown much kindness to Maryska, but the afternoon had merged into evening before any answer was brought to them.

CHAPTER III
THE MARIGOLDS TO THE SUN

I

Maryska had been out and about London with Harry Lassett upon more than one occasion, and this had been to the knowledge and with the approval both of Silvester and of Gabrielle. Both had known Harry for many years, and he had become almost as the son of the house. Their own duties carried them so much abroad during the terrible days that they were well content when the young man did what he could to amuse the child during the long hours; and they used to hear of the mutual escapades with the interest they would have bestowed upon two children come home from school and eager for the holidays.

Here their trust went out wholly upon their own plane of honor and convention. The boy had been to a public school and to Cambridge. He was of a type which three hundred years of a great tradition have moulded finally and left as a corner-stone of the national society. A firm faith in the blessings of domestic freedom had always been characteristic of Silvester's teaching. Trust your sons, and they will not fail you, he had said.

But, if he knew that Harry had taken Maryska to such places as a young woman of her age (and one who was a stranger to the City) might visit, he would have been astounded and dismayed had he known that she had gone to Harry's lodgings, and latterly had made a practice of visiting him there. This was concealed by both as a secret between them of which no whisper must be heard. It was the first scene of an act of drama speedily to follow. Maryska would never forget that day. They had been to Madame Tussaud's, where a wretched group of people were sheltered from the cold, and tried to forget the shadow which lay upon the City. Returning towards five o'clock, Maryska had told him that she knew the truth about England at last, and that it was the arctic land of which her dead father had told her.

"They come here in little ships," she said, "and it is to find *le Pôle Nord*. There was a café of that name in Dijon, and once when we were very poor

I danced there and got money for him. He beat me when he found it out, and that night I hated him, and went back to dance once more. That is what a girl should do when a man beats her! Ah! I shall run away from you yet, *bête sauvage*."

He laughed in a great boyish way, and drew her arm the tighter within his own. How good it seemed to have these bright eyes looking up into his own, to hear the little savage prattling, and to know that she was happy. Though the kingdom of England had perished that night, these two would not have cared a scudo. The eternal voice of youth called them, and they bent to it as "marigolds to the sun."

"Do you think I shall beat you, Maryska? Is that in your head? You are a rum little devil, I must say!"

She took it rather as a compliment.

"I do not know what you will do when you are angry. The English are difficult to understand. I think they are afraid of women. Mr. Silvester runs away when I stamp my foot. I have heard him shut his door when I come down the stairs. *Bon Dieu!* what a cat of a man—and he is a priest, and the people do not know that he is afraid of women! Shall we go to your lodgings, Harry—shall I make you some coffee there? It will be ripping,—and they would be so angry if they knew. Let us hurry on, for it is late—to your lodgings, I say."

He was a good deal taken aback, and argued with her while she trotted by his side; all her strength returned, all her youth triumphant. To his rooms! That was a new proposition, to be sure. And what would Gabrielle say if she knew of it?

"Look here, Maryska, people will talk if you come to my lodgings!"

"Will they not talk if I stop away?"

"They'll say rotten things. I shouldn't like to have them said about you."

"But, Harry, do you always live alone in your rooms?"

"I don't take ladies there, Maryska."

She was amazed.

"It is not wicked to be with you in the street, then, but wicked in your rooms. *Ecco!* what a country! And all the people are frozen and the wind eats them up, and they are so frightened of us they lock us out of their lodgings. How *he* would have laughed! Why, all the ladies in Ragusa came to his room, and he would sing and laugh all day. It was not wicked there! He would not have done it when I was with him, if it had been."

He tried to tell her that countries have different customs, and that what is done in the south may not be done in the north with impunity. But she was wholly unconvinced, and the spice of daring being added to the dish of her thoughts, she led him insensibly towards Holly Place and not towards Well Walk as they approached Hampstead.

"Just to see what this wicked place is like, Harry. Surely, I may stand at your door and see you go in? They will not punish me, these horrid English, for that. Oh, yes, I shall stand at your door and see you go in, and you will give me some wine. Do you know that we have nothing but syrup at the Silvesters'? Oh, *mon pauvre*! it is all ice inside as well as out. I go thirsty all day—there was wine always when *he* was alive, and now there is none! I shall wait upon your doorway until you give me a little wine, Harry."

This idea pleased her very much, and she danced and sang her way through the silent streets upon it. Even the searching cold of the early night did not affright her, nor those suggestions of loneliness and isolation which usually attended her journey northward. She was going to see Harry's rooms and to drink some wine when she got there! The fact that he had nothing but good Scotch whisky did not enter into her calculations.

As for Harry, the proposal annoyed him at the beginning, but grew upon his sympathies as they went. He tried to follow her logic, and to think that it would be absurd to treat her otherwise than as a child. What harm could there be after all, and was not her view of it safer than his own? The Silvesters were too busy looking after impossible people in the East End to do their duty by this little exile. What forbade him to treat her as a sister? Upon this there came tumbling many a picture of that bewitching apparition as sympathy could frame it. What a riot she would make in his puny lodging! And how good it would be to watch her swinging her shapely legs on the edge of his pet arm-chair! She filled the whole house with visions already.

They marched up Heath Street forlorn, wind-swept, and deserted, and came at last to his door. He remembered how easily she took possession of the place, marching here and there as though she were its mistress—setting this or that in order instantly; tidying his desk; looking reproachfully upon his joyous negligence. When a lean landlady asked her genially if she would take a little tea, she answered immediately, "No; you are to go to the café for the wine, Mr. Harry will give you the money!"

And Harry gave it, as though it was the best of jokes, and one in which he must now play his part.

II

The first of many visits—how soon it was forgotten, that others more intimate should be remembered!

She came almost every day during the final week of the tribulation, and would sit with him, smoking his cigarettes and drinking his claret as though his house had been a café! He discovered that she had many talents, was a rare dancer of the wild, uncouth dances of the East, and could draw with a wonderful sense of portraiture. Her pictures of Silvester should have gone to *Punch*, but her portraits of Gabrielle were full of feeling. One day, when she had been sitting upon the arm of his chair, using his broad back for an easel, she asked him, à propos nothing at all, if he were in love, and when he looked at her astonished she seemed insistent.

"Are you in love with her, Harry? Why do you not answer me?"

"Why, you know that I am. Aren't we going to be married, little Gipsy?"

She put the pencil down and laid her head quietly upon his shoulder.

"I shall never believe it; you do not love her—she is nothing to you."

"Oh, come, Gipsy! What do you know about it?"

She sighed, but did not raise her head.

"If you loved Gabrielle Silvester you would not let me come to this house."

"Why not, Gipsy?"

"Because I love you, Harry."

So there it was, in a flash, and both her arms were about his neck and her lips hot upon his own. She loved him and had no shame in the avowal. Destiny gave him to her. The little wild girl who came God knew whence, was not this her haven at last? She entered into her heritage fiercely as one who would not be dispossessed.

Of course, Harry treated it as a good joke, or perhaps attempted so to treat it. He could not resist her kisses and made no effort to do so; but when she had calmed down a little and he had pulled her on to his knees so that he could look deep into her black eyes, he said:

"We mustn't tell Gabrielle about this; we mustn't say a word just yet, Gipsy."

She thought about it, pulling at the button of his vest.

"Do you wish to love me in secret, Harry?" she asked presently. He laughed again at that, and said it would be a good joke.

"Gabrielle will never marry me; I know that, Gipsy. She's gone on your American friend, and is too proud to tell him so. Our affair was all a mistake. Time will put that right, and then you and I will be free. Let's keep it secret, and have the laugh of them all. Will you do that, Maryska?"

Her eyes were wide open; she made an effort to understand.

"You do not forbid me to love you, Harry?"

"Certainly not; aren't we pals?"

"I may come here just when I like?"

"As long as Silvester doesn't get mad about it."

She thought upon this, but half satisfied.

"Will you take me to Paris some day? I want so much to go to Paris. There is life there—life, life, life! One sits in the door of the hotel and sees all the world. These English people make me hate them, but I love the French as my father did. They said in Paris that he was a great artist; I know it was true. He could have compelled all the world to say so if he had not been so idle. There were whole weeks in Ragusa when he lay in bed; sometimes we had no food in the house; then he would paint, and I would go with the picture to the Jew with the beard and bring the money home. That night was always a *festa*. It was better in Paris, where he had many friends who would come and say, 'Work, beast!' and he would laugh at them and take up his brushes. You know that he was a prince in his own country, Harry? Once when he was very ill, he told me so and gave me some papers. That was at San Gimignano—oh! so many years ago. When he got better he took them away again, and we travelled and travelled, just like two gipsies, together upon the lonely white roads. At last we reached Granada, where there is a mountain with gipsies, running in and out of their holes like the rabbits in the forest. We lived with them a month and he painted many pictures; then we took ship and went to Italy, and he was so ill that I knew we should never go over the white roads together again. Ah, dear God! what a life I have led! and now you—you are the only one in all the world, Harry."

She hid her face from him and put her arms about his neck again. Her passionate story moved him strangely and seemed to set her in a new aspect before him. Was it possible that this waif was what the dead artist had proclaimed her to be? Beneath all the sorry veneer of the *Wanderjahre*, would he find at last the grains of nobility and of a precious birthright? That would mean very much to a man of his temperament; to one whose whole career had taught him to esteem these things. The mystery of it all fascinated him strangely—she frightened him in such moods as this.

He did not promise to take her to Paris, but, comforting her with fair words, they went round together to Well Walk and he saw Gabrielle for a few brief moments. The talk between them was quite commonplace, but, as often before, the name of John Faber quickly crept into it. Harry turned his heel upon that, and went back to Holly Place in high dudgeon.

"Good God!" he said. "That man again!"

Why did she not tell him frankly that her ambition lay here and would not be rebuffed?

III

He had been very proud of Gabrielle in the old days, and was proud still in a vain boyish way. He knew that she was a beautiful woman, and could suffer chagrin when he admitted that the measure of her intellect was far beyond his own. A sportsman and little else, all this cant of movements and causes and social creeds stirred him to ebullitions of temper of which he was secretly ashamed. Nothing but the influence of years forbade him to say that both of them had made a great mistake, and that he must end it. He resolved to do so after Maryska's avowal, but his courage was not responsive. He could not bring himself to what must seem in Gabrielle's eyes but a vulgar affront upon her loyalty—and so the days drifted. In the end he made up his mind to leave London for a week or so and trust to new scenes for inspiration.

By all accounts John Faber was about to sail from England, and, having altered his plans at the last moment, Maryska had been left with the

Silvesters—to her great grief but not to Gabrielle's dissatisfaction. Harry knew little of the circumstances, for his friends at Hampstead were secretive, and latterly had become unaccountably vague in all their plans. That John Faber's departure was a great disappointment to them Harry guessed, though his vanity suffered by the admission. He knew now that things must come to a head between Gabrielle and himself directly he returned to London, and the very fact kept him in Brighton. It would have been good to be alone but for his longing after Maryska. He missed her every minute of the day—there was hardly an hour from dawn to dark when her image did not arise before him and her black eyes look into his own.

Brighton had always interested him in the old time, but he found it insupportably dull during this brief and almost penitential vacation. His club, one of the "brainiest" in the country, as he used to boast elsewhere, was filled by earnest men who could discuss nothing but the passing of the frost and the danger which the country had escaped almost miraculously. Standing upon the breezy front, where a warm south wind rattled the windows of the old houses, it seemed impossible to believe that a man might have picked ice from that very shore but a few short weeks ago. Now Brighton was as ever a compound of stones and stucco; of square lawns and of wide windows as methodical; of a tumbling sea, and elderly gentlemen in weird waistcoats to gaze upon it.

All these had plans for their country's salvation, and few of them did not mention the name of John Faber at some time or other. Harry would sit in the corner with the old priest, Father Healy, and listen contemptuously to the talk of one who, as he said, had earned immortality by cornering the wheat market and then giving away a few sacks for the sake of making a splash! When the kindly old priest would say, "Come, come! he has done very much more than that," the good sportsman admitted that perhaps he had; but he would invariably round it off by saying, "Well, he's gone now, anyway!" and would ask upon that: "What are we going to do to help ourselves; that's what I want to know?"

It opened fine possibilities of debate in which many joined. The militant section had but one panacea: "We must prepare for war!" Civilians, equally confident, harped upon a system of national granaries, and asked what imbecility of the national intellect had prevented us building them before? "Provisions against a siege," they said.

The priest was almost alone in desiring that a siege should be made impossible.

"Build granaries of goodwill, as John Faber has advised you," he said. "Let the builders be your best intellects. There is no other surety!"

Harry liked the doctrine, but had not the wit to support it with success. He was constantly depressed, and even the cheery spirits in the billiard-room could do little for him. The futility of his flight and the cowardice of it became apparent as the days rolled by. Why had he left London and what was he doing in this place? Was not Maryska alone, and was she the one to be left safely to her own devices? He began to be afraid for her, and to say that he must return. His courage shrank from the ordeal, but his desire would face it.

And that was the state of things when, without any warning at all, "the little gipsy" came to Brighton, and, presenting herself immediately at his rooms, declared with conviction her intention not to depart therefrom without her lover.

CHAPTER IV
SURRENDER AND AFTERWARDS

I

She looked very tired; there were deep black lines beneath her eyes, and her dress was muddy. Incidentally she told him that she had walked from the station—a feminine coup to deceive possible adversaries, and one greatly to her liking.

Harry occupied a bedroom and a sitting-room in that Boulevard St. Germain of Brighton, Oriental Terrace, opposite the club. The sitting-room had a window, from where you could see the pier if your neck were long enough; the bedroom was dark and gloomy, and suggestive of the monastic habit. Neither apartment had any ornament to speak of—the pictures wounded the gentlest critic; the chairs were mid-Victorian and covered in leather. Yet when Maryska came, he would have sworn that this was a house of Arcady. One wild question he put to her: one loud word of remonstrance which brought the tears to her eyes. Then she was in his arms, her heart beating like a frightened bird's, all her nerves quivering when her lips sought his own.

"Maryska, what have you done?"

She snatched her hat from her tousled hair, and threw it on the shabby sofa. Squatting upon the corner of the table, her luggage in her hand, she tried to tell as well as laughter and tears would permit.

"It was after breakfast—Gabrielle had gone down to the church to see the organist. I ran out with all my money in my purse, and went round to Holly Place. She would not tell me where you were until I frightened her—*Dieu de mon âme*, what a woman she was! But I stamped my foot, and I said the things he used to say, and then she wrote it down for me. At the bottom of the wide hill I saw the *voiturier*, and called him. When I said that it was to Brighton, he laughed—the *gamin* that he was! But I was angry once more and I got into the carriage, and I would not get out again. That seemed to please him. He said that he would vote for women, and he took me to the *gare*. I did not know that you must go by the railway to Brighton, and he laughed when I asked him—but the *facteur* was there, and he said I was on time. So I came right along—and *ecco*, I am here! Are you glad that is so, *bête sauvage*? Are you not pleased that I have come to you?"

He had not an idea what to say to her. The world seemed to be turned upside down in an instant. There was no such town as Brighton in all the kingdom. How the sun shone into that gloomy room! What diamonds of light were everywhere! He had come suddenly to the palace of his dreams and the mistress of it was here. And yet his talk must be a commonplace. The whys and wherefores would not stand aside even in an hour pregnant of such wonders.

"Do you mean to say you bolted, Maryska—just biffed off without a word to anyone? My hat! what will the Silvesters say? What shall we tell them when we go back?"

She swung a little bonnet by the strings and shrugged her shoulders determinedly.

"Do you suppose I am going back to that house? *Jamais de ma vie*—I am here, and I shall stay. If you do not want me, please say so. I have money and I shall do very well. It is there, and you can count it; the American is my friend, and he has given me money always. So, you see, I do not wish you to work for me; and when the money is all spent, I will go out to the cafés and they will let me dance. Then we shall do very well, you and I, Harry, but not in such an apartment as this. *Dio di mi alma!* was there ever so dreadful a lodging? And you have lived here three whole days as the woman told me! Three days in such a house—*madre mia,* what a life! But now we shall go away to the hotel until the money is spent. Say that we shall go, and make me happy, for you know that I could not live here. Will you not say it, Harry—please, at once?"

She put her arms about his neck again and kissed him, while her round eyes looked deeply into his own. He was her lover, and all her creed, learned in the nomad's church, taught her that she was sacred to him and he to her. Upon his side was the swift realisation that he must play the game. He would take her back to London immediately. There was no alternative.

"I'd say anything I could to please you, Maryska, but don't you see that we must think of what other people will say? Why, we're not even engaged, little Gipsy, and if we went to a hotel together, all the idiots we know would shout at us. I can't have that for your sake. If we were married, it would be different. Let's go to London at once, and tell the Silvesters what we mean to do. Now, don't you see, it's the very best thing we can do?"

She did not see, but sat there, a rueful picture, with fifty golden sovereigns on the table beside her and all her worldly possessions in a little unopened parcel. A terrible fear of the return to the gloomy house in Hampstead consumed her. Her eyes filled with tears.

"I will never go back," she said coldly; "if you do not want me, Harry, I will go where no one shall ever see me again. If you love me, why cannot you marry me? I am ready to go to the priest this instant. *He* said it was all d—d palaver, but I do not refuse to go because of that. Take me now, and I will be your little gipsy wife. Do you not wish it, Harry?"

Of course he wished it, and yet what should he say to her? Being a mere man and knowing something of such a nature as this, her threat had a meaning he did not dare to ignore. What if she refused to go to London with him? Would people blame him? He heard already the horrible malice of those who would declare that he had decoyed her from her home. The world, so far as it concerned him, would say that he was a scoundrel; his whole life had taught him to care for such censure when the greater issues were at stake. Oh! she had put him in a pretty fix; and yet he loved her and had discovered that he could not leave her though ten thousand railed upon him.

"Don't you understand, Gipsy," he protested in despair, "these things cannot be done just like that? I'm going to marry you, and no one alive shall stop me. But I can't do it in five minutes. We shall have to get a licence and swear we've lived in Brighton heaven knows how long. Then there's the church people to see—and, of course, the Silvesters must know. It would be shabby to keep them in the dark. My dearest, why do you cry? Don't you see I can't make it different just because I love you? Won't you understand?"

She looked up at him through her tears.

"You do love me, Harry?"

"More than anything on earth, little Gipsy. So help me God! it's true. I couldn't leave you now if I wanted to. Put your arms round my neck and tell me you believe it. There, just like that—and don't say another word about going away, or I don't know what will happen to you."

He pulled her on to his knees and held her close to him. She had twenty schemes in her head, but the one she liked best was the suggestion that her fifty pounds would bribe the priest to an immediate ceremony. For herself, the thing was of little account. *He* had taught her that it did not matter as long as a man loved a woman, and beyond that was a knowledge of the world almost terrible in its savage conceptions of right and wrong.

"In my country," she said naïvely, "we go away to the hills when we are in love, and no one thinks we have done wrong. I have seen dreadful things, Harry; I saw them at Ranovica when 'the boss' went there with my father. Oh! do not think I am the simple baby that you English like their wives to be. The world was very unkind to him and to me. Sometimes, for many days together we have slept at the hotel of the Belle Étoile, and he would sell our clothes for bread. Once, at Perpignan, we were put in prison, and I did not see him for a week. It was there he met a fellow-countryman who bought us from the judge and took us to Scutari. His relations were great people, but he would never ask anything of them, he was too proud. Some day, when you and I are rich, we will go to Bukharest and tell them who we are. Perhaps we will walk all the way, as he and I did from Dijon to Nîmes, when the money was gone. Dear heart! what a walk it was, and all the acacias were blooming and the scent of the hay in the fields and the white farms at night—and, yes, the old abbé who was so gentle and good. He called me 'little daughter'—it was near Valence, and I know that if you and I had gone to him, he would have married us. Perhaps, if you cannot bribe the priest here, we will take the steamer and go now. Oh, how good it will be in the warm hay when the sun shines! And we could get money at the cafés and perhaps in Bukharest; it would be true what he told me, and his friends would be a little kind. Will you not take me, Harry? Shall we not go to the sun together, away from this dreadful country? Oh, how happy I would be! How my life would be changed if you would go. Dearest, will you not do it when Maryska asks you?"

She pressed her hot cheek upon his hand and held his hands as though she never would release them. If her confessions startled him, he perceived in them an acquaintanceship with life and its realities far surpassing his own. He had led a humdrum existence enough apart from his cricket; but here was one who could lift the veil of romance as no story-book had done. The word pictures of the joyous life moved him strangely by their suggestions of a freedom which was all-embracing; of a garden of love whereon the sun would ever shine! And from that, it was like him to tumble suddenly to realities and to remember the loaves and the fishes. She must be very hungry, he thought. What course more obvious than to take her to the hotel, and to give her some food?

"By Jove! I forgot all about it," he cried, lifting her on to her feet, and so snatching at her hat. "We'll go to the Metropole and have some grub, Gipsy!

Aren't you hungry, little wild cat? Don't you think you could eat me? Come along, then. It will be time to talk about all this afterwards. We can wire the Silvesters as we go; let 'em do what they like, Gipsy. I shan't part with you now; never again, I swear."

She shook her head, and was but half satisfied. The kindly minister of the gospel stood to her for an ogre who would make light of the Belle Étoile, but much of that ancient office beginning with "Dearly beloved," and ending with the ecclesiastical blessing.

II

Gordon Silvester was a man who had lived forty-five years of his life without excitements, and had then been plunged into them headlong.

It was a great thing for a man, whose only diversion hitherto had been the weekly disputations with the deacons or the quarterly disagreement with the organist, to find himself suddenly upon public platforms, cheek by jowl with the great men of the world, who pleaded for the supreme blessing which could come upon humanity, the blessing of peace. The notoriety had fallen to the plodding minister after many years, and henceforth he had been up to his eyes in the papers, the pamphlets and other paraphernalia of the pacific propaganda. The *réclame* of it all delighted him. He became almost a hustler, and was at war with every whisper which deplored the ancient habit and the paths of ease.

There were many worries, to be sure. Bishops would send mere archdeacons to his meetings. His letters to the Press were shockingly mutilated. He had the suspicion that certain worldly millionaires merely considered him a pawn in the game, and were quite unwilling to admit that Hampstead was the hub of the universe. Upon this, came the gradual conviction that his daughter, Gabrielle, was the real agent of much of the fame that he won, and that his meetings were a success or a failure in just such a measure as she chose to make them. If this had been the case before the great tribulation, he found the position even more intolerable when the danger was past. All England spoke now of fact and not of theory. The demand for brains to save the nation from another panic was universal. Men said that arbitration had become as much a necessity as vaccination. You could not starve thirty-seven millions because the frontier of a swamp must be delimited or a possible mine in a bog be possessed! The phantoms of the living death had hovered over the country during the terrible weeks and the lesson had been learned. But for that master-mind—the mind of the great American, whom destiny had sent in the critical hour—the end of all things had come! It was supererogatory now to preach mere platitudes from ancient platforms.

So Silvester fell a little to the background and suffered an unmerited obscurity. The common ills of the domestic life cropped up again, and must be doctored. He had to pay rents, rates and taxes, and to remember that Gabrielle was about to marry a boy whose income, at the best, could not be more than five hundred a year. And she might have done so well! Some recollection of his old time ambition upon the steamer filled him with vain regrets now that John Faber had left England. The compensation was a cheque for £5,000, to be employed to Maryska's benefit until she should set out for New York. Meanwhile she was to remain at Hampstead to learn all that Silvester could teach her of the social amenities and the elemental faith. An unstable patronage, to be sure, but very characteristic of that restless brain. Silvester paid the cheque into his bank, and declared he would do his best. Three days afterward he knew that he could do nothing at all.

III

Harry sent the telegram from the General Post Office at Brighton at half-past two exactly. It was laconic, and evaded the issue somewhat cleverly.

"Maryska is at the Metropole Hotel at Brighton with me. All well. Return as soon as possible."

He had written it when fortified by the child's black eyes, and some excellent Rudesheim she had insisted upon drinking. It was all up between Gabrielle and him—it had been all up long ago, and well enough for both of them that it should be. She would marry the American and spend his money like one o'clock! Harry was sure of this, though he had some qualms when he remembered that Faber had sailed from Southampton and intimated very plainly that the date of his return was distant.

It was wonderful how frankly he and Maryska discussed this very matter. The daughter of Louis de Paleologue knew little of the sacrament of marriage but a great deal of the sociology of the studio. Her doctrine recognised the passion and the pathos of love, but the bonds it inspired were personal, and had little to do with the priest. If a man did not love a woman, he left her and sought another. There were neither scenes nor scruples. Sometimes the woman would rage fearfully for a day, but her anger soon passed and calm fell. In this case she did not think there would be any anger, and she was right. There was merely humiliation.

Verily a heavy blow fell upon that little house in Hampstead when the telegram came. It was so like Gordon Silvester with his large faith in human nature, and his habit of making a fetish of a public school education; so like him to believe it all mere high spirits and to declare that the pair of them would be home to dinner. Gabrielle knew the truth from that moment. The ship that drifted upon the ocean of a "boy and girl" infatuation had come to harbour. She would not hide it either from her father or herself, whatever the cost to her pride.

"I expected nothing less!" she said to Silvester, when he ran into her boudoir with the telegram and tried to make a jest of it. "It was in the child's blood. We cannot be responsible."

Silvester threw himself into an arm-chair, and began to swing a leg as was his habit.

"Responsible for what? Don't you see it's a childish freak? Of course, they ought not to have done it. I must cut down all this liberty now that Faber has gone. She's to give me an account of her day, and no going out at all unless you or I know. Really, it's too bad of Harry!"

Gabrielle went to the window, still holding the telegram in her hand. Her lips quivered, but she spoke apparently without emotion.

"At least, he will behave honourably," she said. "I have no fear upon that point. He will marry her at once, father; he cannot do less."

Silvester laid back his head upon the cushion and surveyed a ceiling not ill-painted by a one-time zealous amateur.

"Marriage is a great institution, my dear; I don't find it a fitting subject for jest."

"Oh, my God!" she said, wheeling about and facing him so suddenly that he sat bolt upright. "Don't you see what it means? Has it not been going on under our very eyes? And you talk of a 'boy and girl' escapade! I tell you they are madly in love. She sees no one else when he is there—he cannot take his eyes off her. Why, they are married already for all I know—or you care," she added with almost savage emphasis.

The outburst frightened a man by no means blessed with much pluck where women were concerned. Silvester turned as white as a sheet. It was as though a pit had been opened at his feet, and he had looked in to see enormities.

"You don't mean to tell me—God forbid!" he gasped. "You don't mean to tell me that this is sin, Gabrielle? You don't think that, surely?"

"I don't know what to think," she said in despair. "It is our business to act at once. You must go to Brighton. What will Mr. Faber say if you don't? Telegraph to Southampton in case the yacht has not sailed. Have we no responsibilities? Oh! don't you see? It's madness, madness! And it's our fault. Both of us are to blame. We have just gone our own ways and left them to themselves. What else could have come of it when they were lovers?"

He stood before her utterly abashed.

"My dearest girl," he said, "I will go to Brighton at once."

And then he said:

"But it's of you I should be thinking. God bless you, Gabrielle!"

IV

He left by the half-past four o'clock train from Victoria, and did not return that night. When he was gone, Gabrielle shut herself up in her own room, and asked herself what new thing had come into her life.

A turn of fortune had cast her down from the heights to the old abyss of the suburban monotonies; and now it had put this affront upon her. She perceived already what sport the teacup brigade would make of it, and how her pride must suffer just because of the very littleness of her surroundings. All Hampstead would point the finger at her, and there would be kind friends in abundance to offer their sympathies. Thus had her destiny punished the brief hours of an infatuation for which her youth had been responsible. As others, she had known a day when she had desired the love of man and had desired it passionately. Thus had she come to be the betrothed of one who had never loved her, and for this she must repay.

She had thrown aside much, to be sure, to fall upon such a penalty. John Faber would have made her his wife could she have escaped the meshes of a net she herself had tied. He would have lifted her above all these sordid creeds of a puny society to the heights of freedom and of opportunity. She believed that she could have risen with him and upheld a position his money would have won for them. She saw herself the mistress of a splendid house; heard her name in high places; believed that she was born to rule and not to serve. And opportunity had passed her by for this. The man who would have ennobled her had sailed for America, and she did not believe he would return. In any case, she did not dare to think of him now. As she had sown, so must she reap.

Something of an intolerable despair afflicted her now, and drove her to silent tears. The stillness of the house, the measured chiming of the church bells, the monotonous fall of footsteps upon the pavement, how they all suggested the round of the insufferable days she must live! It had been so different a month ago, when her name had been honoured and her activities abundant. How full her life had been then, when many had honoured her, and she had gone proudly in and out among the people. Such an opportunity could not recur; and she reflected that it had been made for her by one who had been willing that she should wear the laurel his brains had won. He was on the Atlantic now, and all must seem but an episode in his story.

Here, perchance, she did herself less than justice; for her aims had been noble and her faith quite honest. She had desired the supreme gift of peace upon earth, and much that she had done was the fruit of an enthusiasm which had brought this very shame upon her. She would not think of it now nor remember her sacrifice. Enough to say that the night of her hopes had come down, and that the day would never dawn again.

So the long hours passed wearily. At eight o'clock there came a telegram from her father in vague terms, but such as she had expected:

"Am doing all possible. Everything will be well. Shall not return yet. Writing."

She crumpled the paper in her hand and fell to wondering what the message meant. Had Silvester discovered such an escapade as his faith discerned or something of which he would not speak? She knew not what to think, but remembered her last words to him, that he should telegraph to John Faber in case the yacht had not sailed.

In case it had not sailed!

Her face flushed and her heart beat faster when she repeated the words.

And yet, God knows, it could matter little to her whether the *Savannah* was still in Southampton Water or had passed the Lizard Light upon its way to the great Atlantic.

V

The lunch at the Metropole was altogether different from any lunch Harry had eaten in all his life. It was as though something had transformed Brighton in a twinkling, making of its commonplaces a paradise, and melting its shadows in a rain of gold. Never had he realised what a town it was: how bright, how inspiring, and how typical of a joyous life. And this is to say that a pride of possession had come upon him so that he walked proudly by Maryska's side—he who had known hundreds of pretty girls, and had flirted with many of them. Now the recklessness of a young passion took charge of the situation, and would not be denied. The tears had passed from the child's face, and the sun shone down upon them.

"We shall go to Paris to-night," she said triumphantly, "and afterwards to Italy. *Bien entendu,* you do not wish to tease me any more, Harry. It is all over, is it not—this gloomy England and all the sad people? I shall never see them any more, shall I?"

He laughed loudly, so that many in the room turned their heads to look at him.

"But, Maryska," he rejoined, "we're not married yet, my dear. How can I take you to Italy when we are not married?"

She thought upon this, her pretty head poised upon her hand. For herself that would have been no obstacle at all, for had not *he* said that marriage was something which the priests did to keep the wolf from the door? Harry, however, must be considered, and for his sake she would think about it.

"You shall pay the priest and he will marry us," she said at length. "Show him the money and he will not turn us away. It is not necessary to show him too much at the commencement. Afterwards you can put more upon the table, and he will see it. That is what my father did when his friend, the Abbé of Dijon, wished that I should be confirmed. He wanted to paint a picture in the church there, and he said that it did not matter a damn one way or the other. So, you see, it can be done, Harry; and what you can do in Dijon, you can do in England. Go to the priest and learn if I am not wise."

"Oh!" he cried, laughing as he raised his glass, "you are the last word in originals, and that's sure! Don't you know that there are twenty things to be done before people can be married in England? It's almost easier to get hanged. No priest would marry us unless he had a license, Maryska. I suppose I can get a special in two or three days, but we shall want all that. Meanwhile, had you not really better go back to Hampstead?"

Her spirits fell. The rose-bud of a mouth drooped pathetically. She did not believe a word of it, and was driven to the thought that he renounced her after all! Thus she came upon the borderland of a scene even in the dining-room of the great hotel, while he shrank in despair from the task of persuading her.

"I will never go back to Hampstead; I will throw myself into the sea first!"

"Don't talk rot, Maryska. You know I want to do the best I can for you."

"Is it the best to send me away when I love you?"

"I'm not sending you away; I'm only keeping you out of the reach of silly tongues."

"What do I care for them? What does it all matter if we love?"

"It won't matter for more than two or three days. After that, we'll go to Italy."

"Then I shall stay in Brighton by your side until the permit arrives. I will never go to Hampstead again, so help me God!"

"Oh, but you mustn't swear! Let's talk about it after lunch, dearest girl. I want just to look at you and see you happy. Do you know you're frightfully pretty, Maryska?"

She flushed with pleasure upon that. Many a man had called her pretty in the old days; but she shrank from their words then, knowing well what they meant.

"*He* used to say that it would be so, if ever I loved a man. I have been so lonely since he died, and that has made my face sad. Now it is different. I do not mean to be sad any more. I shall go to Italy, and we will laugh in the sun together. Cannot it be to-day, Harry? Here is the sea, and there are the ships. Let us take one and sail away! We can think of the priest in France, where there are many who will be glad of our money. Will you not please me, *sauvage bête*? Then take me upon the ship immediately."

He could not answer it. The problem became more embarrassing every hour, and when lunch was done, and they were out on the parade together, it began to seem beyond his wit altogether. Not for a kingdom would he have brought tears to those bright eyes again. How prettily she babbled at his side; how quick, how clever, how beautiful she was! A pride of possession prevailed above all prudence, and drove him far from considered resolutions. He was content to go, hand in hand with her—God knew whither!

In the end, it all came back to the priest. Let them see the priest! He knew but one priest in Brighton, and that was the excellent Father Healy, with whom he had fraternised at his club. Divine inspiration. Let them call upon him.

VI

Father Maurice Healy lived up at the back of the town in an old windmill, skilfully transformed and built about so that it had become a veritable bungalow, with more than one pleasant room and a little chapel which his lady friends declared was too divine for words. He had been smoking his afternoon cigar, when the amazing pair burst in upon him, and never in all his life had he laid down good tobacco to listen to a tale so wonderful!

"Ye'll have to wait," he said dryly. "I've no power to marry ye at all as the State understands the term. Ye'll get a special licence, and then come to me. 'Tis wise advice, my dear, that ye should go back to your friends in London until things can be put straight. Make up your mind to that. I'm no better off in securing you to legal marriage than any man ye may stop in the street. Mr. Lassett knows that well, and he'll have told ye as much."

Harry nodded his head in unison with the words as though this was just the counsel he had expected. Maryska, thinking that she knew priests well, clasped her precious bag firmly in both her little hands and looked the enemy squarely in the face.

"We will pay you money," she said with much dignity. "I have ten pounds here, and you shall have it. What you say does not matter to us at all. We are not frightened of the judges, Harry and I. If you marry us to-day, we shall go away to Italy, and the gendarmes will not find us. He has said that I must go back to Hampstead, but I will never do so. I will kill myself if you do not marry us. Harry knows that it is true, and that is why we have come here. Perhaps, if you married us, he has some money and will add it to mine. There are other priests, but we do not wish to go to them. Oh, sir, will you not do it for those who love? Will you not make us happy? It is nothing to me this ceremony, but to him it is so much. And I have the money here; I will show it to you if you wish."

She began to fumble with the bag while the good father and Harry regarded her with an amazement beyond all words. Never had Maurice Healy heard such an address or seen so pretty a bargainer in that little room. And the horror of it all—her ignorance, her childish faith, her frank confession! He was as clay in her hands already—and she, a heathen.

"But, my dear young lady, 'tis far from understanding ye are," he gasped at length; "not a penny of your money would I be touching anyway. Don't you see I can't marry ye because the law will not let me? 'Tis not me, but the Parliament that has the making of it. Ye must take your money to them."

Maryska looked at him almost with pity. Harry's appeal to her might as well have been addressed to the stucco walls of the bungalow.

"I do not believe you," she said; "you have a little church there, and you can say the words. The money will buy you many things that this poor house is in need of. Please to marry us at once, and then we can go and be happy. Oh, sir, if you knew what it was to love! But priests do not know that; they have no hearts. You will let us sail to Italy without your blessing, and will remember it afterwards. Is it kind of you to do that when you think that you serve God?"

"But, my child, I will give ye my blessing freely; 'tis to marry you I am unable."

"We do not care for that; nothing matters to us but our love. We go to Italy to forget this dark country and its people. If you will not do as we wish, we shall ask no other. Is it for religion to refuse us, father, when we have come here as the Church would wish us to do?"

"God be good to me!" he cried in despair, "but I don't know what to say to you, and that's the truth. I'll see your husband, my dear, and have a talk to him. Will you come into the dining-room while I have a word with ye, Mr. Lassett? 'Tis beyond all argument and reason—God knows it is."

She did not demur, and they went away, leaving her before a superb crucifix, which seemed to speak of the country for which she sighed. The argument between the good father and the equally good sportsman was both long and at times explosive. "Nothing easier," said the priest, "than to take her back to London and be married in three days' time." "Nothing more impossible to do any such thing," urged Master Harry, who thought that he knew the patient. She would never go to London, and if she were left alone in an hotel at Brighton, he would not answer for her. Had she been an Englishwoman, the whole situation would have been impossible. But she was just a waif and stray from the wilds of Bohemia, and her creed had been learned under the kindly stars. Would Father Healy take charge of her until a licence could be got? The father said "No," most emphatically; he would have no woman in the house. What, then, did he suggest?

Of course, they were both very frightened of her, and they spoke in low tones as though she might burst in and accuse them. Impossible to face that little fury and declare, "There is nothing to be done." When Harry suggested that common humanity would marry them and trust to the licence afterwards, Father Healy asked, "Would ye have me in prison?" None the less, both plainly perceived now that it must be done. A licence could be obtained immediately, and the civil marriage celebrated at the office of the registrar. The good father, vague about the law, followed Harry back to the room with a protest on his lips. It was none of his doing—and yet he did it after all. And Harry must swear solemnly, and she must follow with her pledged word, not to leave Brighton until the affair was made legal. Oh, the change in her when she knew the truth!

So they got the priest's blessing before the little altar in the oratory, and when the brief ceremony was over, they went away together, back to his rooms. But they were no longer gloomy rooms, for now the two saw nothing but each other's eyes, and little it mattered to them that the oleographs were mid-Victorian and that the mahogany chairs matched them. Maryska had found the heart of a new world, and she dwelt there for just two hours in good content until there came a knock upon the door, and Gordon Silvester, tired, pale, and wonderfully earnest, entered softly into their paradise and began to speak of men and cities.

"I have telegraphed to Mr. Faber," he said. "He must know immediately."

Maryska laughed in his face.

"He is on the sea," she said. "You will have to send the telegram which flies."

CHAPTER V
TWO SHIPS UPON THE SEA

I

Faber had expected such a telegram; but he had not thought that it would be so longed delayed.

He told Gabrielle once upon a time that she was drifting upon a tide which would carry her to unhappy seas; but he himself had been doing the same thing since his work in England was finished. This was a man who had learned to love a woman, but was a very novice, none the less, in all the arts of love.

Had it been a business affair, with what zeal would he not have plunged into it? Being far from that, a situation in which the whole soul of the man was at stake, he did as the woman had done—drifted upon the tide of circumstance, and was content to wait.

Be sure that he had read the secret of Harry Lassett's passion for Maryska almost at the beginning. Because of it, he left her in the little house at Hampstead, and would have sailed to New York without her. If Harry had the courage, he would cut the knot, and the treasure ship would float upon a kindly stream to the harbour already prepared. But would he have the courage? One excuse and another kept Faber at Southampton, but the news did not come. The order to weigh anchor had been given, and recalled a dozen times in as many days. The yacht would have been in the Solent that very night, but for Gabrielle's instructions to her father. "Telegraph Mr. Faber," she had said. He received the message while he was writing to Sir Jules Achon in the little cabin which served him for library, and there being no train to serve his purpose, the fastest motor-car in Southampton was on the road to Brighton within the hour.

It was half-past eleven when he reached Oriental Terrace, and five minutes later when he burst in upon a dismal company. Having taken possession of "the assets of respectability," Gordon Silvester had refused to budge an inch; and having exhausted his homilies upon "honour," "the married state," and the "scandal of the whole proceeding," had fallen to a sullen silence. Harry and Maryska, no less obstinate, declared their intention of remaining in Brighton until a registrar had married them, and then of leaving for Paris immediately. An appeal to the girl to consider her obligations toward John Faber met with the characteristic answer that she recognised none. She was sorry for this a little later on when Faber himself appeared just like a fairy godfather to a scowling Cinderella. His coming gratified her vanity; his dominant will never failed to subdue her. She remembered the hours they had spent together upon the road to Ranovica and all they had meant to her.

"Why, little girl, and what has been going on here, now—and Mr. Lassett, too? I guess I'm on time for the party anyway. Will someone just tell me what it's all about before we begin? Don't move, Mr. Silvester. I'd have you all be comfortable and I'll light a cigar if Miss Maryska doesn't mind. Now, will no one tell me the story?"

Maryska ran to him just like a child to a father. He was plump in an arm-chair with her by his side before a man could have counted ten, and she lit his cigar with a little hand which trembled while it held the match.

"Harry and I are married!" she said, "you must not be very cross; *he* would not have been. We went to the priest this afternoon—then that man came, and will not go away! Will you send him away, please? We do not want him here."

Even Silvester laughed at this; all the conventions went into the melting-pot at the bidding of the child. It would have been impossible for Melpomene herself to have resisted her. The minister puffed hard at his pipe, and forgot her ingratitude. John Faber stroked her hair, and said to himself that her love had changed her wonderfully.

"Why, my dear, that's not very kind to your good friend nor to me!" he said gently enough. "Don't you think you might have told us something about it all? Perhaps we should have been able to help you if you had come to us. Was it right to keep us all in the dark like this?"

Of course, Harry blurted out that it was all his fault, and that she was not to blame. There were three speaking at once presently, and all the while Faber had Maryska's arms about his neck. They had not meant to do it all—circumstances drove them; they thought that he had gone away. To which was added the truly feminine dictum that they could not help loving each other, and were not to blame. When Silvester obtained a grasp of the situation, and declared that she must have known she was doing wrong, Maryska responded that she did not care a d—n; which finished the worthy pastor, and sent him in high dudgeon back to his hotel. It was nearly midnight, and he feared that he would be locked out!

When he was gone, Faber took Harry aside and had a long talk with him. This was a very different affair, and set every nerve in the young man's body tingling. To begin with, there was the charge upon the honour of the man. Why had he not had it out with Gabrielle? A man who cannot talk straight to a woman, whatever the circumstances, is worth very little in the world. Then, what did he propose to do? To keep house and wife and children upon his paltry three hundred a year? What selfishness was that; what a confession of idleness and vain folly! He, Faber, would let Maryska remain with no man who would not work himself for her, and bring ambition to his task. Harry should have twelve months to justify himself! If he needed capital, it was there—but he must prove his worth. "Show me," said Faber, "that you earn five hundred pounds honestly at the end of twelve months, and I will make it five thousand!" Failing that, he swore very solemnly that he would have Maryska back with him at Charleston, and defy the consequences. "She'll be glad to come," he said; "she's just the kind to discover whether a man has grit in him or no—and God help you, if you haven't."

To the little wife, his farewell was in a kindlier mood altogether. She must know that she had a friend in him always; send for him whenever she was in trouble. He would try to cross the Atlantic to see her sometimes; the years were speeding, and he did not mean to work as hard as he had done. He would have her always in his thoughts, his fellow traveller upon the drear road of death. The present that he gave her brought the hot blush to her cheeks. Oh, the days of joy it would buy in the south, where the sun would shine upon her life. She kissed him again and again. "*He* will know that you have made me happy," she said.

He saw her last through the uncurtained window, showing her treasure to Harry. The boy drew her close and kissed her. They were alone at last.

But John Faber returned immediately to Southampton, through a sleeping country for which his genius had done much in the days of tribulation.

II

Sir Jules Achon's yacht was in dock when Faber awoke late next day, and he learned with some surprise that it had reached the Solent yesterday, and was anchored a little while in Portsmouth harbour, until, indeed, Rupert Trevelle went aboard with news of the *Savannah*. Then Sir Jules sailed for Southampton immediately, and so the master minds met at last, each with his own story of the tremendous days. Faber thought the baronet a little worn by his labours; but his zeal was unchanged, and he still looked toward that goal of life where the peace of the world should be won. The Tsar, he said, was still unwilling to come in; but he had obtained much encouragement at the minor courts, especially those of the south-east of Europe. For England herself, he had little hope in the matter. The old imagination had failed his countrymen. The petty issues, not the greater, were discussed in the market place.

"This should be a story of three kings," he said, "and they must recreate the world. In your country, you have built an altar to humanity which never can be cast down. We learn slowly in Europe, for we are blinded by the glitter of ancient arms. In more material things, the shopkeeping instinct is the foe of progress. When I can throw down the commercial barriers, I can cast out war. The field is mighty, but the labourers are few. If I were not already in my sixty-fourth year, I would hope to see the noblest day in the story of man. As it is, I can but sow and leave those who come after me to reap."

Faber said that none of them could hope to do more.

"We are up against the animal instinct, and that is as old as Eden. You know my view. If peace is to be won for humanity, it will be by the brains and the money of those who lead humanity. This country has had a terrible fight, and everyone is crying out for this or that to be done. I shouldn't wonder if it all ended in nothing being done. Men talk the old platitudes the while they read their newspapers and ask what Germany or Spain has the intention of doing. I don't blame the war party, for it is its business to make war. God knows, I've seen enough of that to last me a lifetime, and when I go back to New York, it will be to live on the hill-top. But others will carry on my business, and it will have to be carried on. The day when any European nation disarmed for reasons of sentimentality would be the last day of its freedom. We must deal with facts as they are; we cannot run ahead of the great company of men, for assuredly we shall fall if we do."

Sir Jules was in accord with all this. He spoke fervently of what the big men were doing. Andrew Carnegie and Taft and Bryce at Washington. An atmosphere was being created, but he feared its artificiality. Commerce was the key, he repeated; remove the commercial bias and the day was won. For Faber's promise to become one of the presidents of the Federation League, he was very grateful. "You have done much for this country," he said; "your name will mean a great deal to me."

They fell afterwards to talking of their more domestic affairs. Sir Jules said that his daughter Eva had gone to Winchester to lunch with a friend, but he expected her to dinner. The same hesitation which had led Faber to defer his departure upon so many recent occasions, now prompted his acceptance of the suggestion that he should join the party, and he went over to the *Savannah* immediately to dress.

"I'll weigh to-morrow anyway," was his word at parting. "My skipper doesn't like these waters in the dark, and I've got to consider him. Eight o'clock, I think you said, Sir Jules? You'll be alone, of course?"

"My daughter and I; it will be a pleasure to both of us."

III

The night fell warm and murky with a soft and southerly breeze.

All the lanterns of the ships in Southampton Water shone clear and steady as Faber paced the quarter-deck of the *Savannah* until it should be time to keep his appointment.

A month ago how different the scene had been—the frost everywhere; the frightened people; the menace of a peril from which the bravest shrank. Now this had become a scene of England's maritime habit—a scene wherein the great steamers moved majestically, their sirens hooting, their crews to be welcomed home or bidden God-speed, as the occasion demanded. In the background were the red and green lamps of the railway, the busy streets of the town, the coming and going of citizens whose day's work was done. As a tempest drifting, the storm had passed. The ramparts beloved of the nation had made of this again an island kingdom.

John Faber dwelt upon such thoughts for an instant, but anon they turned to a woman. Would he leave England and seek no more to reason with Gabrielle Silvester? Would he be justified in going to her in an hour of some humiliation? He had no young man's impetuosity, no virile passion of love which would break all barriers rudely. A real and generous sentiment toward her, the belief that she was for him the one woman in all the world had become a habit of his life. She would be the ornament of any man's home. Her dignity, her wit, her womanliness—in what precious jewels would he not set them if she had but come to him? And all this might have been if Harry Lassett had had the courage to tell her the truth and the little witch of Ragusa had been as other women. Now, all had been put to the hazard. It might be that all was lost.

The boat came alongside at last, and he went aboard. It was very silent all about him, and when he heard a woman's laugh, coming from the deck of a ship, he wondered that it should seem to speak to him across the waters. The *Savannah* herself lay warped to the quay of the dock, but they put a ladder down for him, and he climbed it slowly. A steward said that Miss Achon was in the boudoir, and he went there—to see neither Sir Jules nor his daughter, but another figure and one whose wide eyes expressed all the hope and the fear of that tremendous encounter.

"But," cried Gabrielle, "Eva told me that you had sailed."

"Ah!" he said, refusing to release her hand, "she's not the first of your sex who always tells the truth."